The Diamond

OF

DRURY LANE

A CAT ROYAL
ADVENTURE

BY

JULIA GOLDING

Roaring Brook Press
New York

For Peggy Chowns—my great
great-aunt who loves reading

Bowles's New Plan of London map courtesy of the British Library

Copyright © 2006 by Julia Golding
First American edition published by Roaring Brook Press
Roaring Brook Press is a division of Holtzbrinck Publishing Holdings
Limited Partnership
175 Fifth Avenue, New York, New York 10010

Library of Congress Cataloging-in-Publication Data
Golding, Julia.
The diamond of Drury Lane / Julia Golding. — 1st ed.
p. cm.
Summary: Orphan Catherine "Cat" Royal, living at
the Drury Lane Theater in 1790s London, tries to find
the "diamond" supposedly hidden in the theater,
which unmasks a treasonous political cartoonist, and
involves her in the street gangs of Covent Garden
and the world of nobility.
ISBN-13: 978-1-59643-351-9
ISBN-10: 1-59643-351-5
1. Drury Lane Theatre—Juvenile fiction. [1. Drury Lane Theatre—
Fiction.
2. Orphans—Fiction. 3. London (England)—History—18th century—
Fiction.
4. Great Britain—History—1789-1820—Fiction.] I. Title.
PZ7.G56758Di 2008
[Fic]—dc22
2007023604
10 9 8 7 6 5 4 3 2

Roaring Brook Press books are available for special promotions
and premiums. For details, contact: Director of Special Markets,
Holtzbrinck Publishers.

Book design by Brand X Studios
Printed in the United States of America
First American edition June 2008

THE CRITICS

"Cat Royal has no Rivals!"—R. B. SHERIDAN

"Capital! (apart from the bit about one's underwear)."
—GEORGE, H.R.H. THE PRINCE OF WALES

"Far too dangerous to be put in the hands of innocent children! Burn every copy!"—THOMAS BOWDLER

"Too short."— JAMES BOSWELL

"I have made it required reading for every midshipman." —ADMIRAL NELSON

"Write on, sister."—MARY WOLLSTONECRAFT

"Scandalous."—HANNAH MORE

"It made me realize what bliss it is to be alive today, but to be young is very heaven!"—WILLIAM WORDSWORTH

"Utterly insane!"—H.M. KING GEORGE III

"Revolutionary stuff. Charge her with something quick!"—THE RT. HON. PRIME MINISTER, WILLIAM PITT

"Electrifying!"—BENJAMIN FRANKLIN

"I haven't had time to read it, but I'm sure it is very good anyway."—GEORGE WASHINGTON

"This book should be banned."
—THE LORD CHAMBERLAIN

❧ A NOTE TO THE READER ❧

Be warned, that the story you are about to read is not for the squeamish. I intend to bring you life as I live it. This is not the world of the drawing room and country estate, but backstage at Drury Lane and on the streets of London. If you want to survive in my neighborhood, you have to be prepared to use coarse language that packs a verbal punch. I include a glossary at the back to assist you. But are you bold enough to follow me? If so, read on.

Catherine "Cat" Royal

Contents

✦ Principal Characters ✦

IN THE THEATER

Miss Catherine "Cat" Royal—ward of the theater

Mr. Pedro Hawkins—gifted African violinist, former slave

Mr. Sheridan—playwright, politician, theater owner

Mr. Johnny Smith—the new prompter, with a secret

COVENT GARDEN MARKET

Mr. Syd Fletcher—boxer, leader of the Butcher's boys

Mr. Billy "Boil" Shepherd—leader of rival gang, handy
with the razor

Mr. Jonas Miller—hog-grubber clerk

THE DUKE'S HOUSEHOLD

Lord Francis—son of a duke who wants to be
a chimney sweep

Lady Elizabeth—intelligent and pretty daughter of the duke

Duke of Avon—pro-reform peer and friend of Mr. Sheridan

Mr. Marzi-pain Marchmont—acquaintance of Lord
Francis, a real pain in the arse

The Earl of Ranworth—a nice old gent

Actors, boatmen, rioters, boxing spectators, maids, etc.

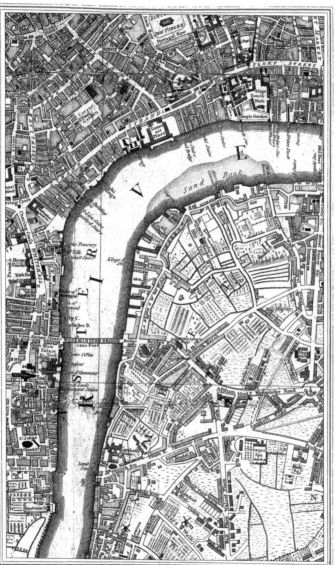

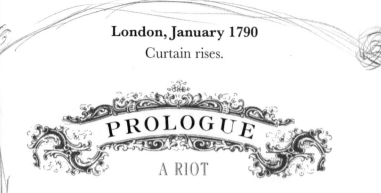

PROLOGUE

A RIOT

Reader, you are set to embark on an adventure about one hidden treasure, two bare-knuckle boxers, three enemies, and four hundred and thirty-eight rioters. It is told by an ignorant and prejudiced author—me. My name is Cat Royal, though how I came to be called this, I will explain later. For the moment I will start with the riot, for that was where the story really began.

It was the opening night of Mr. Salter's new play, *The Mad Father*. I sat as usual curled up behind a curtain in the manager's box, watching the audience as much as I watched the stage. I love a full house: there is always so much to see. The vast auditorium was packed: all London was there, from the flash dandies in the pit to the ha'penny harlots high up in the gods. Candles blazed in the chandeliers, catching on the jewels and polished fans of the ladies in the boxes. It was a gorgeous display.

Tonight the mood of the crowd was dangerous. There was a low buzz in the room like a hive of angry bees threatening to swarm. The theater owner, Mr. Sheridan, was sitting hunched over the box rail, looking like thunder. In the candlelight, the red flush across his face burned brighter than ever. His dark eyes glinted. I am never quite sure what he is thinking, but I guessed that this evening he must be feeling very foolish. In my humble opinion, it had been a mad idea for him to agree to put the play on in the first place, but even I didn't dare mention this to him. I had seen it in rehearsal—an arsy-varsy affair, not a patch on Mr. Sheridan's own comedies, which were guaranteed to have the audience in fits of laughter. Mr. Salter's play by contrast was not worth a fart.

Prejudiced though I was against it, I was alarmed to see that the gentlemen of the pit were exceedingly bored after the first act. Mr. Kemble, our leading actor, had to struggle against a hostile shower of orange peel. I could tell that it would not be long before a more dangerous rain of bottles and rotten vegetables would fall. Some in the audience were climbing over the benches in an attempt to reach the forestage. Leading the vanguard was vile Jonas Miller, from the lawyer's office across the road. You should know, Reader, that he is a real hog-grubber, that one. He thinks so highly of his own taste that he believes he has a right to praise or damn a play by forcing the actors off the stage. Ducking out of the shadows of the box, I filched Mr. Sheridan's opera glasses from his hand and took a swift look at the other parts of the house. The galleries, particularly the footmen in the balconies, were on the point of revolt, giving a crude Anne's fan to the actors, with their white-gloved hands and wigs askew as they pushed and shoved to reach the rail. The ladies were gathering their shawls about them in anticipation of the riot to come. I noticed one party directly opposite was already on his feet, heading for the exit.

"It's not looking pretty, Cat," Mr. Sheridan remarked over his shoulder. He too had read the signs. "I suggest we make a tactical retreat before the oranges are aimed in my direction."

With a nod of agreement, I uncurled from my comfortable lookout. Jonas and his cronies had now reached the spikes guarding the stage from audience invasions. Poor Mr. Kemble faltered in his speech, sensing that he was about to be upstaged by the frenzy of an audience demanding their money back.

"I hope Kemble can turn the play around and stop them ripping up the benches: it cost hundreds of pounds to repair the damage after the last riot," Mr. Sheridan muttered half to himself as I followed him down the dark corridors leading backstage. "I can't afford it. Mr. Salter is costing me far more than he's worth."

I rejoiced inwardly to hear my enemy so criticized by his employer. Ever since Mr. Salter got off the Norwich mail coach and knocked on the door of Drury Lane looking for work as a playwright, he has been no friend of mine. In my defense, I should point out that he started it by calling me a "dirty beggar" and suggesting that the Foundlings Hospital was a more suitable place for an orphan like myself than a theater. Since then, I am not ashamed to admit that it has been open war between us. And as he has been angling for the job of prompter for weeks after Old Carver got too deaf to carry on, he knows that I've been using all my influence with Mr. Sheridan and Mr. Kemble to stop him getting the job.

Leaving the noise of the bellowing, braying audience behind, Mr. Sheridan ducked into the shadowy labyrinth backstage and made his way deftly around the scenery, ropes, and barrels that littered his path. This was the world never seen by the paying public—workshops, storerooms, dressing rooms, and cellars: the underbelly of the theater. You could get lost in here for hours. But Mr. Sheridan did not put a foot wrong; we both knew this place like the back of our hands. We passed Mr. Salter, who was quivering in the wings, his old wig scrunched up in his hands as he gazed in agony at the destruction of his hopes onstage. Mr. Sheridan barely spared him a glance but pressed on without offering a word of comfort, a bitter smile on his lips. He seemed to have forgotten I was with him as he was now striding along, hands clasped behind his back, whistling "Rule, Britannia" under his breath horribly out of tune. His mind had clearly turned to other things. And there were many things that he could be thinking about—in addition to owning the theater, he is a member of Parliament, a leading figure in opposition to Prime Minister Pitt's government, as well as best friend of the Prince of Wales. He has made himself into one of the first men in the country—which is no mean feat for an Irish actor's son, you must agree. I admire him more than anyone I know—though even I am not blind to his shortcomings. You could not spend five minutes among my friends backstage without knowing that his inability to pay wages is probably his chief fault. He is distinctly devious about money matters and always in trouble with someone about his failure to pay up.

With all this on his plate, I could not even begin to imagine what business might be on his mind, but that did not stop me trying to find out. Curious to know where he was going in this purposeful manner, I followed him, slinking behind like his shadow.

Perhaps he was only going for a breath of fresh air? Sure enough, Mr. Sheridan stopped at the stage door and said a few friendly words to Caleb, the doorkeeper, offering him a pinch from his snuffbox, which the old man gratefully received. I lingered in a dark corner, wondering if there would be anything more interesting to see. A stray rioter perhaps?

"Has my visitor arrived yet?" Mr. Sheridan asked Caleb quietly, though I thought his expressive eyes twinkled with more than usual interest to hear the answer.

"No, sir," Caleb replied hoarsely. "Not a sight nor sound of anybody around the back tonight. All the excitement's out front from what I 'ear." The night breeze carried with it the sound of breaking glass and raucous voices; the protest at Mr. Salter's execrable writing had spilled over onto the street.

"Oh, he'll be here all right," said Mr. Sheridan, looking out into the bleak January evening. "He has no choice but to be here. Go get yourself a drink, Caleb. I'll watch the door for a few minutes." There was a chink as he dropped some coins into the doorkeeper's gnarled palm.

"Thank 'ee very much, sir," wheezed Caleb. "I don't mind if I do." He shuffled off in the direction of Bow Street in search of a warming mug of porter.

As soon as the old man had limped out of sight, there was a cough in the darkness beyond the doors. Mr. Sheridan took a step outside.

"Marchmont, is that you?" he called.

Something scuffled over to our right behind a stack of barrels but it was too black to see anything. A rat?

"Anyone there?" challenged Mr. Sheridan, moving toward the sound.

A gentleman stepped out of the night behind his back. He was much taller and slighter than the stocky Mr. Sheridan, swathed in a black cloak and had a three-cornered hat pulled low on his brow, giving him a most villainous appearance. I shrank behind the door curtain, keeping out of sight but within call in case Mr. Sheridan should need help.

"Sherry, my old friend, of course it's me. Why, were you expecting someone else?" the man replied. His thin, high-pitched voice would have sent a shiver down my spine if I hadn't already been trembling in the bitter wind blowing through the open door. I hid deeper in the folds of the door curtain, trying not to sneeze as my nose rubbed against the musty material.

Mr. Sheridan ignored his question. He shifted uneasily, looking about him into the shadows.

"Do you have the diamond?" he asked, speaking so low I could barely hear him.

I swallowed my expression of surprise. No wonder he had sent Caleb away! He did not want anyone to hear this. This was evidently a conversation on which I should not be eavesdropping—that of course made it all the more tempting to listen.

Marchmont must have also noticed Mr. Sheridan's agitation for he laughed in a shrill neigh. "Don't be so worried, old friend. The riot has distracted everyone, as you predicted. The diamond will be with you later tonight. We can slip our jewel across town without anyone noticing."

So Mr. Sheridan had not been as deficient in taste as I thought: the choice of play was deliberate, I noted.

"Good, good," said Mr. Sheridan, relaxing a little. "Would you like to come in for something to take off the chill? I have a few bottles stashed away in my room."

"Of course you do," Marchmont said, with a knowing leer at one of England's most celebrated drinkers. "I dare say I could force down a drop of something. The river was damned cold tonight."

The two men stepped back into the theater. I kept very still, hardly daring to breathe. I would have got away with it too if the fastening of the man's cloak had not snagged on the curtain. He turned to tug it free and caught sight of a pair of white-stockinged legs peeping out.

"What's this?" Marchmont barked. I felt my arm seized in a fierce grip as I was wrenched into the open. Two fingers pinched my ear, dragging me upward so I had to stand on tiptoes or part company with my earlobe. I squealed with the pain and tried to push him off. "A spy? What have you heard, girl?"

Behind Marchmont I could see Mr. Sheridan looking back at me, his face white with shock except for the inflamed patch across his nose that was flushed red like a warning flag.

"Nothing!" I lied.

"I don't believe you! Why were you hiding there? Who's paid you to follow me, eh? Tell me quickly or you'll find yourself at the bottom of the Thames with only the fish to spy on."

He twisted my ear, causing me to yelp in pain a second time.

Mr. Sheridan took a step forward and grabbed Marchmont's wrist, making him release his grip.

"Don't frighten the child, Marchmont. It's only my little Cat. No one's paid her to spy on us." He turned to me, his eyes sparkling with anger at my presumption. "What are you doing here, Cat? What did you hear? Everything, I'll be bound."

I nodded miserably, eyes trained on the shiny caps of his shoes. "Sorry, sir. I just followed you when we got backstage."

"And?" he said threateningly.

"And I stayed to see who you were meeting."

"And?"

"And I heard you talking about the diamond." I looked up to see if I could read my fate in his face.

Surely he wouldn't throw me out onto the

streets after all these years? "But I promise I'll not tell anyone, sir," I ended lamely.

Mr. Sheridan's expression was enigmatic. I could not be sure, but there seemed to be a ghost of a smile hovering around his lips.

"You'll keep my jewel safe for me, won't you, Cat?"

I nodded my head vigorously. "Yes, sir."

"You'll let me know if anyone comes sniffing around for my treasure—anyone that shouldn't be here?"

"Of course, sir."

Marchmont laid an unnaturally white hand on Mr. Sheridan's arm. "Is this wise, Sherry? The girl already knows too much. You should get rid of her."

Mr. Sheridan ruffled my hair. "They've been saying that to me for years but somehow Drury Lane would not be the same without its Cat." He pushed me out of Marchmont's reach. "Run along now and keep your ears open for me, won't you?"

"Yes, sir!" I saluted him before darting away, eager to escape from the presence of Mr. Marchmont. He made my skin crawl.

The conversation I had overheard gave me plenty to think about that night as I settled down in the Sparrow's Nest, the costume storeroom on the top floor of the theater where I was allowed to sleep. The place was misnamed—the magpie would have been a more suitable bird, in view of the treasures that lay scattered through the wardrobe. It was like a museum of curiosities: the regalia of heathen kings lay next to those of Christian saints; chests were filled with the castoffs of Roman emperors and Egyptian queens, now mingled in democratic abandon with the rags of laborers and shepherdesses. I made my bed on the couch with Lady Macduff's velvet cloak for my blanket, careful to blow out my candle as instructed, for one spark in here would set the whole theater ablaze.

So, I thought, staring open-eyed into the darkness, listening to the raucous noises of the night revellers outside as the four hundred and thirty-eight rioters ended their evening smashing bottles and shouting in the street, Mr. Sheridan wanted to hide a treasure in the theater? And he had tasked me to protect it. It was a charge I was determined to take most seriously.

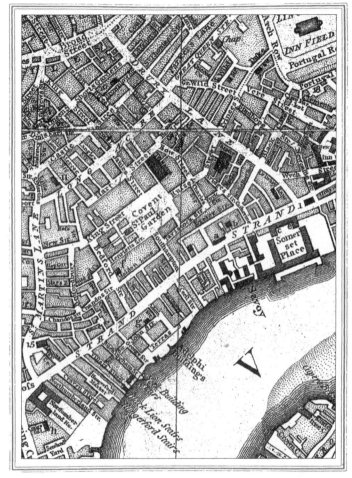

*Act I - In which a spectacular
stage effect goes spectacularly wrong...*

ACT I

SCENE 1—A BALLOON RIDE

It occurs to me now, Reader, that you may be wondering who I am and just what I am doing living in a theater.

My full name is Catherine Royal, known to almost everyone but the vicar and Mr. Salter as Cat. I am four foot four, have long red hair and green eyes, and not a penny that I can call my own. But I am not asking for your pity: I think I am more fortunate than those heiresses of many thousands a year that you read about in sentimental novels, for I live in the most exciting place in the whole wide world: the Theater Royal, Drury Lane, London. Forget everything you've heard about our rival house, Covent Garden, for Drury Lane undoubtedly has the best actors, backstage hands, musicians, and dancers. And I should know, for there is nothing that happens in our theater that I am not aware of—well, almost nothing, as my tale will show.

Why do I live in a theater? you ask. Why am I not at home with my mama and papa? Well, you see, I seem to have lost my parents, or rather, they lost me. Mr. Sheridan himself found the infant me on the theater steps one cold January night in 1780. Rather than hand me on to the Foundlings Hospital, where a scrawny scrap as I was then usually dies in the first few days, he decided to take me in. He even named me after his theater, which explains why my surname is Royal. Mrs. Reid, the head seamstress, says that Mr. Sheridan was drunk at the time or he would never have done anything so soft-hearted. This is probably true. But drunk or not, he picked me up, transported me over the threshold of his theater, and I have not left since. The theater has become my family, and I have become its Cat. It has fed and clothed me, taught me to read and write, and given me employment. There is many an abandoned child who freezes to death on the streets of London in winter—but I was lucky.

And what do I do in the theater? Well, Reader, you may think of it this way. The theater is a kingdom. Mr. Sheridan is our King George (without the fits of madness); Mr. Kemble his prime minister; the actors and actresses the royal family. The different departments in the theater are like the various ministries of government, providing costumes, scenery, music, and dance to keep the royal family in fine form. You could call me the mail coach, running messages about the kingdom. Johnny says I am more like the oppressed masses doing the jobs no one else wants for no wages. He told me to write down that he is the Archbishop of Canterbury as, in his role as prompter, he administers the word to those in need. I wasn't sure if this was blasphemous or not, but he instructed me not to be so lily-livered and put it down in any case.

This brings me to Johnny. Or Mr. Jonathan Smith, as I suppose I should call him if I am to make a proper job of the introduction. I first met him the day after the riot. He was waiting outside Mr. Kemble's office early the next morning when I came down from the Sparrow's Nest with a pile of washing. He was kicking his heels in the corridor and whistling "Rule, Britannia," just as Mr.

Sheridan had the night before, with the difference that his rendition was far more tuneful. He did not see me, perhaps because I only come up to his chest, so he managed to trip me up as I passed.

"Clothead!" I squealed at him as the washing tumbled onto the floor with me on top of it. "Fool!" (You see that I was brought up in the politest society and know how to introduce myself to a gentleman in the most agreeable way.)

Johnny almost fell over himself in his attempt to right his wrong. He hauled me up and began to load me down with the clothes, practically burying me under Miss Stageldoir's smelly stockings.

"I am so sorry, I did not see you there, Miss . . . ?"

I sniffed disdainfully, then regretted this immediately as it brought a rather overwhelming whiff of feet to my nostrils. "Miss Catherine Royal," I said with dignity.

"Miss Catherine Royal," said Johnny, making a low bow, his eyes gleaming mischievously as he squinted up at me. "Will Miss Royal ever forgive her humble servant?" He remained bent over, his face contorted, half-laughing, half-pleading.

I had to smile. "Of course," I said, trying to curtsy to show him that I too could be refined if I tried. Unfortunately, my bob sent the clothes tumbling back to the ground. We bent down together to pick them up. "But you'd better call me Cat, because no one will understand you if you call me Miss Royal."

"Your wish is my command," said Johnny, like the genie out of the Arabian Nights.

I took an instant liking to him: a tall youth with long black hair tied behind in a blue ribbon. His eyes were so brown they were almost black and seemed to dance with laughter. He was also very handsome. I guessed that the girls backstage would all be swooning over him before too long.

"And who are you?" I asked when he did not introduce himself.

"Mr. Jonathan . . ." he hesitated for a moment, "Smith—at your service. Though you can call me Johnny." He gave me a wink.

"Well, Johnny, what are you doing here? Mr. Kemble doesn't usually get in this early."

He fortunately found my impertinent curiosity amusing. He laughed. "Oh, I have an appointment.

You're looking at the new prompter." He stood up and gave another bow, this time as if to an imaginary audience.

"Oh good!" I exclaimed, thinking how angry Mr. Salter would be. "I'm so pleased they've appointed you."

Johnny gave me a queer look. "I'm glad to hear it. Thank you for your vote of confidence. From what Sheridan—Mr. Sheridan—told me, I have to secure your blessing if I am to succeed behind the scenes."

This made me wonder. It was strange to think that someone as important as Mr. Sheridan had thought to mention me to Johnny.

"I'd better get these to the carrier. I'll see you later," I said, a little embarrassed as I clasped the washing tightly to my chest.

"See you later, Catkin."

I could feel his eyes on my back as I made my way down the corridor. I had a warm glow inside, a wonderful sensation like being allowed near Mrs. Reid's fireside on a frosty day.

After sending the washing off on the carrier's cart to the laundress in the nearby village of

Islington, I slipped into the auditorium to see what the damage from last night's riot had been. Long Tom, the tallest of the stagehands, was sweeping up the debris left in the pit. There was a dank, unpleasant smell left by too many bodies crushed together down here night after night. It needed a good airing. How strange to think that somewhere among the squalid splendors of Drury Lane, Mr. Sheridan had hidden a treasure—a perfect diamond, a real jewel in her gilt crown. I wondered where he had put it. The stone would not be large; it could be almost anywhere.

"Much harm done, Tom?" I asked, clambering over the upturned benches to reach him.

"Morning, Cat," he greeted me, gesturing to the pile of rotten vegetables and crumpled-up playbills he had collected. "Not too bad. I'd say we got off lightly seeing what rubbish we inflicted on them last night. We'll be able to open tonight as usual."

I began to help him right the benches but then a door behind us banged open, and a white-haired man with a cloak lined with scarlet flapped down the central aisle. Enter Signor Angelini, musical director.

"*Vivamente*! Quickly now!" he called over his shoulder, clapping his hands rapidly twice.

"*Buon giorno*, Signorina Caterina," he said as he swept past me to the stage.

"*Buon giorno, maestro*." I bobbed a curtsy.

Behind him trailed the members of the orchestra, the cellists carting their instruments under their arms like reluctant dance partners. The orchestra strongly resented being made to rehearse before noon. I spotted Peter Dodsley, a tall, thin man, never seen without his immaculate white wig. He played first violin and was an old friend of mine. He gave me a wink and suppressed a yawn.

"You're up early," I teased. Peter would probably have slept for only a few hours after earning a little extra on the side playing at some fancy party until the small hours of the morning.

"Apparently," said Peter, nodding toward the maestro, "he has something *special* for us."

"I see," I grimaced back. We both knew that this probably meant that Signor Angelini wanted to inflict one of his own modern compositions on the orchestra, some wild piece full of unrestrained emotion. He'd then spend the rest of the day trying unsuccessfully to persuade Mr. Kemble and Mr. Sheridan to let him play it that evening. He'd been turned down so often that they were said to shout "No!" as soon as they saw him darken their doorways holding a sheaf of music.

On this occasion, I heard raised voices coming from the stage. I turned from Peter to see Signor Angelini head to head with the stage manager, Henry Bishop, a powerfully built man with a shock of red hair peeping out from under his ancient wig.

"Absolutely not, sir!" Mr. Bishop was shouting. "You cannot rehearse now. I've got a hot-air balloon descent to practice for tonight's musical farce."

"*Dio*! You think spectacle of stupid balloon dropping from ceiling more important than music?" protested Signor Angelini, pointing at the flies, where the scenery and lighting were suspended.

Mr. Bishop put his hands on his hips and fixed the musician with his one good eye, the other being hidden by a leather patch, a casualty of a special effect with brimstone that went wrong a few years back. "Yes, I do. It's what the public wants and we're going to give it to them. After last night, we can't afford to disappoint them. Mr. Kemble has ordered that we prepare for the farce—and unless I get this contraption working, there will be hell to pay." He stared down the Italian so that even the usually indomitable Signor Angelini withered like a plant in the hot sun.

"*Chiaro*," the signor said, bowing to the stage manager's authority, "but I can practice down there, no?" He pointed to the cramped orchestra pit.

"Of course. You tootle away as much as you like—it won't disturb me and the men."

"If they are men, what are we then?" Peter whispered to me archly. "A bunch of daisies?"

With an irritable flick of his wrist, Signor Angelini directed his players to their places in the pit. Peter gave me a nod of farewell and settled himself down at his usual station at the front of the orchestra.

Behind him, ropes began to creak as Mr. Bishop's team started dropping and raising the mock air balloon, a copy of the amazing Montgolfier craft that they say really flew over Paris in 1783. Imagine, Reader: men taking flight like a bird for the first time since Icarus! We are living in exciting times. The balloon was a sumptuous piece of scenery—a circular frame draped in blue and yellow silks over a large wicker basket which was to hold the actors. I was most desirous to have a ride in it ever since seeing it under construction, so I perched hopefully on the edge of the stage waiting to see if Mr. Bishop needed any volunteers for a test flight.

"So, maestro, where is the music?" asked Peter with a hint of resignation in his voice as he bowed to the inevitable.

"No new music," said Signor Angelini, rifling through his sheets, scattering them to the floor like seed corn. I jumped down to gather them up for him. "No, today we 'ave a new player to join us. "'E will be performing in the play."

Peter looked about him but could spot only the familiar faces of his colleagues.

"Where is he? What does he play?" he asked.

Signor Angelini did not answer; he clapped his hands twice again and barked, "Pedro, come!" The main doors to the auditorium swung open and a small figure could be seen silhouetted against the daylight streaming in from outside. The newcomer made his way confidently down the aisle to the orchestra pit and bowed low to Signor Angelini. With lightning swiftness, he then undid the case he held clutched under his arm, took out a violin and bow, and stood, feet apart, ready to play.

The new player was a boy no older than me, but he had the darkest skin of any child I had ever seen. Dressed in yellow and blue livery, his skin gleamed like the ebony keys on the pianoforte. I realized then that he must be from Africa, one of the people taken forcibly from their homes to work as slaves on the plantations of the West Indies. You've doubtless read about them since the recent exertions of the Abolitionists to bring their plight to the public's attention. But how he had ended up in Drury Lane with a violin under his chin was anyone's guess.

"Who's the boy, maestro?" asked Peter dubiously, eyeing the violin as if it might explode at any moment.

"Is this a joke?" muttered the horn player, an unpleasant fellow who played his instrument most crudely (Peter has nicknamed him the brass-belcher but I would be grateful if you did not pass this on). "It's bad enough with those bare-legged hoydens flitting about in the ballet; surely you don't expect us to play with performing monkeys too?" He scowled at Pedro, but the boy did not flinch. Pedro kept his gaze fixed on the conductor, his posture confident and dignified, though from the tightening of a muscle in his jaw I could tell he was offended.

"Tcht!" hissed Signor Angelini, waving an angry finger at the horn player. "Enough of your rudeness, barbarian. The boy can play like an angel. Pedro, start at the first movement."

The horn player snorted scornfully. Now firmly on the boy's side, I watched with bated breath as he took a moment to compose himself. He then launched into the piece, making the notes dance and flutter about the strings in a cloud of butterfly melodies, wiping the sneer off the face of the horn player.

"Enough," interrupted Signor Angelini, cutting the stream of music off abruptly with a flick of his baton. "The opening of the second, if you please."

Pedro took a deep breath, eyes closed, and now made his violin sing with such sweet sadness that I felt a sob rise in my throat. After only a few passages, Peter wept unashamedly into his white handkerchief, his shoulders heaving with emotion. Even the noises from the stage crew had stopped as Mr. Bishop and his men stood still to listen to the performance.

"Now the end of the third," said the conductor, looking around at the subdued audience with a triumphant smile.

The boy raised his bow and set off at a terrific pace, a virtuoso dash through the music, taking every obstacle in his path like a thoroughbred horse. Sweat beaded on his brow as he came to the conclusion, making the bow fly so fast that it became a blur. He finished on three victorious notes and was rewarded by the spontaneous applause of the orchestra and stage crew, as well as myself.

"Very impressive!" said Peter loudly. "That was Mozart as he should be played."

Pedro, who had been studiously avoiding anyone's eye but Signor Angelini's, now shot a grateful look toward the first violin. The two musicians had come to a mutual understanding.

"Indeed, Mr. Dodsley," said the signor. "But, *tristemente*, Pedro will not be sitting with you to play Mozart. 'E will be playing the part of the Mogul Prince in the farce." The signor tapped his music stand with his baton. "Attention, gentlemen! Let us start at bar thirty."

The music rehearsal now properly under way, I drifted off to see how work on the balloon was progressing. The stagehands were groaning in the wings as they tugged like mariners hoisting a sail, making the machine rise and fall slowly. I approached Mr. Bishop with caution.

"Will it work?" I asked tentatively. I was never sure of my reception from Mr. Bishop. Mostly he tolerated me, but occasionally he would scold me as a useful vent for his anger if he was having a bad day.

Perhaps the music had mellowed him, but he appeared to be in a good humor.

"It might," he said, thoughtfully scratching his chin, examining the ropes and pulleys stretching up to the galleries above.

"Can I be of assistance? I mean, would you like to try it with someone inside?"

Mr. Bishop looked down at me, calculating my weight. "That's not a bad idea. You're a fraction of the weight of Mr. Andrews, so it would give the lads something to practice on before we try the full burden. In you go, Cat."

With a shout to his men, he lifted me into the basket and stood back.

"Take her away!" he ordered.

With a jolt, the basket began to move slowly up from the floor, ropes creaking in the blocks above. This must be what it is like to fly, I thought. I could see the will-o'-the-wisp lights of the orchestra in the pit below, the gleam of the whites of the African boy's upturned eyes as he watched me rise above him. Even the vast stage began to look very small. The white cross that marked the trapdoor in the floor looked tiny from up here.

"One more heave and that should do it!" bellowed Mr. Bishop, standing underneath to monitor my progress. I leaned over the side to give him a cheery wave.

"Aargh!"

It was my scream that echoed around the stage as the rope holding the front of the basket came away from its fastening, tipping its contents—me—out forward head over heels. As I fell, I just managed to grab onto a handle on the rim of the basket and ended up dangling twenty feet from the ground.

"Stop!" yelled Mr. Bishop.

The balloon lurched to a standstill. There was another jolt, and the tackle holding a second rope gave way, snaking to the floor like a whip. The orchestra ground to a dissonant halt.

"Hang on, Cat!" Mr. Bishop shouted quite unnecessarily. As if I was going to do anything else.

"Can you lower her?" he shouted into the wings.

"The block's jammed," Long Tom shouted back.

There was a hubbub of noise below me as people ran across the stage. Swinging like a pendulum, my skirts billowing in a most undignified manner, I clung on with my fingers, praying rescue would come quickly. Taking a terrifying glance downward I saw one of the stage crew running on with a big piece of canvas, passing it out to the rest to form a net to catch me. Half the orchestra had also climbed onto the stage and were grabbing hold of the canvas. I felt sick with fear. Surely it was too far for me to fall, even if they caught me?

Someone else must have been thinking the same thing, for a new voice piped up.

"She will break her neck if she jumps from there." It was the boy violinist. He leaped lightly onto the stage.

"He's right," chimed in Peter, climbing up beside him. "Don't you have a ladder?"

"Not long enough," said Mr. Bishop.

"No need for a ladder," said Pedro.

As I twirled in the air, I watched the boy bound across the stage, nimble as a squirrel, leap onto the rope Long Tom had used to haul the basket into the air, and begin shinnying up it.

"Somebody stop the boy. 'E'll kill 'imself!" shrieked Signor Angelini, but Pedro was far out of reach before anyone grabbed the rope.

He climbed right up into the roof to the jammed block of the pulley system and leaped across to transfer to the rope leading down to the basket. I gave renewed shrieks as the basket began to sway alarmingly, my grip sliding on the woven wicker. Calmly, Pedro slithered down the rope to stand on the upturned edge of the basket. Twisting one leg around the rope, he stretched over the side and held out his arm to me.

"Here, take my hand," he said, holding it out inches from mine.

"I can't!" I whispered, now almost paralyzed with fright. "I can't let go."

With an impatient whistle between his teeth, Pedro let himself slide a little farther over the edge so that he was now dangling upside down alongside me.

"Is that better?" he asked cheerfully, grabbing both my wrists in his hands. "Trust me now?"

"Yes," I gasped. I let go.

Like some bizarre circus act, we swung there for a few moments, Pedro upside down, me dangling in his grip, before he heaved me up onto the upright side of the basket.

"Here, hold on to this," he said, placing my hands on the rope. "I'll see if I can unblock it above."

Now that I was no longer hanging by my fingertips, my pride was returning. If Pedro could climb the ropes, then so could I.

"No, I'll follow you," I said, kicking off my leather shoes for a better grip. They tumbled to the ground, hitting someone in the crowd gathered below. The victim cursed loudly.

Pedro shook his head. "English girls don't climb," he said. "Sit still."

"This one does." Not waiting for him, I started to shinny up the rope as I had seen him do. It wasn't easy: I had to fight off the silk canopy of the balloon as it billowed around me. But I'd been playing backstage all my life, climbing over bits of scenery and scaling the odd rope, if never one so high, so I refused to be put to shame by this newcomer. After all, I was the girl who had perfected the one-armed cartwheel during many hours playing alone on the empty stage. I could do it.

Or perhaps not.

I had clambered up to the tackle and seen what was to come next. I bit my lip. The jump that Pedro had made looked a very long way from here. A one-armed cartwheel was one thing; a leap across this chasm another.

"Stay there, Catkin!" someone shouted below. "Don't do anything stupid."

But I could now feel Pedro's breath literally hot on my heels. For the national honor, I had to do it. I held out my arm over the void, preparing to leap.

"No good like that," Pedro panted below. "Swing closer."

The rope began to sway. I glanced down and saw Pedro hanging off it to make it move to and fro, each time bringing us closer to the rope at the side of the stage. Catching on quickly, I began to copy him. The balloon and basket creaked ominously below. I could hear Mr. Bishop clearing the stage in case something larger than my slipper fell on a head. But now the rope was almost within reach.

"Ready?" asked Pedro. "Next time, we go. I count to three—one, two, three!"

And we were off, both letting go with one hand to stretch across and hook the rope. Like acrobats, we hung straddled between the two ropes before swinging over to hold on to the one leading to the ground. Pedro slid down as if the rope was greased; I followed gingerly, having no desire to make a mistake at the last moment.

Mr. Bishop was waiting to lift me to the floor.

"I think you'd better not let Mr. Andrews try it just yet," I panted with relief as my feet hit firm ground.

Mr. Bishop scratched his head, pushing his wig onto the back of his head. "No, you're right there, Cat. Back to the drawing board on the ropes."

"I didn't notice that in the script," said Johnny Smith, coming forward to pat Pedro on the back. Johnny handed me my shoes with a rueful grin. I noticed that he had a red heel-shaped mark on his forehead.

Pedro shrugged; his face resumed its disengaged look. It made me think that he was probably used to being treated badly and found it safest to keep himself to himself. He didn't know yet that he was among friends at Drury Lane. As he turned to leave the stage, I darted forward and caught him by the arm.

"Thank you," I said, trying to coax a smile from him.

He looked at me with his large brown eyes and seemed on the point of saying something when the horn player blurted out:

"What did I tell you? Performing monkeys— and now we've got two of them. And one of them wears a skirt!"

"Hold your tongue, Harding," said Peter, his pale eyes flashing angrily at the offender.

I wheeled around, fists balled, ready to lash out at the horn player.

"I didn't see you risking your neck to save me," I said tartly. "At least there was one gentleman brave enough to do so."

"Gentleman! Pah!" mocked Mr. Harding, leering at me. "I saw no gentleman."

"Yes, gentleman," I said defiantly.

"She's right," chipped in Johnny from behind me. "It's the manners that make the man, not the color of his skin."

The other musicians murmured their agreement, forcing Mr. Harding to back down this time. He retreated to the orchestra pit, grumbling loudly. Satisfied that I had won this bout of verbal sparring, I turned back to speak to Pedro, but he had gone.

SCENE 2—GANG LEADER

"Where is 'e?" asked Signor Angelini. "We still 'ave much to do!"

"Perhaps he has gone to have his costume fitted?" suggested Peter with a languid wave towards the rear of the stage. "You did tell him that Mrs. Reid wanted to see him."

"Shall I go and look for him?" I asked, eager to find out more about my rescuer.

Signor Angelini nodded. "If you would, Caterina. We 'ave wasted enough of time already this morning. If we do not want the music to be a farce as well as the play, we must work very 'ard."

"Wasted!" protested Peter, putting an arm around my shoulders and giving me a comforting squeeze. "Only so we could save our Cat!"

"Then she can help repair the delays by finding 'im for me," Signor Angelini said briskly, ushering the orchestra back to their places. "Run, Caterina. Tell the boy 'e won't be in trouble if 'e gets back in the next quarter of an hour. After that, 'e will regret it." He swished his baton, giving me no doubt that he intended to apply it to Pedro if he was still missing after that time.

I ran as fast as I could up the rickety stairs leading to the Sparrow's Nest. Mrs. Reid was sitting with Sarah Bowers, heads bent over a long velvet train that had got ripped in the scuffle to leave the stage last night. A shaft of smoky light fell across their laps from the window above their heads, dust motes dancing in the beam like tiny fairies. Their needles twinkled as they plied them in and out of the cloth with great skill—a skill I had never been able to acquire despite all of Mrs. Reid's lessons.

"Is Pedro here?" I asked breathlessly.

Mrs. Reid looked up, her mouth full of pins. "Who, dear?"

"Pedro. The Mogul Prince."

She still looked blank.

"The black boy."

"No, dear. We've not seen anyone. But if you do see our prince, tell him his costume is ready for fitting."

"I will," I shouted as I clattered back down the stairs.

What had become of him? He was much in demand but nowhere to be seen backstage. True, Reader; there were plenty of places to hide if you knew your way around, but Pedro had never been here before as far as I knew, and in any case, why would he be hiding? He seemed too serious a character to indulge in such childish play, particularly when no one else was in the game. It was a puzzle.

I sat on the bottom step for a moment, thinking. If he wasn't hiding and he wasn't backstage or front of house, then he must have gone outside. Yes, that was it. The brass-belcher's remarks must have upset him more than I had realized. Pedro had deserved praise, not insults for doing what he did. He had probably gone outside to get away from us all.

I ran to the stage door. It stood open, but there was no sign of Caleb. This was unusual, for if Caleb were called away for any reason, he would not leave the door like that. This confirmed my theory. I emerged into the little courtyard that led onto Russell Street. It too was deserted. Where would he have gone? Left toward Covent Garden, or right toward Drury Lane? I stood indecisively, trying to see the place as he would have seen it. He probably had not meant to go far. Perhaps he just wanted some air? Well, if he wanted open spaces, he would have headed for the market. There, despite the constant din of the fruit and vegetable sellers crying out the latest bargains, the wagons passing to and fro, not to mention the clucking of the poultry on the butcher's block, the only uninterrupted view of the sky in this part of town opened up. I felt a sudden stab of concern for him. A boy in fine livery would stick out like a sore thumb among the tough apprentices of the market—I should know, for most of them were my friends.

I had a bad time negotiating the busy crossing on Bow Street. It was packed with people going about their business. A bailiff hurried by with his men, loaded down with goods they must have just seized from some poor debtor. A hawker of ballads stood on the corner crying out his latest wares.

"You 'eard it 'ere first, ladies and gents: the dying speech of John Jeffreys, traitor, thief, and murderer. "'Ot off the press! 'Ear 'ow 'e laments 'is wicked crimes afore 'e took the drop at Newgate last week."

I gave the ballad maker a wide berth, having no taste for such grisly songs. In any case, they were all pure invention: the unfortunate Jeffreys would have had no time for long versified speeches before the trap opened, and certainly no time afterward unless he revived on the table before the anatomy men dissected his body.

My attempt to steer a path through the crowd gathered around the ballad seller had the unfortunate consequence of bringing my feet plumb into the middle of some freshly dropped horse manure. I cursed. To add insult to injury, a black coach and four with a ducal crest rattled by, spraying me with the icy water from a puddle outside the Magistrates' Court. I hopped back too late, colliding with one of the Bow Street runners, our local law enforcers. He pushed me roughly away.

"Watch where you're going, you idiot!" he bellowed, brushing down his uniform.

"That goes double for you, you old fogrum!" I replied, and dashed across the road before he could box my ears.

(I should perhaps explain here for the more delicate among my readers that a different deportment is required on the streets of London than is usually taught to young ladies and gentlemen. Believe me when I assure you that I would not have survived long in my present situation if I had not learned this early on. I hope you are not unduly shocked, for there is much more of the like to come.)

I ran as fast as I could out onto the piazza and dodged under one of the arches of the houses flanking the marketplace. I shook out my skirt and scraped my shoes on a piece of old sacking lying in the corner. Thankfully, the cold weather had quelled some of the riper odors of the street: the refuse, piss, and dung that gave our streets their distinctive odor were noticeably less overwhelming this morning. This was just as well as I was now carrying most of it on my shoes and skirt. But the cold had another consequence: having neglected to put on a shawl over my woolen dress, I was already shivering. Time to find the violinist and get back into the warm.

I looked around the piazza. It was a crisp winter's day—the painted houses stood out gaily against the bright blue sky, each roof ridge, each chimney pot sharp and distinct. At first I saw nothing unusual; just the normal collection of servants making purchases, stallholders waylaying the naive with rotten fruits hidden under their most gleaming articles for sale, apprentice boys lounging outside the inns finishing a late breakfast, gentlemen passing in and out of the coffeehouses.

Then I spotted him. I had not seen him at first because he was, as I had feared, surrounded by a crowd of some of the roughest boys of the market, pushed up against the stone monument in the center of the square. Foremost among them was a tall, thin youth of about seventeen with a close-cropped head of dark hair. It was Billy Shepherd, the leader of one of the gangs that vie for control of the market underworld. I've known Billy ever since I first played on the streets: he was a bully then and shows no signs of improvement as he gets older. Of course, he is by no means the only tyrant in Covent Garden. The thing that makes Billy different, that has thrust him to the head of his gang, is that he is clever. He links a total absence of moral scruples with the cunning of a fox. Let me put it this way: if the Devil challenged him to a sinning match, and they were taking bets, I'd put my money on Billy to win. You don't believe me? Well, here's my shilling, Reader: put yours down on the table and we'll see who's the richer at the end of the adventure.

Knowing Billy as I do, I looked anxiously around, wondering if Syd's gang was anywhere in sight. Syd was Billy's rival for mastery of the square. Though a gentle giant, Syd had a mean pair of fists when roused to defend his territory. If I could persuade him to take Pedro under his wing, he would look after him. Unfortunately, I could see neither hide nor hair of my friend. I was on my own if I wanted to return Pedro to the theater in one piece. And I had better act quickly, for Billy now advanced on Pedro and grabbed him by the jacket. Pedro stared back at him in disbelief, confused by the attack he had done nothing to provoke. He didn't understand that Billy needed no excuse.

"'Oi! Billy!" I shouted, running over the cobbles to reach them. "Leave him! He's with me!"

Billy leaned coolly against a pillar, pinning Pedro by the throat. A couple of his burly mates chuckled as I came sliding to a stop at the bottom of the steps to the monument.

"Found yourself a beau, 'ave you, Cat?" he sneered. "Scraping the barrel with this one, ain't you? What's wrong with one of us?" His eyes, pieces of ice in his pasty face, sparkled maliciously as he looked down at me.

"Oh, hold your tongue!" I snapped back, annoyed to feel that I was blushing. "He's not my beau. I met him only this morning but he saved my neck at the theater just now."

"Saved your pretty white neck, did he?" said Billy. "Well, ain't that nice to 'ear. I tell you what, if you give me a kiss, I'll let him go." He puckered up his ugly fat lips and waited. His gang all laughed as if Billy was the sharpest wit in London.

"Kiss my arse, you toad! I'll smack you in the face if you don't let him go this instant!"

"Ooo! I am scared!" Billy said in a mock whine. "The little cat will get out her claws, will she? 'Elp, boys, I'm terrified."

His cronies sniggered again. One with a sharp nose like the snout of a ferret made a meowing sound behind me, plunging them into fresh paroxysms of mirth.

"I'm warning you!" I said, taking a step toward Billy. I did not know what I was going to do, but anger was driving me recklessly on, like a runaway horse pulling a carriage downhill.

But at least my rage produced one good effect: Billy released his hold on Pedro and swaggered toward me as if he owned the whole market and everything in it—including me. "Or what? Are you askin' for a beatin'? 'Cause I'll give you one, even though you are a girl. Mind you, you're no lady, so it don't count." He gave me an evil grin, displaying his row of blackened teeth. "You're just a daggle-tail 'oo can speak like a duchess when it suits but can't wash off the stink of the gutter no matter 'ow you pretend to your fine friends in the theater."

"A daggle-tail cat!" repeated Ferret-Features with an appreciative chuckle.

I was searching for a suitably tart response when Pedro, his fists raised, scrambled in to stand between me and Billy.

"Don't you dare touch her!" he challenged.

Even I had to admit, my champion's threat was not very impressive. He looked as if one stout blow would knock him to kingdom come. But I appreciated his courage all the same.

"Or what, Blackie?" jeered Billy. "You want a gob-full of claret too, eh?"

"Leave him out of this!" I said angrily.

Billy flicked a contemptuous look at Pedro. "Wot ya think, boys? Our Cat 'ere 'as fallen for 'is dusky charms." Billy pushed Pedro aside and tucked me under his sweaty armpit. "We can't 'ave our English girls messin' with no African slave boys, can we now?"

I struggled to free myself from his arm, but he continued to tow me away. If I didn't do something quickly, he would bring his boys in against Pedro in a lynch mob. There was nothing the London youth liked better than a bit of foreigner-bashing. I had to think of something to draw their fire away from him.

But the African wasn't helping. "I'm no slave!" declared Pedro proudly, standing up erect.

"Let me go, you fathead!" I protested, punching Billy ineffectually in the ribs to get him to release me. "Back off, Billy *Boil*!"

Billy winced. He did indeed have the misfortune to have a large inflamed spot on the end of his nose. I had not realized that he was so sensitive about it—if I had, I would have employed the insult sooner. He shoved me roughly away, onto the cobbles, and called me a name that you do not hear in polite company. He then aimed a kick at me.

"Run!" I yelled at Pedro as I picked myself up and made a dash for home. I did not even look around to see if he was following. I had done my best by distracting Billy; Pedro would have to rely on his own wits for the rest. At least in part the trick had worked, for I could hear the thunder of footsteps on my heels: Billy and his boys were after me. I leapfrogged over a grocer's stall, knocking over a crate of apples as I passed through. A boy cursed behind me as he fell to the ground, feet forced from under him by the green ammunition I had let loose.

"Come back 'ere, you vandal!" shouted the unfortunate owner of the stall, but I was not fool enough to obey him.

Out of the corner of my eye, I saw Pedro running parallel, chased by two of Billy's thugs. He was outstripping them easily and appeared to stand a better chance of getting home in one piece than I did. I could hear the panting breath of someone hot on my heels. If I didn't get out of sight, it was all up for me. I took a sharp right, dodging out of view of my pursuers for a few precious seconds, and dived under the cheesemonger's stall. Mrs. Peters was minding the shop—a lucky thing for me, for she was known to be a kindhearted woman.

"Hide me, please!" I hissed to her plump ankles.

"Lawd love us, Cat!" she muttered. "What scrape 'ave you got into now?"

I had no time to reply, for Billy Shepherd had arrived at her stall. I shrank close to a churn, hoping he would not think to look under the table. My hiding place had the sour smell of milk about to spoil, but in my present situation I could not afford to be too particular.

"'Oi, missus! Which way she go?" asked Billy, panting hard.

"'Oo's that?" Mrs. Peters replied with forced cheerfulness, though I could see her knuckles were white as she clenched a cloth by her side. All of the stallholders had reason to fear Billy Shepherd. He was a nasty piece of work who would not think twice about wrecking their business if it suited him. They had been appealing to Syd to do something about Billy, and we all knew a confrontation was brewing.

"Don't be clever with me," growled Billy. "Cat—that red-'aired girl from the theater. 'Oo else d'you think I mean?"

"Oh, 'er," said Mrs. Peters as if the daylight of understanding was just dawning in her benighted mind. "I saw 'er run off down Russell Street as if the devil 'imself were after 'er."

Billy swore. "I don't believe you, you old cow. She couldn't get so far so fast."

"If you don't believe me, search my stall then— and 'is—and 'ers." She waved her cloth at the other stallholders. This was a high-risk strategy on her part. I slid as close as I could to the churn, feeling the metal cold on my cheek. "I've got nuffink to 'ide from the likes of you."

"Watch it, woman, or my boys will be paying you a call one of these nights."

Mrs. Peters fell silent. Would Billy take up her invitation to search the stall? If he did, I was dead. But perhaps the thought of poking around through the highly smelling cheeses deterred him. He hesitated just long enough for one of his boys to come running back to him.

"Billy, Blackie's been spotted. Over 'ere!"

The hobnailed boots thundered off across the cobbles on the scent of a new quarry. I waited till the din had died away completely and then scrambled out of my hiding place.

"Thanks, Mrs. Peters," I said gratefully, gulping breaths of fresh air.

"Don't you do that to me again, Cat!" she said, venting her fury by hacking at a round cheese the size of a cartwheel axle.

"Sorry. I didn't mean to get you into trouble."

She wiped her forehead with the back of her hand and stood looking at me, her hands on her hips. "I know, dearie, but you stay out of 'is way, won't you? Or you'll be found in the gutter one mornin' with your throat slit like wot 'appened to poor Nat Perkins." She looked around the edge of her stall, checking that the coast was clear. "You'd better get out of 'ere while you can."

I nodded and headed off southward, intending to circle around and enter the theater from the Drury Lane side. I just hoped that Pedro had managed to get away too.

I found him leaning over a water fountain near the stage door. His fine livery was in tatters and he had a bloodied nose and black eye. He looked up as I approached and gave me a nod, his white teeth stained with blood from a cut to his mouth.

"You got away too then?" he asked.

"Better than you, by the looks of it."

He shrugged. "I took a wrong turn but there was only one of them by the time he caught up with me—the small one. I soon sorted him out and got away before the others arrived."

"Sorted him out?" I asked incredulously. I'd not put Pedro down as a street fighter.

"I can look after myself, you know."

"So you didn't need my help then?" I asked sarcastically. "I wish you'd told me, for I'd've spared myself a lot of trouble. I s'pose you'd've beaten them all single-handed, would you?"

"Well, I have to admit that it wasn't looking promising until you showed up." He shook the water off his face and dusted down his ruined clothes. "Shall we go in?"

He didn't seem to realize just how close we had come to serious injury. "You may have dealt out one beating this morning," I told him grumpily, 'but we both face another when they see what a state you're in."

"Beatings are nothing new. Thank you for coming to help me, Miss Cat." He gave me a mocking bow.

I could not help but smile at his flamboyant flourish. He had bowed as if I were a duchess.

"It's just Cat, Pedro. You saved me from the balloon; I rescued you from the Boil. So, we're even then?"

"Yes, we're quits."

It was only as we reached the safety of the theater that it really struck me that we hadn't heard the last of this morning's escapade. I had made myself a very formidable enemy in Billy "Boil" Shepherd—and his enemies had the unfortunate habit of meeting sudden ends down dark alleyways. Not a pleasant thought.

SCENE 3—A TRIUMPH

As I had predicted, we were both soundly beaten for arriving back at the theater covered in mud and, in Pedro's case, blood. No one wanted to hear our explanations. As far as Signor Angelini was concerned, the only thing that mattered was that Pedro had missed an hour of rehearsal time and returned having spoiled both his clothes and appearance. As for me, Mrs. Reid did not look kindly upon my mud-spattered skirts nor on the part she assumed I had played in ruining her Mogul Prince.

"It's all very well for you to cry, missee," she scolded as I nursed my hands, raw from the blows she had just inflicted, "but you should have thought first before you led the boy off into the streets. If you want to stay at Drury Lane, you have to start acting like a lady, not like a street beggar's brat."

"I didn't lead him anywhere!" I protested, outraged by the unfairness of her accusations.

"I was saving him from being mobbed by the market gangs!"

"Well, you didn't do a very good job, did you?" she replied, stabbing a pin into Pedro's costume as he stood patiently waiting for her to finish. He had been thrashed by Signor Angelini but I will not tell you where. Suffice to say that the beating will not interfere with his violin playing nor be visible to the public. He winced as she tugged on a red silk sash but then, seeing that I was watching, he gave me a wink when her back was turned.

Sarah Bowers entered carrying an enormous confection on a tray. I looked again: it wasn't a dessert as I had at first thought but a lavishly decorated turban of pale pink.

"'Ere you go," said Sarah, ramming the hat on Pedro's head so that it covered the cut on his right temple. "I've gone to town with the jools—they should take eyes off that there black 'un of yours."

Indeed the twinkling gemstones were dazzling even in the pale light of the Sparrow's Nest; it was not hard to imagine them in their full splendor under the chandeliers. But Sarah's talk of jewels reminded me of another subject I had almost forgotten in today's adventures.

"Are those real?" I asked, stretching up to tap on the big ruby set in the center of the turban. A white ostrich feather bobbed over Pedro's head like a swan's neck dipping into a silken stream.

"I certainly hope so," said Pedro, squinting at himself in the mirror, "because then I'll be on the first boat to France and will live off my riches for the rest of my days."

Mellowing a little as she admired the effect of the costume over which she had slaved so hard, Mrs. Reid laughed. "You won't get far with those, my lad; they are all paste. Gimcrack rubbish the lot of them. The feather's worth more than they are put together—all the way from Africa, would you believe it! So mind you see that no harm comes to it if you don't want a second beating!" Her nearsighted eyes glared a warning at him in the mirror as she fixed a single pearl earring in his lobe.

Pedro nodded, sending the ostrich feather into a swaying dance.

"Mind you, you rarely see the real thing, Cat," added Sarah, arranging the folds of the turban. "When the ladies sit in the boxes with ropes of pearls and diamonds around their necks, you know they're mostly fake. There's many a duchess with her jools laid up in lavender, if the rumors be true."

"Laid up in lavender?" I asked.

"At the pawnbrokers, dear," explained Mrs. Reid, "to pay gambling debts usually. So think about that if ever you are tempted to try your luck at the card table." She gave Sarah and me a cautionary look over the top of her glasses.

I was very unlikely to face that temptation. No one could possibly think I had money to lose in a card game, let alone jewels. But perhaps Mrs. Reid could help me with the mystery of Mr. Sheridan's diamond.

"Mrs. Reid," I began, passing her the tape measure that had fallen to the floor, "if you had a real jewel, where would you keep it for safety?"

"Locked in a big iron chest in the Tower of London, guards on the door day and night," she chuckled. "If only . . ."

"Forget the chest," said Sarah, throwing a shovelful of coal onto the fire. "Just give me the guards, six foot tall and 'andsome as can be." She stood up and mimed flouncing across the hearth rug like a fine lady, swinging a jewel on the end of a chain around her neck.

"You bold madam!" laughed Mrs. Reid. "You'll come to no good, you will, if you carry on like that. Now, young man, take off your finery, and Cat can show you where to get something to eat before the show starts. You've not got long."

Grabbing some small beer, cold meat, bread, and sweet wrinkled apples from the table laid out in the green room, Pedro and I made our picnic in my favorite hideaway of the manager's box. Already the early arrivals were taking their seats in the pit, and a number of servants were lounging in the galleries, saving places for their masters and mistresses. The stage was empty—the balloon (now repaired) was well hidden in the flies so that it could descend unheralded to the amazement of the crowd. Pedro had a lot to play against if he was to make his mark tonight.

"I'll watch you from here if Mr. Sheridan lets me," I told him. He had gone very quiet, and I suspected that nerves were beginning to have an effect on him. "Are you nervous?"

Pedro shook his head, the pearl earring that he had not taken off glinting in the candlelight. "No, I'm not nervous. I was just thinking about all the other theaters I've performed in. This one is undoubtedly the grandest." He looked about him, taking in the raked seating capable of accommodating thousands of London's finest citizens—as well as some of her worst. "You really live here?"

"All my life," I replied simply. "And you?"

He shrugged. "I don't remember much about the early years except . . ." He paused, thinking back, ". . . friendly faces and a hot sun."

"So how did you get to drizzly, cold London?" I asked, encouraging this new mood for shared confidences.

Pedro's face took on a hardened, embittered expression.

"When I was still an infant, my people were sold by our enemies to the slavers. We were split up. I got lucky, I suppose you would say, for on the voyage to the colonies I caught the eye of a gentleman, a Mr. Hawkins. He saw me playing on a sailor's pipe one day—I'd managed to get out of the hell belowdecks by entertaining the crew. He bought me and spent a few years training me up as a violinist. Then he got some of his money back by sending me on tour in the southwest, performing in theaters and private houses. That lasted for a couple of seasons and then I was sold on to Signor Angelini last month."

"Sold? So you are a slave then?" I asked curiously.

Pedro flashed me a dangerous look. "I am no such thing. I am an apprentice musician under articles to Signor Angelini. Once on the shores of your country, I became free—as free as you are."

"Sorry," I mumbled, realizing I had offended him. "So you can leave when you like? You can go home?"

He gave a hollow laugh. "Home? Where is that, pray? My family were all sold for slaves. If they are still alive, how could I ever find them? I can't even remember my proper name." He looked at me angrily, as if I was somehow partly to blame for his misfortune. He wasn't to know that, though describing a very different life, it sounded to me as if Pedro and I shared much in common: we had both been thrown out into the world at an early age and were now cut off from our origins. I had often wondered what name my mother had given me. I had vague memories of a woman caring for me—I sometimes dreamed of her but no image remained in my waking mind. But at least I knew exactly why I had ended up as Cat.

"So why are you called Pedro?" I asked.

"That was the name of my first master's dog—you see how highly he valued me," Pedro replied with an ironic smile. "My second name is Hawkins, after him. But I'm going to make my own name now. I won't be anyone's performing monkey any longer. Now I've reached London, I'm going to make my name as the best musician in Europe." He held his head proudly, glaring down at the audience below as if challenging them to refuse his claim.

"I can believe it," I replied.

He raised his mug of beer to acknowledge my remark and took a swig. Wiping his mouth, he then asked:

"And what about you? What are you going to do when you are too old to live here?"

I was taken aback. I had never considered a life when I was not living backstage at Drury Lane. But he was right: a day would come when I could no longer bed down on the costumes in the Sparrow's Nest. I did not want him to think that I was completely without talent, unable to take care of myself.

"I'm going to be a writer," I said on impulse. "I'll write for the stage." Pedro gave me a skeptical look. "I've been taught to read and write by the old prompter. He always told me that there was no better education to be had anywhere in the world. Shakespeare, Dryden, Johnson—I've read them all. I speak French with the ballerinas—and I can read it too."

"But you're a girl," he said dismissively. He clearly didn't think very much of my talents.

It was my turn to get angry. "So? Women can make a lot of money from writing. Look at Mrs. Radcliffe and Mrs. Inchbald."

He snorted. "And what have you got to write about? Have you traveled the world? Have you been to the Indies and the Americas? Have you moved in high society like I have?"

"No, but at least I wasn't carrying a tray of drinks at the time!" I answered angrily.

He laughed. "Touché."

"What do you mean by that?"

"Touché—a hit. It's from fencing—a hobby of my old master."

"Oh." I was feeling quite out of spirits now. Compared to the worldly Pedro, learned in the gentlemanly arts of music and swordplay, I knew nothing. But I still refused to accept defeat. "For your information, I've got plenty to write about. Like Mr. Sheridan's diamond, for example."

"Diamond?" It was his turn to look impressed, but even so I instantly regretted that I'd even mentioned it.

"I shouldn't have told you that. Forget it."

"Of course I can't forget it! You'd better tell me now—or I'll ask Mr. Sheridan himself."

"You wouldn't!"

"Would!" His face was determined, ruthless even. I believed him capable of anything at that moment.

"I'll tell you if you promise to keep it a secret." He nodded, giving me a solemn bow, hand on heart. "Well, Mr. Sheridan has hidden a treasure in the theater and I'm looking after it for him."

"Where is it?" he asked eagerly.

I then remembered what Pedro said about running away to France with the jewels from his turban and was therefore thankful to be able to deny all knowledge of its exact location.

"I don't know. But I'm to tell him if anyone comes sneaking around to look for it."

He gave me a queer look, perhaps wondering if I meant him. "I'll help you," he said. "It sounds exciting. Perhaps we'll get a reward if we catch someone who's after it."

I shrugged. "Maybe." I looked away to the auditorium and saw that it was almost full. "Hadn't you better get changed? The performance is about to start."

Pedro brushed the crumbs off his lap and bowed again.

"Tonight I will play for you, Cat," he said gallantly as he left the box.

As I watched him go, I wondered about my new friend, for I supposed that was what he was after all we had been through today. Pedro was the most unusual boy I'd ever met and I wasn't talking about his skin color. I couldn't forget the music that poured from his violin that morning: he seemed to be in touch with something much greater than anything I knew, something almost holy. That was it, I thought with a smile as I realized what image I was feeling my way toward: he was like a priest, a priest of music, superior to the rest of us who had never gone beyond the veil into the Holy of Holies. That was until you mentioned money to him—that brought him straight back to earth among the rest of us. I wouldn't be encouraging him to think any more about the diamond—that had been a big mistake.

Mr. Sheridan had not yet arrived, though I expected him to come for the first night of the balloon farce, *The Mogul's Tale*, after the main play. This meant I had the delicious luxury of the box to myself. I sat in his chair and played with the opera glasses. I trained them on the pit, picking out the men on the seats below as they chewed on handfuls of nuts and oranges. Jonas Miller, the clerk from across the road, a pinched-nose youth with straggly fair hair and a poor complexion, was here again, sitting at the end of the bench just under my box. He must spend all his wages on tickets. Jonas was a fanatic about the theater and was famous for his devotion to Miss Stageldoir, sending her weekly offerings of nosegays and other tokens of his affection. She ignored him, of course, saying that he was only a clerk with ideas above his station. I could have added that he was a louse who never missed an opportunity to insult those below him. As I was somewhere near the bottom of life's pile, that meant he treated me cruelly when our paths crossed, either directing some foul remark in my direction or pushing me roughly out of his way.

Jonas was at present sitting next to a dark-suited young man, both with eyes trained on a pamphlet in their laps. Deciding to have my revenge by abusing my position of power, I focused the glasses to spy on the paper they were looking at. It was only a caricature—some crude picture lampooning the government or the royal family. I bent closer to the edge of the box to listen to what they were saying.

"Captain Sparkler's been at it again," cried Jonas. "Look at what he's done to the king. He looks like a sack of Norfolk potatoes. What's this? He's only gone and drawn him squatting on 'the dung heap of history.' Ouch! That's a bit bold, ain't it?"

"The French king doesn't look very happy though," said the other. "I'm not sure French liberty is to his liking."

"I'm all for a bit of French revolutionary spirit here, aren't you, Reuben? Shake up the old orders—give us young men a chance. After all, *we* are the future of this country, not that old German fart, the king."

Reuben looked about him nervously. "Ssh!" he hissed. "Someone might hear you! They've got people out looking for troublemakers. You know you could be carted off to the Tower for insulting the king? Not to mention being hanged, drawn, and quartered for treason."

"They wouldn't dare," bragged Jonas, though I noticed he had dropped his voice despite his bold words. "They're too scared of us—afraid we'll do to them what the Frenchies have done to their king, making him come at their beck and call. And we might." Jonas tried to swell impressively, but to my eye he just looked like a bullfrog, croaking out empty threats.

He was wasting his breath. The mob would never treat King George as the French had their Louis. And as for putting him on the dung heap, that was impossible! Britain without a king was as inconceivable as London without its theaters. Hadn't we tried it with Cromwell and decided we rather liked royalty after all? It was just a shame Jonas's concern for the underclasses did not stretch to those under him, I thought, turning my attention to the more interesting events on the stage. The orchestra filed in. It had gone six-thirty: the performance was starting at last.

I had a long wait to see both Pedro and the balloon as I first had to sit through *The Haunted Tower*, a dark Gothic opera that I did not rate much higher than the productions of Mr. Salter's pen, but at least the audience seemed to like it. Mr. Kemble made sure there was plenty of fake blood and screaming to keep them happy.

A door opened behind me in the fifth act, and I had to scramble out of my chair to make way for Mr. Sheridan. He was accompanied by a gentleman and two young people, a boy and a girl a few years older than me, both finely dressed. As I ducked out of the way, I caught a glimpse of the sky blue silk of the girl's lace-edged gown and felt a pang of envy. I had never owned anything so beautiful in my entire life.

"Keeping my seat warm for me, were you, Cat?" joked Mr. Sheridan.

"Yes, sir." I bobbed a curtsy, knowing better than to presume upon his kindness in the presence of outsiders. The boy was staring at me with undisguised curiosity, as if I was something intriguing in a cage in the zoological garden.

"Run along then," Mr. Sheridan said, shooing me away. "Make room for Lord Francis and Lady Elizabeth."

Not needing to be told twice, I quit the box. The rich masters had come to throw out the servant. With no revolution here to change the old ways in my favor, I would have to find another vantage point from which to watch Pedro.

Sneaking downstairs, I crept through the door into the pit. Respectable girls did not usually come down here, so I grabbed a pile of theater bills from Sally Hubbard, the doorkeeper, and stood by the entrance, pretending to be there to sell them.

Things were not going well for me if I was to get my wish of seeing Pedro and the balloon. It was now so crowded (standing room only) that I could barely see the stage, being several feet shorter than the men surrounding me. One portly gentleman standing at the very back noticed my predicament as I hopped from foot to foot. He offered his assistance in a most gentlemanlike manner and lifted me up onto a pillar by the entrance, where I could hang on by the candle bracket. I now had a superb view over everyone's heads to the stage. I smiled my thanks to him and he tipped his hat most courteously to me.

At last the curtain rose. The stage was empty. On realizing this, the men in the pit began to mutter angrily to each other. They had been promised a spectacle such as they had never seen before in the theater, and now it looked as though they had been duped. I smiled to myself, knowing they were about to witness something that would rival the feats of the most daring rope walkers at Bartholomew Fair.

The orchestra struck up an Eastern tune, evoking an exotic Asia, a land of moguls and tigers, diamonds and spices. The grumbling died away. Then, from the very roof of the stage, a long rope tumbled down, a small anchor at its end. It fell on the stage with a clatter. Next came a creaking of ropes and shouts of "Ware below!" and the basket of the balloon appeared suspended above the stage, swaying slightly. The crowd gasped. Slowly, without a hitch, the basket came down, Mr. Andrews, its sole passenger, saluting the audience as it inched to the floor. I held my breath: had Mr. Bishop really solved the problem with the ropes? I wondered. Now the silken canopy came into sight, and the crowd cheered and began to applaud wildly, standing on the benches to whistle their approval.

"Capital!" bellowed my kind gentleman, mopping his forehead with his handkerchief. The heat of the audience's enthusiasm was making the pit quite sultry.

The basket touched down and Mr. Andrews, a tall man famed for his comic roles, leaped out and bowed. Everyone whistled and clapped.

"Encore! Again!" cried many voices around me.

Mr. Andrews held up his hand for silence. The hubbub was quickly stilled.

"I am one John Smith, a poor English balloonist. I earn an honest living by offering rides in my craft in Green Park in that greatest of cities, London." (A cheer from the partisan London audience.) "But one day, as I mounted in my balloon, I was blown by a sudden wind to the east. I wonder to what fair country I have been carried? I shall explore before *I return*." He gave the last words special emphasis and winked at the front rows, in effect promising them another balloon ride at the end of the piece. Placated, the gentlemen resumed their seats and gave him their attention.

The farce was absurd and simple: John Smith has landed in the harem of the Great Mogul and is caught by the palace guards. Threatened with death, his only hope is to persuade the Great Mogul himself to spare him. The mogul, played by Mr. Kemble, turns out to be not a monstrous tyrant but a man of learning and mercy. He frees John Smith in return for a balloon ride. Straightforward enough stuff, providing plenty of opportunities for the ballet and musicians to show off their prowess at the exotic style now much in vogue. But where was Pedro? I wondered as the minutes ticked by. The play was nearing its end and he had still not done his turn.

"And now," declared the mogul, interrupting my thoughts, "I will show you the greatest wonder of my kingdom. My son and heir will entertain you before you depart." He clapped his hands and two pantalooned slaves entered, carrying a chest built on poles to resemble the bulbous towers of an Eastern potentate's palace.

What an introduction! Pedro had been pitched against the balloon. If he wanted to make his mark, he would have to produce something to rival that silken ball of hot air. I clenched my fingernails into my palm, my heart pounding for him.

The slaves lifted the lid of the casket, and there was a blinding flash as two firework fountains burst into flame, spilling glowing white sparks onto the stage. With great agility, Pedro leaped over the trail of hissing embers and landed neatly center stage. The silks and satins of his robe gleamed richly and the jewels in his turban flashed with fire to match the scintillating sparks of the fireworks. With the same swiftness I had seen him use that morning, he produced his violin as if from thin air and tucked it under his chin. He then began to play, a new piece full of such haunting melodies and strange harmonies that I was at once transported to the

India of my imagination: a land of palaces, unimaginable riches, heavily laden merchant ships at anchor, a beating sun. I cannot have been the only one so transfixed, for the audience was absolutely silent, hanging on every note that issued from his instrument like a stream of liquid gold sound.

Pedro finished and there was a pause. Had I misjudged the audience's reaction? Then the house erupted into tumultuous applause, stamping, cheering, and whistling, crying for an encore. Pedro was ready. He launched himself into a new melody, spinning faster and faster as the tune gathered pace. The audience cheered and clapped in time to the beat until it got too fast for them to keep up. The music and Pedro's wild spinning came to a stop at the same triumphant moment, and applause rang out once more.

It took some minutes before the play was able to resume. When the noise had simmered down, Mr. Andrews gave his farewell speech and climbed into the basket.

"Farewell! See you in Green Park!" he shouted, waving cheerfully to the audience. They waved back and then waited. We all waited. It became clear something was wrong with the pulley system once more. The play was about to end with a flop.

Suddenly, Pedro leapt into action. Abandoning his violin in the hands of a startled Mr. Kemble, he jumped into the basket and shinnied his way up the nearest rope. The audience began to murmur, wondering if this was all part of the act. Mr. Kemble seized the moment.

"Look, my son goes to ask the gods to allow the balloon of the Christian barbarian to return to his damp island," the Great Mogul declaimed, waving the violin bow at the ceiling.

The crowd laughed and cheered the Mogul Prince as he climbed up and disappeared under the silken canopy. Then the slack ropes of the grounded balloon began to shake. I guessed that Pedro was adjusting them in the tackle above. Only a minute or so had passed, and Pedro reemerged, sliding rapidly down the rope to spring to the floor.

"Are the gods content to let this heathenish contraption rise again?" asked the mogul.

Pedro gave a nod, his ostrich feather agreeing with him vigorously over his head.

"Then, farewell, stranger!" cried the mogul. He clapped his hands twice, Mr. Andrews gave a slightly nervous wave to the spectators, and the balloon creaked once more into action. As it disappeared up into the roof, the actors and audience all tilted their heads to watch and the curtain fell.

"Amazing!" cried my gentleman, clapping and cheering with the best of them despite his advanced years. "In all my days, I've never seen the like! Did you enjoy it, my dear?"

"It was wonderful!" I said sincerely, accepting his hand to jump down from my vantage point. "And Pedro was brilliant."

"Pedro?" he asked, his eyebrow cocked with interest.

"The little prince—Pedro Hawkins."

The man straightened up and started to chant, "Bravo Pedro! Bravo the prince!"

Those near us took up his call and soon the whole theater was ringing with Pedro's name. As the curtain rose again, he was ushered forward by Mr. Kemble to take his own bow.

Pedro Hawkins had made a name for himself.

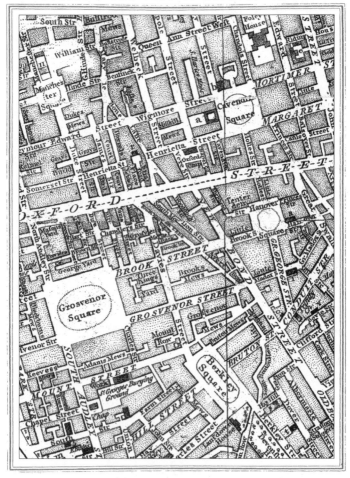

Act II - In which the world is turned upside down at a boxing match between the Bow Street Butcher and the Camden Crusher...

Act II

SCENE 1—THE DUKE'S CHILDREN

I ran as quickly as I could to the green room so I would be the first to congratulate Pedro on his London debut. In the end, I need not have hurried, because I had a long wait—the crowd must have demanded a further encore. Finally, the performers piled into the room, talking loudly in their exhilaration at being in a hit. Mr. Andrews and Mr. Kemble had their arms around each other's shoulders, faces glowing with high spirits. Mr. Andrews was mimicking his companion's extemporized lines about calling on the gods for permission, making the actor-manager roar with laughter.

I looked in vain for Pedro. He had not come in with the others. The green room was already stifling with the heat of so many bodies crushed together, the clink of wine glasses being raised to toast the success, the odors of greasepaint and perspiration. I wormed my way to the door, ducking through the crowd of Eastern beauties and slaves in curling slippers. There, on the threshold, was Pedro. He was having his hand shaken by each of the stage crew in turn. Long Tom thrust a mug of foaming beer into his hand, and Mr. Bishop slapped him on the back as he made to drink it, slopping beer everywhere. The stage crew howled with exuberant laughter. Pedro smiled uncertainly, wondering if they were mocking him or merely having a lark. But the friendly smiles on their faces told him that they now considered him initiated as one of the boys, so he grinned and downed the rest in a gulp.

I hovered shyly to one side, waiting for my opportunity to congratulate him, but before I could get a word in, Mr. Kemble had come forward and steered Pedro into the thick of things, shouting out to the crowd, "Here is the man of the moment! What a performance!"

"Indeed," agreed Mr. Andrews. "Without your quick thinking the crowd might have hanged us all from that damned balloon."

Pedro accepted the adulation with dignity, bowing to those who came up to compliment him. I still could not reach him—so thick was the press—but I noticed that he was looking around, perhaps trying to spot me in the forest of grown-ups.

"Pedro!" I shouted from the corner I had been backed into. Peter Dodsley was embracing Pedro with great emotion. "Pedro, over here!"

My voice must have carried to his sharp ears for he turned and waved. He broke away from the first violinist and began to duck and weave his way through the crowd until finally we were together again.

"Did you watch?" he asked eagerly. "I played to your box but I couldn't spot you."

"No, you wouldn't've. Mr. Sheridan arrived with guests and threw me out." Pedro's face fell. "But I watched from the pit. I had a splendid view. And you were magnificent!"

Pedro's face cracked into a wide smile. "So no one noticed my black eye then?"

I laughed and shook my head. "Absolutely not."

There was a loud call for silence at the door. We turned to look and saw Mr. Sheridan standing framed in the doorway, flanked by his three smart guests who had ousted me from the box.

"Ladies and gentlemen," Mr. Sheridan called. A hush spread from the front of the room to the back like a wave rippling over a peaceful lake. "I have the great honor of presenting a very special visitor to you. The Duke of Avon expressed the desire of personally conveying his appreciation of tonight's performance to you all."

The Duke of Avon, a stately gentleman with white locks brushed forward from a receding hairline, stepped into the room and cleared his throat.

"As my honorable friend here says, I thought you excelled yourselves tonight—none more so than our little African. Where is he? My children in particular would like to meet him."

"Go on," I hissed, pushing Pedro forward.

Arriving before the duke, he gave an elegant bow.

"An unforgettable debut!" declared the peer. "Well done!"

Mr. Sheridan then steered Pedro to one side to meet Lady Elizabeth and Lord Francis.

Conversation in the green room picked up again as the private interview commenced, but I stayed close to the door, watching the fictitious prince meet some of our country's highest nobility. Lord Francis looked younger than his sister; I guessed he was probably only a few years older than me. He had a head of unruly dark brown curls and vivid blue eyes. I noticed that he could not stand still; he fidgeted from foot to foot with barely suppressed excitement, looking at everyone and everything that passed. By contrast, his sister stood serenely and listened to Pedro as he recounted what he had done to save the balloon flight. I liked her expression: at once intelligent and gentle. She did not seem to think it beneath her to spend time giving her attention to a mere player.

Lord Francis then spotted me. He nudged Lady Elizabeth.

"Look, it's Sheridan's Cat, Lizzie," he said, grinning over at me. "I wondered what had become of her."

I would have slipped away, but Pedro strode over and hooked me by the arm. "Allow me to introduce you to her."

He dragged me over. "You say, my lord, that you want to know about the theater; well, here is our resident expert." He waved his hand toward me in a flourish like a conjuror producing a white rabbit from a hat.

I blushed at the introduction and curtsied.

"So, Miss . . . ?" began Lady Elizabeth tentatively.

"Miss Catherine Royal," I supplied, thinking it the moment to use my full title.

"Miss Royal, what do you do at the theater?" she asked.

"Do you sing?" asked Lord Francis eagerly. "Do you play?"

I hesitated. Message-runner did not sound very impressive faced with the cream of English society who expected me to dazzle them as Pedro had done.

"She writes," said Pedro quickly. "Oh yes, the first production of her pen will soon be on all good bookstands—a story of mystery and intrigue from a child prodigy. She is the bookseller's dream, a gift to the journals!"

I gaped. Fortunately no one noticed as they were now discussing my forthcoming work eagerly.

"Well, I am impressed!" exclaimed Lady Elizabeth. "Will it be full of banditi and haunted castles?"

"Or highwaymen and thief catchers?" asked Lord Francis.

They both turned expectantly to me. I could not help smiling at the absurd tale Pedro had spun, but I was not going to let the theater—or myself—down in front of them. I would prove that I was worthy of their respect.

"Oh no, nothing like that," I said with a superior air. "It is set here, in Drury Lane, and will go from the lowest ranks of society to the highest, from the gangs and barrow boys to the baronets and beauties. My themes will be—" (I cast around for some suitably Shakespearean language to impress them, not having in truth a clue what I was talking about) "the wickedness of treason, the sting of revenge, and the noble disinterestedness of love, all set behind the scenes."

"Excellent!" said Lord Francis, clapping his hands with enthusiasm. "And what's it to be called?"

I went blank for a moment, floundering around

for a title appropriate to the medley of themes I had just described.

"*The Diamond of Drury Lane*," Pedro extemporized quickly.

I vowed to kick him later for his recklessness. I had much rather he had not mentioned the diamond. Neither of us seemed to be doing very well in keeping Mr. Sheridan's secret. If Pedro had his way, it would be splashed all over the bookstalls and magazines.

"That sounds wonderful," said Lady Elizabeth, addressing herself to me. "Perhaps you and Mr. Hawkins would accept an engagement to entertain a gathering of our friends next Friday—if you can be spared from your other duties, that is?"

"What kind of engagement?" I asked hesitantly.

"Mr. Hawkins to play, of course, and you to read us a chapter of your most interesting work."

"Capital idea," said Lord Francis.

"Yes, we will," answered Pedro before I could think up an excuse.

"Then we will expect you around six," said Lady Elizabeth, making a note in a small notebook with a tiny pencil that she had taken from her reticule.

"But . . ." I began.

Pedro interrupted, stepping on my toes to stop me saying any more. "What Miss Royal means to say is, 'Thank you, but where exactly should we come?' "

"Grosvenor Square," said Lord Francis, stifling a yawn as if the very thought of home was wearisome to him. "South side. You can't miss it."

Grosvenor Square! This was sounding more and more daunting. Grosvenor Square was the most desirable address in the West End. Only the very best families lived there. If you did not have some kind of title, you need not even think of presuming to pollute this hallowed turf with your presence. The families even had their own private garden square in the center—a rare luxury in the crammed streets of London—which was barricaded from the riffraff by railings. I remember once, when an errand took me into that part of town, how I stood gazing longingly into the forbidden garden, watching the rich children playing on the unsullied green lawn—that was before I was rudely moved on by a footman.

"We most willingly accept your gracious invitation," said Pedro with a bow.

Lady Elizabeth clearly considered the matter settled and turned to look for her father. He arrived, reeling a little unsteadily, flushed-faced and happy. I suspected he had been partaking of the champagne Mr. Sheridan had ordered in.

"Come along, my dears, time you were in your beds," he said, offering his arm to his daughter. "Did you get what you want, Lizzie?" he asked, chucking her under her chin.

Lady Elizabeth nodded, her blue eyes sparkling up at him. "Indeed, Papa, more. Miss Royal has also agreed to entertain us."

The Duke of Avon gave me a skeptical look, which took in my patched dress and tumbled appearance.

"She writes the most wonderful stories, sir," said Lord Francis quickly.

"Oh? A writer, is she? How extraordinary for a girl of her class!" the duke exclaimed. Once again I had the impression that this noble family thought I was a curiosity, like the two-headed calf, to be put on show at the fair. "I will be very interested to hear more about this. Perhaps you need a patron to get published, young lady? I am all for encouraging the lower orders to rise above the disadvantages of their station in life—as long as it is consistent with womanly virtues, of course," he added as an afterthought.

Pedro was not slow to pick up on the offer of monetary support. "I can vouch for Miss Royal, your grace. I expect it can be arranged for her to leave a sample of her work when we come on Friday so that you may peruse it at your leisure."

"Excellent," he said. "Till Friday then."

With a slight nod of dismissal, the duke swept off to return to his carriage, taking his children with him, Lady Elizabeth on his arm, Lord Francis lagging behind, still enraptured by the world behind the scenes.

As soon as they were out of earshot, I turned to my friend. "Pedro! What were you thinking of?"

"Your future, Cat," he grinned, "and mine. Offers like that don't come by every day, believe me."

"But I haven't written anything suitable for a duke's eyes, nor the ears of his children!"

"Oh, that's no problem. They don't want to hear about people like them; they want a bit of the rough and raw world of the common people. It's like a voyage to a foreign country for them."

"But I haven't got anything ready for Friday!"

"Then you'd better start burning the midnight oil, Cat. I don't want to hear any more excuses. You'll never realize your ambition to be a writer if you don't put pen to paper. Besides, I'm counting on you to support my first private engagement in London. You won't let me down, will you?" He gave me an appraising look that suggested he still had his doubts about me. Well, I'd show him!

"Oh," I sighed irritably, "all right. I'll do my best."

"You'd better get started then," he said, pushing me in the direction of the Sparrow's Nest. "I'll expect to see at least four pages by tomorrow. Good night."

"Good night, slave driver," I muttered under my breath.

SCENE 2—HIGH SOCIETY

When Mrs. Reid heard about my invitation to Lady Elizabeth's tea party, she was almost as thrilled for me as if she were going herself. Appointed by my patron to keep an eye on me, she took her duties seriously, chastising me for wrongdoing, seeing to my food and clothes. She usually acted toward me like a strict mistress to a servant, so I was particularly touched when she promised to make me a dress suitable for the occasion.

"You'll be representing the theater, mind," she said to excuse her softheartedness. "We can't have you letting the side down."

Johnny also thought it a splendid opportunity. I told him all about it the next morning as we sorted through the old scripts for Mr. Kemble. Johnny bent over the table, a pen tucked behind his ear, no jacket on, the sleeves of his fine linen shirt rolled up to his elbows, displaying his ink-stained fingers.

That made me wonder if he was an aspiring author too.

"Johnny, do you write?"

He laughed. "Not *write* in the sense you mean, Catkin. But if you want to show me what you're doing, I'll be able to help with grammar, spelling, and so on."

"So why do you have ink stains on your fingers?"

He looked down at his hands, turning them over to contemplate them. "You are a sharp one. The Bow Street magistrate could do with your help. No villain would escape your beady eye."

"Oh, he doesn't stir out of doors," I said matter-of-factly. "If you want anything solved around here—stolen property returned, revenge for assault, runaway wives tracked down—you have to go to one of the gangs. They know everything that's happening on their turf."

"Hmm," said Johnny skeptically. "I suspect they mete out a rather rough justice, that lot."

"Some do," I agreed. "Billy Shepherd's boys, for example, are a bad bunch, more likely to be the cause of the problem than a help. And if you do something that makes them lose face, then you're in trouble. They have a keen sense of honor. . . ." I faltered, remembering what I had done the day before.

"Honor? That's a strange word to use about a bunch of thugs."

"It's not just gentlemen that fight if they think they've been insulted, Johnny," I explained. I had to put him straight for he wouldn't last long on our streets if he didn't know about the code of honor that prevailed out there. "But not all gangs are like Shepherd's. Thankfully, there's my friend Syd and his lads. They help keep Shepherd's lot in check. If you need help, go to Syd: he's always fair. And remember, it's Billy Shepherd you have to watch. He'll steal a blind man's stick if it takes his fancy— and kick him into the gutter in the bargain." Having delivered my little lesson, I realized Johnny had successfully diverted me from asking about his inky fingers. "So, tell me."

"Tell you what?"

His air of innocence as he rifled through the papers did not fool me.

"Tell me what you've been up to."

He looked about him. "I don't suppose it will do any harm to let you in on the secret," he said. "I draw."

"Draw? What, likenesses? Could you draw me, for example?"

He nodded. "Though I doubt I could do justice to your freckled nose and scruffy long curls." I hit him. "Ouch!"

"Will you illustrate my manuscript for me? I'm sure the duke's children would love to see more about what life is like backstage."

He looked at me for a moment, considering my request. "Of course I will," he said at length. "Avon is a decent fellow, I believe. The son also. And Lady Elizabeth is . . . is everything a lady should be. No, I don't mind entertaining her friends."

It seemed a strange way to put it, but at least I now had something new I could offer on Friday.

Hopefully, the young lords and ladies would excuse the writing if they were diverted by the pictures.

Pedro was able to escape from his rehearsal at noon so I decided it was high time to introduce him to Syd Fletcher. He needed the protection of Syd's gang now that he had had his meeting with Shepherd. I also wanted to tell Syd about our good fortune. Syd was bound to be very impressed: his father, a butcher, could only dream of supplying the likes of the Avon household, whereas Pedro and I were actually invited indoors! Perhaps this would at long last make Syd change his refusal and let me in as a member of his gang.

Two of Syd's boys were watching the street outside the back entrance to the Fletchers' butcher shop, lounging in the wintry sunshine. Nick was spitting wads of tobacco at the wall while Joe practiced a flamboyant shuffle of his pack of cards, letting them arch from one hand to the other.

"'Ello, Cat," said Nick in a friendly tone, eyeing my companion with interest. "Come to see the big man, I s'pose?"

"Of course. Why do you ask?"

"I's 'opin' that you might've come to call on me and Joe, that's all," he laughed. "Well, you can go on in—'e's almost done for the day."

They waved us through into the gang's inner sanctum: the slaughterhouse at the back of the shop. We found Syd washing down the bloody block where many a creature met a sudden end, his blond hair flopping over his face as he scrubbed hard with a bristle brush. As all parts of the animal were put to use, the room was full of red-stained buckets containing every organ and cut known to man—from ox tongue to tail, as Syd would put it, guffawing loudly at his own wit. The place had that curious odor of sawdust mixed with the surprisingly sweet smell of carnage, a scent that hung around Syd even when he was away from home. He looked up and smiled when he saw me.

"Well, if it ain't our little ray of sunshine! How's tricks, Cat?"

"Good, Syd, thanks." I always felt comfortable with Syd—I'd known him so long that he was like the older brother I'd never had. Even as very little children playing in the streets, he'd looked out for me and taught me so many things.

I introduced my companion. Syd wiped his palms on his blood-stained apron before shaking Pedro's hand, dwarfing the musician with his six feet of muscular body.

"I 'ear you were quite the sensation last night, Prince," said Syd admiringly. "The 'ole market's abuzz with it."

Pedro shrugged, but I could tell this was pleasant news for him.

"And there's more," I said quickly. "We have both been invited to a duke's house!"

"Whatever for?" asked Syd, shooting me a concerned look. "You're not going for scullery maid, are you, Cat?"

"Of course not, you oaf!" I snapped. I am the only one Syd allows to talk to him so irreverently. "We are to entertain Lady Elizabeth and Lord Francis."

Syd gave a snort of laughter. This was far from the awed expression of amazement I had been anticipating. He moved across to a sack of sawdust that hung suspended from the ceiling and gave it a punch with his calloused knuckles. "I can see what the boy can do, Cat, but what about you? Are you goin' to give 'em a bit of your sharp tongue and show 'em 'ow to fight like a wildcat?" He gave the sack a quick double jab. "That's all you're good for, ain't it?"

This fairly took the wind out of my sails. "I'm going to read to them—read a story I've written," I said quietly.

Syd could see that he had offended me. He gave an appreciative whistle, hugging the sack to still its pendulum motion. "Now ain't that just grand: a girl that can 'old 'er own in the market place 'oo can also read and write like a fine lady. I never knew you 'ad it in you, Cat. You'll knock 'em dead, you will."

"Thanks, Syd," I said in a gloomy tone.

Pedro could tell I was beginning to worry again about our visit to Grosvenor Square, so he changed the subject.

"Tell me, Syd, how do things work around here?" he asked, picking his way like a peacock across the sawdust in his shiny buckled shoes. "I met Billy Boil yesterday, but it seems I would have been better off meeting some of your boys."

"Billy *Boil*?" Syd gave a loud guffaw of laughter, which attracted Nick and Joe in from outside. "You 'ear that? The prince has met Billy *Boil*!"

"That's what Cat called him to his face," Pedro continued.

"I like it!" said Syd appreciatively, turning in my direction. "You called 'im that, did you, Cat? I bet 'e weren't pleased."

"No, he tried to beat her up but she escaped him," Pedro explained.

I would have made Pedro shut up if I could, but it was too late. I had had no intention of confiding in Syd, knowing the likely consequences.

"'E threatened my Cat, did 'e?" asked Syd, his blue eyes now cold with anger. "'E'll regret that, 'e will."

"I don't want any trouble on my account," I said quickly. "He was after Pedro really."

"Was 'e now?" Syd strode over to Pedro and gave him a long, searching stare, gauging his uses.

"Well, you can tell Boil next time you see 'im that the prince's in," said Syd.

"He's what?" I asked.

"Prince's in the gang. One of us."

"What!" I protested. "I've been asking to join for months and months, and you let him in not five minutes after meeting him. That's not fair!"

Nick and Joe began to laugh until Syd gave them a stern look.

"I don't 'ave girls in my gang, Cat, as I keep tellin' you."

"But you have African violinists?"

Pedro gave me a glare that implied I'd insulted his origins. I hadn't meant it like that—it was the violinist bit that I'd really meant to draw Syd's attention to.

"Yeah, 'e's a boy, in case you ain't noticed."

"Of course I've noticed!" I said stamping my foot with anger. "But I'm as good as any of you!"

"No, you're better, Cat," said Syd with a wink, "which is why I don't want you in my gang."

"Pedro, tell him! Tell him how I saw the Boil off for you!"

Pedro shrugged. "You ran away quick enough, that's true."

The rat! I'd done far more than that and he knew it! His words served to confirm Syd in his decision that I was not fit to number among his boys. I was sure Nick and Joe were laughing at me. I felt hot with embarrassment and anger, but Syd had dismissed my request and turned his thoughts to other matters.

"As for Billy Boil," he continued, perching on the block, swinging a cleaver absentmindedly in his right hand, "'E's planning a big fight for Monday night, and now I've got a new reason for wanting to beat 'im to a pulp. The gang's meeting at the Rose at ten. Will you be there?" he looked at his newest gang member.

"Of course," agreed Pedro at once.

I moved quickly to dissuade him. "But Pedro, you'll get in trouble again. You don't know how nasty these fights can get!"

"I'll see 'e doesn't come to grief," promised Syd. "'E's our lucky mascot, 'e is. No other gang 'as the star of the stage in their ranks, do they now?"

"No," I said shortly, "because all the other stars are too sensible to get involved."

Pedro gave me a dig in the ribs. "Don't fret. I'm not afraid of a beating. And if you make sure everyone sees that you are safely tucked up in bed, then you'll not be held to blame for whatever happens."

"Perhaps," I grumbled resentfully, "but I wouldn't put it past Mrs. Reid to find some way of making it my fault."

Syd chuckled. "Well, I'll 'ave a word with 'er then." He swung the cleaver in a menacing fashion. "Make 'er see sense."

"Oh, you're both hopeless!" I exclaimed as Pedro, Nick, and Joe fell about laughing.

Syd, who I knew would be the last person to threaten a lady, threw the cleaver aside with a clatter and stood up. "I must go. I 'ave my trainin' this afternoon. You'll come and see me in my boxin' match, won't you, Cat?"

I nodded, though feeling very reluctant. I was not eager to watch two grown boys beating each other up for money, particularly when one was my good friend. "Sunday morning, isn't it?'

"That's right, in Marylebone Fields. You'll 'ave to dress as a boy, like last time."

"Can I come?" asked Pedro eagerly.

"Of course, Prince. All the gang's goin' to be there. You can look after Cat for me."

As if I couldn't look after myself!

"Who are you fighting?" I asked, trying not to show them how angry I still was. They'd only put it down to me being a moody girl if I did and laugh about it when I'd gone.

A worried frown passed across Syd's face for a moment. "The Camden Crusher."

"Is he good?"

"Not as good as me," Syd said proudly, flexing his muscles and rolling his bull-sized neck to warm up. "I'll set 'im to rights, you'll see." He rocked lightly from foot to foot, making a few practice punches at the air.

"I hope so, Syd. Better that than having the surgeon set you to rights afterward."

"Should we knock at the front door or use the tradesman's entrance?" I asked Pedro nervously, clutching my manuscript under my arm.

We both looked up at the tall sandstone house rising four floors above us. The large windows were all lit, shining out into the cold January evening in an opulent display, telling the world that money was no object as far as candles were concerned. An imposing flight of six marble stairs ran up to the black front door. The knocker—a brass dragon's head—gleamed balefully at us. To our right, partially hidden by the spiked iron railing, was a mean, narrow staircase that ran down to the lower floors: the tradesman's entrance.

Pedro looked back at the front door. "We're not bidden to the kitchen; we're here to see the family." He mounted the steps before his courage failed, seized the knocker, and thumped it twice. Almost immediately, the door swung open, and a white-wigged, liveried servant stood there, looking down his long nose at us.

"Yes?" he said dubiously, holding out his hand for a message.

"We're from Drury Lane. Lady Elizabeth is expecting us," said Pedro, ignoring the out-stretched hand and making to step inside.

"I doubt that very much," said the footman with a sardonic smile, blocking his way.

"We're here for the tea party," I added boldly, annoyed by the man's supercilious attitude. "If you don't believe us, why don't you ask her?"

Perhaps our confidence made him think better of shutting the door in our faces. "Wait here," he ordered. He turned to another footman standing in the hall. "Watch them," he told his colleague. "See that they don't touch anything." He then strode swiftly up the red-carpeted stairs.

We stood under the hawkish gaze of the second servant, waiting for our fate to be decided. Before long, the footman returned and reluctantly opened the door wide enough to allow us in.

"Apparently, you are expected," he said with ill grace. "Would you like to leave your cloak here, miss?"

I took off my hood and handed over my old black cloak, revealing underneath the white muslin dress with a green silk sash Mrs. Reid had made for me from one of the ripped ballet dresses she had stashed away. The footman's manner instantly became more respectful.

"Step this way, miss," he said, bowing me up the stairs.

I winked at Pedro, who was staring at me as if seeing me properly for the first time.

"You look—well, you look different, Cat," he muttered on the way upstairs. "I didn't know you washed up so well."

I grinned. "But I'm still the same Cat underneath, even if my hair is neat for once."

Sarah had spent hours that day taming my red mop into a series of ringlets tied back with a matching green bow. I felt I looked good enough for the company we were about to meet, and that gave me the confidence to continue up the stairs.

The footman stopped by a door on the floor above. Inside we could hear the tinkle of the piano and the laughter of young voices.

"Who shall I say is here?" he asked me.

"Miss Royal and Mr. Hawkins, if you please," I said with dignity.

He opened the door and gave a cough.

"Lady Elizabeth, your visitors have arrived: Miss Royal and Mr. Hawkins."

He ushered us forward and then closed the door behind us.

My first impression was of a sea of pink faces turned curiously in our direction. Then I took in the fine muslin petticoats that seemed so light as if made of nothing but spun sugar, the smart breeches and jackets of the boys, the elaborately arranged hair of the girls. Suddenly my own outfit seemed very tawdry.

"Miss Royal, Mr. Hawkins, we are delighted to see you both," said Lady Elizabeth, rising from a cherry-red silk sofa to greet us.

Lord Francis bounded over, abandoning a group of three sour-faced young people. "Just when we needed livening up!" he said enthusiastically. "Who's to go first, eh?"

Pedro bowed. "I am to have that pleasure."

I nearly giggled. It seemed so funny to hear Pedro putting on a refined act in front of this audience—it was like we were all playing at being lords and ladies for the day. I had to remind myself that we were probably the only ones in the room without a title.

As might have been expected, Pedro's concert was a great success. He played the piece by Mozart I had first heard him perform, and it had the same mesmerizing effect in the duke's drawing room as it had at Drury Lane. The music transported us all. Pedro seemed able to conduct our emotions, using his bow as a baton, making us smile or weep by turns. When he stopped, I knew that he had succeeded in claiming his place in this room as an equal by virtue of his talent alone. Indeed, there was something in his gift that put him beyond our reach. He was loudly applauded. Even the sour-faced trio were impressed.

"Now, Miss Royal, it is your turn," said Lord Francis, taking my hand and leading me to a chair. "We are most eager to hear from you."

My heart was thumping so hard I was surprised he could not hear it. I felt most unwilling to read after the virtuoso display we had all just witnessed—it was like bringing the ballet chorus girl on after the principal dancer. "If you wish, sir," I said, unfolding my papers and giving a nervous cough to clear my throat of the frog that had taken up residence there. I took a deep breath.

"Reader, you are set to embark on an adventure told by an ignorant and prejudiced author—me." I sneaked a look over the top of my papers. Lord Francis and the boy beside him were laughing; Lady Elizabeth smiled. They gave me the courage to continue. *"'Much harm done, Tom?' I asked as I clambered over the upturned benches to reach the stagehand as he cleared away the debris from last night's riot. . . ."*

Ten minutes later, I came to the end of my recital and waited. The room was quiet. In that instant, I was convinced I had failed—I had shocked, possibly scandalized them, and they were just struggling to find the words to tell me so. I had been so stupid even to think that I could pass myself off as an author in this discerning gathering. My hopes of launching myself on a new career with ducal patronage plummeted to the ground as rapidly as had the balloon in the extract I had just finished reading them.

"Heavens!" said a pale girl with long brown ringlets like the sausages in Syd's shop. "To think that people really live like this! Fighting in the streets—can you believe it!"

I could sense all their eyes were fixed on me. I felt like a cadaver on the surgeon's table being anatomized before the gaze of curious students.

"I think it's grand," said Lord Francis, thumping his fist playfully into his neighbor's stomach. "Come on, Charlie, how about it?"

Pedro gave me an amused look over Lord Francis's head: though I had changed a few details to protect the identities of my subjects, any astute listener would have been able to identify him as the boy who ended up with a black eye after outrunning the gang.

"Frank!" scolded Lady Elizabeth, her eyebrow raised in warning.

Lord Francis gave her an apologetic look and helped the winded Charles to a seat.

"Well, it certainly was unorthodox," said a sweet-looking girl with a heart-shaped face. "Though perhaps the subject matter is a little unbecoming for a lady. I would have expected Miss Royal to begin with some witty general observation, a wryly expressed universal truth, for example, on love and courtship—the usual themes for the female pen."

"Oh, Jane!" protested Lord Francis. "How can you be so dull? We don't want none of that girly stuff. Straight into the action, that's what we like and that's what Miss Royal gave us. And I thought the pictures were capital."

The sour-looking fellow, with a face like a weasel and sleek silver-blond hair, piped up from his corner: "The pictures did indeed display an uncommon talent but I'm not sure if Miss What's-Her-Name's outpourings are respectable enough for my sisters to hear, Lady Elizabeth."

Our hostess now looked worried.

"Rubbish, Marchmont!" exclaimed Lord Francis.

Marchmont! The name struck a chord with me. I turned to take a closer look at my critic, wondering if I could trace any family likeness to the dark-cloaked man who had threatened me at the stage door.

"It's stuff like that which leads to anarchy. We see it daily in France; I hope to God we do not see it here," the Marchmont boy continued, like some little politician on the hustings. Tension crackled between him and his host. I had the impression that they were old sparring partners between whom there was no love lost.

"Parroting your favorite Pittite phrases, are you?" said Lord Francis. "You'd better not let your father find out. As a friend of liberty, he wouldn't like to hear that his son's a dyed-in-the-wool reactionary."

"Francis!" said Lady Elizabeth, scandalized.

"I think we had better go," said Marchmont, rising and leading his sisters to the door. "Thank you for a lovely evening, Lady Elizabeth. The *music* was superb."

The Marchmonts' departure was taken as the signal for the party to break up. Pedro and I lingered in a corner, wondering if we should slip out or wait to be dismissed. We had been expecting to receive something for our trouble. I hoped that my audacity in reading my poor stuff to the duke's children had not lost us our bounty. Pedro would never let me hear the end of it if it had.

When the last person had left, Lady Elizabeth turned to her brother.

"Frank, do you have to be so rude to my guests?"

He shrugged. "I don't know why you invited them, Lizzie. Just because Father's friendly with his father, it doesn't mean we have to endure them. You know I think Marchmont a prig. You are too polite to say what you really think of his sisters, but I know you don't like them."

"Yes, but to attack him in our own drawing room—that's very bad manners!"

"And criticizing your brother in front of strangers isn't?" he said with a nod at Pedro and me.

Lady Elizabeth blushed. "I'm sorry. I did not realize you were still here." She nudged her brother. "Go on," she hissed, "pay them!"

Lord Francis strode over to us and bowed. "A token of our sincere appreciation of your talents," he said, dropping a promisingly heavy purse into Pedro's hand.

"Thank you, sir," said Pedro.

Lord Francis turned to me. "I hope our ill-mannered guest did not offend you, Miss Royal? You did splendidly. Tell me: does all this really happen as you describe it?"

I nodded and smiled into his friendly eyes, thinking how much I liked him. "Yes, sir."

"It's even better than she writes it," Pedro butted in, trying to impress the young nobleman. "We have parties and music, boxing and battles."

"Boxing!" Lord Francis grabbed at the word eagerly. "My great passion is the ring! I want to learn how to box, but Father won't let me."

"Well," said Pedro leaning forward confidentially, "Cat here—I mean Miss Royal—just so happens to be best friends with Covent Garden's boxing champion. We are watching him in a match on Sunday. For a small consideration," he chinked the purse suggestively, "we might be able to take you along."

"Pedro!" I whispered in warning. This really did not sound like a good idea.

"Will you? . . . Yes, I might be able to get away," said Lord Francis, thinking aloud. He stole a look over his shoulder at his sister, who was now running her fingers over the piano keyboard in a melancholy love song, lost deep in thought. "Lizzie's a bit absentminded at the moment, mooning over one of her suitors who ran off late last night. She's not as sharp as normal. If I pretend to be ill and get out of church, I should be able to do it."

"We'll meet you on the corner of Grosvenor Square then," said Pedro quickly. "At ten."

"At ten," agreed Lord Francis.

"*If* you are coming," I said sullenly, glaring at Pedro, "you'd better dress down a bit, sir."

"Right you are, Cat—I mean Miss Royal," grinned Lord Francis.

SCENE 3—BOW STREET BUTCHER V. CAMDEN CRUSHER

I was not looking forward to the prospect of trying to smuggle his lordship into the boxing match. It was bad enough that I had to pretend to be a boy to pass unnoticed, but bringing along someone who would have no idea how to blend in seemed pure recklessness. I could imagine what fun the lads would have if they found out that one of their lords and masters was mingling with them. Lord Francis would be very lucky to get home in one piece. Pedro didn't have a clue what he was doing.

I confided my fears to Johnny the next morning over lessons. Having heard from Mrs. Reid how Old Carver had undertaken my education, Johnny had insisted on carrying this on. His choice of reading matter was very different from Mr. Carver's solid diet of English greats: Johnny was improving my French so that I could read

Rousseau in the original, and his idea of English composition revolved around the cream of the crop of the latest political tracts. It was not all hard work, however: at my insistence, he was also giving me lessons in drawing.

We were sketching a bust we had found in one of the airy club rooms on the first floor of the theater when I raised the subject of the match.

"I agree: it doesn't sound like a good idea," said Johnny, lifting his pencil to measure the space between Roman nose and weak Roman chin of Julius Caesar. "But neither do I think it a good idea for you to gad about town dressed as a boy, Catkin."

I scribbled a big proboscis on my drawing, which made the emperor look as if he had a beak. "What were you saying earlier about men and women being equal? How else am I to enjoy equal freedom if I don't disguise myself?"

He looked down awkwardly at his sketch, for he knew that all his counterarguments ran against his own principles. "You've lived too long in the theater, Cat. All these breeches roles for actresses must have gone to your head."

"Don't worry about me, Johnny. I do it all the time. It's Lord Francis you should worry about." I was then struck by what I considered a brilliant idea. "I know, why don't you come with us? If you were there, you could help us look after him."

"I can't do that, Catkin." He gave a vicious twist to Caesar's thin-lipped mouth.

"Why ever not? It's your day off, isn't it?"

"Yes, but I don't want to be seen just now." He sighed.

Now, the only reason I knew for a grown man to hide himself was to avoid those to whom he owed money; many a man lives in fear of hearing the bailiff's knock on the door coming to cart him off to debtor's prison.

"But even if you are hiding from the bailiffs," I said, assuming my guess was correct, "you're free to go out on a Sunday, aren't you? I thought they couldn't arrest people on the Sabbath?"

Johnny laughed and flicked his pencil deftly into the air, catching it as it spun to the floor. "So you think I'm on the run from the bailiffs, do you? It's a likely enough tale. Still, you would agree,

Catkin, that it would not be wise to allow anyone to see me, follow me, and thus find out where I have concealed myself?"

I shrugged. "I suppose not. But is that likely at a boxing match?"

"You'd be surprised," said Johnny, putting the sketch away in his portfolio. "Many gentlemen of my acquaintance are bound to be there for the gambling. I can't risk it. Now, let's see what you have done."

I showed him my drawing.

He chuckled. "You have made the old villain look like one of those anteaters from the Americas. A very good start if you want a career as the first female cartoonist, Cat."

On Sunday morning, Pedro and I waited at the corner of Grosvenor Square for Lord Francis. We appeared to have arrived at rush hour: carriage after carriage was drawing up at the front doors, taking the inhabitants off to the church service of their choice. Only a few families were brave enough to expose their expensive attire to the streets by walking the short distance to the parish church.

I spotted the duke and Lady Elizabeth emerging from their house shortly before ten. Pulling Pedro out of sight behind a carriage waiting on the corner, I watched them walk arm in arm in the opposite direction.

"'Ere, what you playin' at?" protested the coachman, flicking his long whip in our direction. "Get away from my carriage."

Enjoying my breeches role (as Johnny put it), I couldn't resist the temptation to indulge in a bit of unladylike shouting.

"What's your problem, mate? We haven't scratched your precious paintwork." I then stuck my tongue out at him.

"Come on, Cat," said Pedro, grabbing the back of my jacket and towing me into Charles Street, away from the anger of the coachman and the reach of his whip. "You're enjoying this too much."

I laughed. "I can't tell you how good it feels to get out of petticoats! I feel quite a different person."

"I can see that." Pedro looked about him as the church clocks began to chime the hour across London. "Where is he?"

There was a shrill whistle behind us, and a clod of earth hit Pedro on the back of his head. He turned around to shout a protest as out of the alley bolted a tall, scruffy boy, his face blackened with soot like a chimney sweep. He ran straight up to us and presented himself for our inspection, arms thrown wide.

"Lord Francis!" I exclaimed. "I'd never've recognized you!"

Lord Francis the chimney sweep looked me up and down. "Nor I you, Miss Royal."

"Forget Miss Royal," I replied, stuffing a stray strand of hair deeper into my cap. "Call me Cat."

"And you'd both better drop that lord business," said Lord Francis, digging his hands into his breeches pockets. "How about calling me Frank?"

"As you wish, sir," said Pedro.

"Frank," Lord Francis said as he cast an eye across the square to see that his father was out of sight.

"Frank," said Pedro uncertainly.

"Come on, we'd better hurry!" I said, setting off toward Oxford Street. "We don't want to miss it."

As we ran through the streets, dodging the carriages, jumping the puddles, jostling the families occupying the pavement as they walked to church, I felt a great bubble of happiness inside me. Despite my fears, I was looking forward to the adventure ahead. If only I didn't have to watch Syd take a beating!

There was a light drizzle in the air as a cold rain shower tried to dampen the holiday mood. Mixing with the swirling smoke from thousands of chimney pots, the rain settled on the day like a damp blanket, forcing the light to work hard to break through the clouds. Yet despite the gray, dank weather, there was no sign of anyone being deterred—crowds began to thicken with people heading for the boxing match as we drew nearer to Marylebone. You could tell at a glance which ones they were: groups of shouting boys, loud-voiced men from Camden or Covent Garden, crafty bookmakers eyeing the punters to spot the gullible—very different from the respectable families bound for the morning service.

We arrived at the very edge of town. Just beyond Oxford Street the buildings give way to villages, fields, and woods, though every year more acreage is covered with houses as London creeps ever farther north like the tide rising to cover the mudflats in the Thames. Today, as we escaped the bricks and mortar of the city, we were also escaping our everyday drudgery, hoping to be thrilled by the primitive pleasure of watching a trial of strength. Man against man, fighting in an arena where neither education nor money gave you the edge: it was brute force and quick reactions that counted.

"Place your bets, gents!" called out one bookmaker, waving his notebook in the air as he wove through the crowds. "Two to one for the Camden Crusher to beat the Butcher with a knockout!"

"That doesn't sound too good for your friend, does it?" said Lord Francis, looking longingly after the bookmaker. "Shall I place a bet on him winning?" He chinked some coins in his pocket.

"No!" I said quickly, pulling him back. "Just how do you think a chimney sweep could afford to bet gold? You'll be found out in one second flat."

"I suppose you are right," said Lord Francis gloomily, withdrawing his hand from his pocket. "And Father's always forbidden me to bet."

"He's a sensible man," said Pedro, gazing after the toffee-apple seller, a large woman with a tray of glistening wares who was following the crowd through the gates onto the field. Lord Francis saw where he was looking.

"I did take the precaution of putting a few pennies in among my guineas," he whispered, pressing some into Pedro's hand. "Why don't you buy us all one?"

"Thank you very much, sir," said Pedro as he hastened off to catch up with her.

"Not 'sir'—Frank!" I hissed as a man at my elbow turned to look at us curiously.

"Thanks, Frank," Pedro corrected himself and scrambled through the press to the toffee-apple seller. He returned bearing four sticks aloft in triumph.

"Four!" said Lord Francis. "Why four?"

"One for luck," mumbled Pedro through a mouthful of toffee. He swallowed. "She'd seen me at the theater, she said, so gave me one for nothing."

It was then that I realized I had wasted my time worrying about Lord Francis drawing attention to us. Having Pedro was sufficient to make most people turn in our direction. I pulled my hat lower on my brow and said dryly, "Come on. Let's find ourselves a spot before we get mobbed by Pedro's admirers."

The crowd was dividing in two around the raised platform. The arena was surrounded by rails and had a three-foot square—the scratch— marked out in chalk at the center. A number of gentlemen sat on benches at the ringside; the rest of us found the best spot we could at ground level. Diving under arms and through narrow gaps, we managed to push our way through to the front.

Syd was sitting in his corner with his second— his father—listening intently to his advice. He had not yet stripped to the waist but was flexing his bare hands thoughtfully. On the other side of the chalk square sat the Camden Crusher—a lad of sixteen, built like an ox, with a small head and powerful shoulders. He had already stripped and his second, a dandified gentleman in a bottle-green jacket with a sharp face like a fox, was oiling his back for him—and, believe me, there was a lot of him to oil.

Nick, the lookout we had met outside Syd's shop, sidled up to us.

"'Ello, prince, Cat. 'Oo's the soot?"

"Frank," said Pedro, handing Nick the spare toffee apple. "He's new."

Nick gave Lord Francis a curious look. "'E's a bit big for the chimneys, ain't 'e? I thought they only liked nippers of eight 'n' under."

"My master specializes in big chimneys, big houses," said Lord Francis quickly. "My younger brother does the small ones."

"Oh," said Nick, losing interest. "Right you are." He nudged me and nodded over at the Crusher. "Looks bad, don't it, Cat? But Syd'll be glad you came. You're 'is lucky mascot. Oi, Syd! Cat's 'ere!" he shouted.

Syd turned around to look down on us. He gave me a wink. "All right, Cat?" he called over. Seeing him standing up there made me think of him as the victim on the scaffold but, as I would not for any money let him see my concern, I gave him my broadest smile.

"Yes," I called up. "Good luck!"

He gave me a nod and then returned to his preparations.

When I turned to speak to Pedro, I found him and Lord Francis sniggering over a piece of paper Nick was showing them.

"What's that?" I asked, making a grab for the pamphlet. I could see it was a cartoon.

"Nuffink," said Nick, hiding it behind his back.

"Don't give me that!" I said, trying to wrestle it from him. "Let me see!"

"Er, Cat," said Lord Francis in an undertone, "I don't think it's suitable for a lady's eyes."

"Stuff that!" I said, determined not to be left out. "Give it here!"

By tickling Nick in the ribs, I succeeded in making him surrender the paper. Perhaps I should not have done so, for as soon as I looked at it, I felt my cheeks go scarlet. It was a very crude representation of a member of the government squatting on a chamberpot marked "The Oppressed Masses."

"The word is," said Nick, covering for my embarrassment, "old Captain Sparkler's gone too far this time. The beak's after him."

"Beak?" asked Lord Francis.

"Gawd, Frank, wot country 'ave you been livin' in? Beak: ma-gi-strate. Got it?"

"Oh," said Lord Francis quickly. "Of course."

"'E's to be made han heg-sample of, they say. Government's got the wind up. 'E's to be done for treason—'anged or transported most like."

"No!" I exclaimed. "All because he poked some fun at a few people! That's not fair!"

"Wot's fair got to do with it? It's powerful people 'e's takin' on, Cat. They don't like to be made to look like fools. They 'ate 'im for makin' fun of 'em. 'E can draw as many bare bums as 'e likes, but you watch, they'll get 'im for attackin' the king. 'Is last cartoon was plain treason, it was. Banned, I 'ear, so sales 'ave gone sky 'igh as you'd expect."

"So, have they caught him yet?" asked Pedro.

"Not likely," said Nick with evident pleasure. "'E's too clever for 'em, is Captain Sparkler. 'E loves to drive 'em wild by flauntin' these pictures in front of 'em as 'e dances out of their reach. The word is 'e's stowed away on a ship for France."

"So how is the pertinacious captain able to draw a cartoon referring to a political scandal that broke last week?" asked Lord Francis, sounding exactly like the nobleman he was rather than the chimney sweep he was pretending to be.

"Lawd, Frankie boy, you swallered a dictionary or somethink?" marveled Nick. Lord Francis now flushed and began to stammer an excuse. "No, don't you apologize. Nuffink wrong with a bit of learnin'. You be proud of it, mate! Look at our Cat here: 'oo'd think she 'ad all that stuff packed away in 'er pretty little 'ead? Syd's always 'olding 'er up as a model to the rest of us 'alfwits!" Nick began to laugh at the very idea of him and the gang learning to read and write like gentlemen.

I did not quell Nick's overloud comments, as I was still thinking about Lord Francis's question. Yes, how was a man, rumored to be in France, able to be so up-to-the-minute with his cartoons? The obvious answer was that he had never left. He must be in hiding, and I had a shrewd suspicion where.

So pleased was I by my own powers of deduction that I was eager to share my guess with Pedro to impress him with my cleverness. Unfortunately, there were too many people around at the moment: it would have to wait.

"Gentlemen!" The referee stood forward and held up his hand for silence. "I present our fighters to you: the reigning champion—the Camden Crusher!"

The Camden Crusher lumbered to his feet and raised his glistening arms to acknowledge the cheers and whistles of his supporters.

"And our challenger: the Bow Street Butcher!"

Rather more nimbly, Syd stripped off his shirt, bounced to his feet, and bowed to acknowledge the applause. His hair looked very pale against his flushed cheeks.

"Go for him, Crusher!" yelled a man on the far side.

"Let's hear it for the brave butcher!" shouted another.

The crowd cheered Syd again, but rather, I felt, as a crowd for a public execution would comfort a popular criminal with their voices. Everyone was expecting him to be well and truly crushed by the boy from Camden.

"You can do it, Syd!" I cried.

Hearing my high voice over the others, Syd turned in my direction to give me a special smile and a nod.

"Now, you know the rules, gents," said the referee in a voice that commanded silence. "Nothing below the belt. If you're down, you have half a minute to return to set-to at the scratch. If you fail to come up to scratch, then your opponent wins. Are you ready, gents?"

Syd grunted his agreement and raised his fists to chest height. The Crusher nodded, giving Syd a mocking smile.

"You're dead," he mouthed.

"Then . . ." said the referee, moving back, "set to!"

The fight began. The Crusher piled forward and grabbed Syd in a wrestling hold, pushing him back against the rails. Syd took small, quick jabs at his opponent's stomach—one, two, three, four, five—until he collided painfully with the wooden bar. There they stayed, the Crusher grinding down Syd's resistance with a flurry of punches that left great red welts on his skin. Once it was clear that the pair were caught on the rails, the referee rushed forward with the seconds to part the fighters. The seconds led their boys back to the scratch, both hissing encouragement and advice. The boxers set to again, this time exchanging body blows. Head down, arms pumping like pistons, Syd grazed his knuckles as his fist caught the side of the Crusher's ribs. Blood dripped from the Crusher's nose as a second jab caught him in the face. When the fighters circled around, I could see that Syd too was bleeding, in his case from a cut to his temple. Blows rained down fast and furious, bone smacking into flesh, red sweat dripping down their backs. I could hardly bear to watch and was reduced to covering my eyes with my hands. The more bloody and vicious the fight became, the more the crowd cheered. Peeking through my fingers, I could see money changing hands as the gentlemen at the ringside placed new bets. Syd was holding his own. I guessed the odds on him were shortening.

Then disaster struck: the Crusher landed a powerful blow to Syd's jaw, knocking him backward to the floor. Syd rolled over with a groan, his eyes now at a level with our heads only a few feet away.

"One! Two! Three . . . !" chanted the crowd.

Syd's dad rushed over to help him to his feet, but he was not moving.

"Come on, son!" he bellowed. "Get up!"

"Fifteen! Sixteen! Seventeen . . .!"

"Come on, Syd!" I screamed above the jeers and hoots. "Keep going!"

Perhaps Syd heard me, for his eyes locked on mine and, through the trickles of blood running down his face, I thought I could see him smile. Slowly, he heaved himself to his knees, then to his feet. Swaying like a drunken man, he let his father lead him to the chalk square.

"Twenty-eight! Twenty-nine . . .!"

He had come up to scratch just in time.

"Set to!" shouted the referee.

Some in the crowd groaned—an easy victory snatched from the Crusher's grasp. Those of us backing the outsider cheered lustily.

Battle recommenced, now slower as the toll of all those blows began to tell on the combatants. Syd was moving heavily as if he had weights tied to his legs, but the Crusher seemed barely to be moving at all as he stood defending himself in the middle of the scratch. I began to think that maybe, just maybe, Syd could win this one. I stopped peeking through my fingers and joined in with the chant of "Butcher! Butcher!" that Pedro and Nick had started. Next to me Lord Francis was hopping up and down, yelling his encouragement.

"At him, man! Go for him, sir!" he shouted, failing miserably to keep in character. Fortunately, everyone was too engrossed in the fight to notice.

With sweat pouring from his brow, the Crusher struck out with another of the right hooks for which he was famed, but Syd leaped back, out of harm's way. The Crusher lost his balance and, before he could right himself, Syd came in with a blow to his jaw that sent the champion staggering. The Crusher collapsed to his knees, hands on the floor, breathing hard.

"One! Two! Three!" the crowd began to chant again.

"Get up, you lazy oaf!" screamed the Crusher's second. "Get up, you good-for-nothing girl!"

But the Crusher swayed and then fell forward, the side of his face pressed against the floor, eyes glassy, a dribble of saliva trailing from his half-open mouth. He didn't move. The second kicked him with his foot, trying to make him stir.

"Twenty-eight! Twenty-nine! Thirty!" bellowed the crowd.

The Crusher hadn't moved.

A huge cheer went up. Even those who had lost their bets threw their hats in the air to applaud the plucky newcomer. Nick, Pedro, Lord Francis, and I jumped up and down together and cheered with the best of them. Syd, bowing to each corner in turn, gave us a two-handed victory signal when he faced us. The Crusher's second was not looking after his man. He was in a huddle with Syd's father at the side of the stage. As they broke apart, he thrust a purse into the butcher's fist and they gave each other a businesslike nod. Behind them, some friends of the Crusher had rushed into the ring to help the defeated boy to his feet. He did not look badly injured, but he missed his stool completely when he went to sit down, ending up on the floor again.

The referee bounded over the prostrate body of the Crusher and raised Syd's fist in the air.

"Gents, we have a new champion. I give you the Bow Street Butcher!"

SCENE 4—BILLY "BOIL" SHEPHERD

"Come on, let's go and congratulate Syd," said Pedro eagerly as he launched himself against the tide of people now flowing away from the boxing ring.

Nick and Lord Francis ran after him. Being the last in line, I tried to follow, but a party of gentlemen jumped from the ringside into my path, blocking my way.

"Splendid fight!" enthused a man in a black silk hat as he leaped heavily down, practically flattening me as he did so.

"A rare talent, that butcher," commented his friend. "Perhaps I should ask cook to get the meat from him in future—show some support."

"Or perhaps not," said the other, already laughing in anticipation of his own witticism. "You don't know what he does with the ones he knocks out cold. Chop, chop! Meat pies, sir?"

The gentlemen both laughed raucously. I

glared at them and tried to push past, annoyed that they could imply anything so cruel about Syd. The gray-haired man must have noticed me trying to squeeze between them for he looked down and automatically clapped his hand to his watch chain.

"We'd better get back to the club," he murmured to his companion. "This place is rife with pickpockets, they say."

The pair pushed past me, knocking me backward into another bystander. I had no time to be offended, for I now found myself buffeted to the ground by the person I had been thrown against.

"Watch where you're goin', Tiddler," he jeered.

I knew that voice. I kept my head down, eyes trained on the steel caps of his boots, hoping he wouldn't notice. Unfortunately for me, some of my hair had escaped from the back of my cap.

"'Ere, wot's this?" he crowed with delight. I was seized by the shoulder and pulled to my feet. "Well, well, a little pussycat pretendin' to be a tom."

A hand snatched the cap from my head, letting my hair tumble over my face. I pushed it out of my eyes and looked furiously up into the face of Billy

Boil. He was not looking at me now: he stood in the middle of a group of his followers, twirling my cap nonchalantly on an index finger, gazing about him to see if I was under anyone's protection.

"'Ere on your own? That's very brave of you, ain't it? Come to see lover boy fight?"

"Give me that!" I said in a fury, making a grab for my cap.

"Oops!" said Billy with a taunting smile as he sent the hat sailing over my head to a pox-faced boy on the other side. Pox-Face dangled the cap just out of reach, pulling it away each time I jumped to snatch it back. Billy's gang, simple minds all, hooted with laughter. I, however, was not amused. I felt hot with humiliation and was annoyed that I teetered so perilously close to tears.

"Aw, look, boys! The little pussycat doesn't like playing with us!" jeered Billy when his sharp eye spotted me wiping away a tear of anger.

Sick of their teasing, I tried to make a run for it, determined to abandon my hat if this was the only way of escape, but Billy stepped forward to catch me by the back of my jacket. Reluctant though I am to admit this, Reader, I have to say that Billy does have his boys well trained, for his gang quickly formed a ring around me, shutting me in as well as hiding me from any friends who might be looking for me.

"Such a shame she don't like playing with us, for I 'eard Little Miss Cat wanted to be in a gang." Billy pulled me toward him. "I'd even 'eard that the blockhead butcher didn't want 'er, so I thought to myself, I thought, why not let 'er join me gang? Add a bit of class, she would." Billy grabbed my cap from Pox-Face and presented it to me with a bow. "Wot you say to that?"

I took the hat suspiciously, expecting him to whip it away again at the last moment, but he didn't. I quickly stuffed it back on my head and made a dash to escape. He gave another tug on my jacket, bringing me back like a fish on a line.

"Not so fast. You ain't given me your answer."

"Answer?" I asked warily, feeling like a sheep surrounded by a pack of wolves.

"Yeah. Do you want to join my gang?"

I stopped pulling away from him.

"You're joking."

"I'm not."

I gazed up into Billy's hard green eyes but saw no mockery in them, only cold calculation. "Why me?"

He looked away and winked at his followers. "Gawd, girl, I'm not askin' you to marry me nor nuffink! Why not you? You're as good as many a boy I know—and better than some."

Despite myself, I felt a rush of pleasure to hear this compliment from Billy Shepherd, of all people. He was offering me a chance to really belong in Covent Garden, to move from the sidelines where Syd had put me and join in with the boys' adventures, to be party to the secret signs and passwords of a gang. I was tempted, sorely tempted. If only the offer had come from Syd, whom I admired and trusted, and not from his devious rival! I would have to refuse, of course, but . . . I looked around the ring of faces, hard-bitten, tough characters all. What would they do to me when I said no?

"That's very decent of you, Billy," I began, backing away from him, looking for an escape route, a weak spot in the wall. Perhaps if I ducked under the biggest boy's legs? "But you don't want a girl like me in your gang."

He gave me a broad grin and tipped his hat back on his head. He smirked at his boys. "See, I told you I'd 'ave to woo 'er!" He turned back to me. "You're wrong, girl. That's just what I want."

"But I'm useless at fighting—I'd let you down."

His grin, if anything, got wider. It was like looking into the jaws of a Nile crocodile waiting to swallow me up. "Don't believe it, Cat. You're a terror when your blood's up—a real little wildcat with 'er claws out. Anyway, I want other talents in my gang than fightin'. I've got Meatpie Matt 'ere to do the punchin'." He gestured toward a burly lad not much smaller than Syd but with none of Syd's blond good looks to recommend him. "Nah, I need you for somethink else."

I had backed up as far as I could go without actually bumping into the ferret-featured boy with carrot-red hair on my side of the circle.

"What's that?" I asked, curious despite myself to know what had prompted Billy to make so astonishing an offer. I could see how he might derive a twisted pleasure from taking one of Syd's friends away from him, but it still seemed a very unlikely proposition.

"It's obvious, ain't it?" said Billy, rocking on his heels casually, though his eyes were still fixed on me. "Brains, Cat, brains. I want you for what you know— though, as you're bein' so slow on the old uptake, perhaps your reputation for wit and learnin' is a case of *misrepresentation?*" He said the last word proudly, as he rarely indulged in words with more than two syllables.

I was flattered. I had not known that I was so highly spoken of in the market. But his praise did not change the essentials of my position: I would have to rely on some of the brains for which I was famed to extricate myself from this circle. But how?

Suddenly, a sooty boy burst through the outer guard into the middle of the circle.

"There you are, Cat!" exclaimed Lord Francis. "We wondered what had happened to you! I was very perturbed to find that you had not followed us."

"Per-what?" guffawed Billy, grabbing Lord Francis by the lapels of his filthy jacket. "'Oo do you think you are, Sootie? A dook or somethink?"

It was an alarmingly accurate guess. I could tell from the look on Lord Francis's good-natured face that he had only just twigged he had walked in on a dangerous situation. He opened and shut his mouth like a fish landed at Billingsgate, but made no comprehensible sound.

"Queer fellas you're making friends with, Cat," said Billy, discarding Lord Francis by pushing him to one side into Meatpie Matt. Meatpie threw the peer of the realm to the ground like a rag doll. "That'll 'ave to stop, you understand? Can't 'ave a girl in my gang mixin' with the wrong sort."

"Er, Billy," I began, my eyes on the crumpled body of Lord Francis.

"Yeah, Pussycat?"

"I haven't actually given you my answer yet."

Lord Francis started to scramble to his feet. Billy absentmindedly kicked him to the floor again and stood with his hobnailed boot on the neck of the duke's son.

"Wot was that you were sayin'?" he said, his eyes sparkling maliciously. We both knew that if I refused to join him, the pressure of his boot would increase.

"Can I think about your offer?" I asked lamely, though I knew what his answer was likely to be.

"Sadly not. For a number of pressin' reasons." He made Lord Francis gasp as he placed more weight on his neck, "I need an immediate acceptance."

My choices were not attractive. Refuse and face the consequences of being the reason why a member of the nobility is kicked to a pulp; accept and find myself under Billy's leadership. I'd prefer to put *my* neck under his boot than to do that. At least I could try to help Lord Francis, not least because his face was now an unbecoming shade of purple.

"Billy, really it's very decent of you—but no!"

Even as I spoke, I put my head down and ran full pelt at him, taking him quite by surprise. I charged into his stomach, knocking us both to the floor, in the process achieving my aim of getting him away from Lord Francis. In the confusion that followed, Lord Francis scrambled to his feet and had the sense to run for it. I tried to do the same but found my ankle seized by Billy. I froze. There was no kind Mrs. Peters to hide me today.

"Wot you make of that, Billy?" laughed Ferret-Features. "Not a wildcat—a miniature bull, that's wot she is!"

The gang were all now roaring with laughter at the ridiculous sight of their great leader floored by a girl half his size—all except Billy, that is. He did not appreciate the joke. I could feel his hand shaking with anger, but he had to make light of it or risk losing their respect. I knew then I was in deep trouble.

"Look, lads!" he exclaimed, pulling on my ankle. "You saw that: she fair threw 'erself at me, she did. Couldn't resist me!"

"Let go, you beast!" I shouted, kicking at him to release his grip, squirming and twisting on the muddy ground.

Without looking at me, Billy tightened his hold and got to his feet, in effect dragging me up upside down so I was left dangling powerlessly. My ankle hurt hellishly in his fist and I could feel all the blood rush to my head. Billy was now pretending not to hear my protests, play-acting as if I did not exist. This his gang found even funnier.

"Anyone 'ear that cat meowin'?" he asked his gang loudly, cupping his free hand to his ear. "Sounds in a bad way. Perhaps someone should put it out of its misery."

The boys bellowed with laughter; Ferret-Features doubled up with mirth. Then, suddenly, the laughter stopped. I felt the grip on my leg give way as I was dropped hurriedly to the floor. Next a pair of strong hands lifted me to my feet and clumsily brushed me off.

"What you doing to Cat?" asked Syd from behind me, his voice laced with menace.

Billy's grin had frozen on his face. He looked pale, tensing for a fight.

"We were just playin', weren't we, Cat?" said Billy. "'Avin' a laugh." His right hand was feeling for something in his pocket. I caught a glimpse of a blade in his palm.

"I didn't see her laughing," said Pedro, pushing his way forward to stand beside me, Lord Francis with him.

Billy shot Pedro a poisonous look, and I could feel Syd's bandaged hands tighten on my shoulders as he prepared himself for another battle. Panic fluttered in my stomach: I didn't want to be the reason that more blood was spilled.

"It was nothing, Syd. Let's go," I muttered, turning away.

Syd looked down at my upturned face with a strange expression in his eyes: part pity, part understanding. I knew then he'd seen the knife too and was concerned for what would happen to me if this confrontation developed into a brawl. He addressed himself to Billy again. "I've 'ad enough fightin' for one day, Boil, but I'll take you all on if I find you touchin' Cat again. Understand this: no one, but no one, messes with my Cat and gets away with it."

Billy slipped his hand in his pocket for a second, then raised his hands, palms open, as if to say something placatory to his rival, but Syd ignored him, steered me around, and marched me through the silent ranks of Billy's gang. Having just seen him fell the Camden Crusher, no one wanted to chance their arm against him now.

Once we had reached the safety of Syd's party of supporters, I felt relieved but also ashamed of myself. I should not have come to the match. I had run straight into trouble and almost come to grief. Syd's father, a ruddy-faced man with fists like hams, gave me a disapproving stare as he watched his son usher me over to a stool at the ringside.

"Let's see that ankle, Cat," Syd said tenderly, taking off the rough woolen stocking on my right leg. Lord Francis, whom I suspected I had to thank for raising the alarm, hovered behind Syd, looking both embarrassed and anxious. Indeed my ankle was not a pretty sight: you could see the marks made by Billy's fingers now blooming into red and blue bruises.

Syd's frown deepened. "I should've punched his stupid face in 'ad I known 'e'd done this."

"It's nothing, Syd," I said quickly, not wanting him to think I was bothered by so slight an injury. "As he said, he was just teasing."

"Teasing!" exploded Pedro. "He had you upside down. That's torture, not teasing. You shouldn't play his game, Cat!"

"I didn't exactly ask to be treated like that!" I answered, channeling the pain into anger at

Pedro's remark. "If you hadn't all run off so quick, I wouldn't have been left alone and he wouldn't've dared pick on me!" I stood up, intending to make a dignified exit, stamping off back home, but collapsed again as a stabbing pain shot up my leg.

"Cat is right," said Lord Francis, looking abject. "We were most remiss to leave a lady on her own."

"We were what?" asked Nick.

"You shouldn't've run off," I translated, "leaving me with that dung-ball Billy Shepherd."

"So that was Billy "Boil" Shepherd?" asked Lord Francis eagerly.

The knowledge that he had just been wrestling with one of London's most infamous gang leaders seemed to restore his spirits, which had been depressed by Billy's boot.

"Let me make some amends for our lamentable neglect by paying for a chair to carry you home," he said, pulling out a guinea from his well-filled purse.

Nick and Syd stared at him in amazement.

"Where'd you get that?" asked Syd. "I'll not 'ave you friends with no thief, Cat." He rounded on me, assuming that Lord Francis's wealth must be ill-gotten.

"Nothing to worry about, Syd," said Pedro, "it's his. He's not what he seems."

Syd gave the blackened face of Lord Francis a hard stare. He may not be quick, but given time, Syd can usually see his way through a brick wall. "You a gent?"

Lord Francis glanced at Pedro anxiously. He now knew to fear the gang leaders of Covent Garden. He wasn't to know that the mountain of muscle in front of him had a much sweeter nature—few people did.

"He is," said Pedro.

"What d'you mean bringin' 'im along, Cat?" Syd said angrily, immediately assuming it was all my fault. "Didn't you stop to think what might 'appen to 'im if 'e was found out?"

"It was my idea," said Pedro, but he could not draw Syd's fire like that. Syd had got it fixed in his head that I must be responsible for the whole affair.

"So why didn't you stop it?" he continued, still berating me. "You know Pedro's green—'e don't know nuffink yet about the streets, but you do, Cat! I thought you were clever!"

It might have been a good moment to employ one of those moves that Richardson's heroines use in his novels—a good faint or tears might have reminded Syd he was supposed to be feeling sorry for me. But it was beneath my dignity to indulge in such foolishness.

"You're right, Syd, I should've stopped him," I said, feeling quite defeated by the day. "If you don't mind, I'd like to accept Lord Francis's offer and go home." I stood up. Lord Francis offered me his arm and I began to hobble over to the gate.

My avowal of being in the wrong had taken the heat out of Syd's anger.

"You can't walk like that all the way to Oxford Street, you daft kitten. I'll carry you," he said, picking me up as if I weighed no more than a doll. "Come on, your lordship, if you must," he added grudgingly over his shoulder to Lord Francis. "I ain't got the gold for a chair—you'll 'ave to foot that bill."

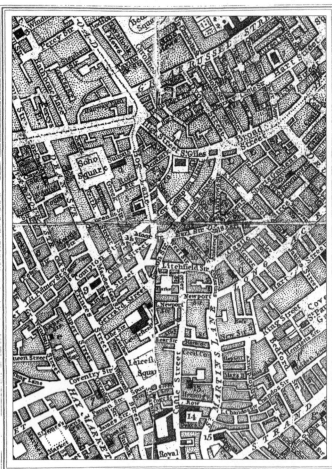

Act III - In which two of our characters have very close shaves . . .

ACT III

SCENE 1—A REWARD

I have to confess that I was in a very bad mood for the rest of that day and did not want to see anyone. I hid in the Sparrow's Nest with my ankle wrapped in a cold cloth, feeling sorry for myself. Covent Garden, my home, had become a dangerous place for me. Now that Billy and his gang bore me a grudge for turning them down, I could no longer take my freedom to roam for granted. What was worse, I had fallen out with Johnny. As I half-expected, I met little sympathy for my injury when he spotted me alighting from the sedan chair. He had gallantly rushed out to check that I had enough money to pay for my ride (the Irish chairmen would not think twice about thumping a passenger who turned out to not have the means to pay for the luxury of being carried across London). Leaning on his arm to hobble inside, I told him about the disastrous turn of my outing.

"If you want to run with the hounds, Cat, you shouldn't be surprised if you get a few nips," he said, helping me through the stage door.

That was rich coming from a wanted man skulking in hiding.

"And I suppose that if you want your wit to *sparkle* brightly, Captain," I said boldly, "you have to take cover under the skirts of Drury Lane to escape the pack baying for your blood?" I enjoyed the quiet revenge of seeing his face drain of color as my words hit home.

The pleasure was short-lived. He tightened his grip on my arm and dragged me around so he could look into my face.

"Who told you?" he hissed, his eyes glinting with anger as he gave me a shake. I felt suddenly scared: here was a Johnny I had not yet seen, determined and dangerous. It was the first time my mild teacher had so much as laid a finger on me.

"No one. I guessed," I explained hurriedly. "Don't worry, no one else knows."

He gave me a searching stare and then let go of my arm. He seemed cold and unfamiliar, not the same man who had spent so many hours with me that week.

"They'd better not hear about it from you, Cat, or you'll be the death of me," he hissed. Turning his back, he strode away, heading for the prompter's office, which he had made his temporary home.

"Johnny! I'm sorry!" I called softly after him, glancing around to check no one was in earshot. "Of course I won't say anything. You can trust me."

He gave a shrug without turning to look at me.

"Can I, Cat?" he said and banged the door closed behind him.

So, Reader, you can understand why I had retreated to my nest in a sullen mood. It was now ten o'clock. The theater was quiet but the streets outside were alive with revelers as the taverns did a roaring Sunday trade. Even from my attic, I could hear voices calling out the name of the Bow Street Butcher. Syd was the local hero and was doubtless being feted by his gang somewhere nearby, glorying in his triumph. All his boys would be around him. Pedro was probably there, leading the singing, perhaps playing for him, spending the money Lord Francis had given him for taking him along on his adventure. Of everyone, I felt most angry with Pedro. He was like the cuckoo coming to throw the chick from her nest: he'd taken the place that should've been mine in Syd's gang. And it was his stupidity that brought Lord Francis to the match in the first place, causing me to argue with Syd! And as for my ankle—well, if I could've thought of a way to blame Pedro, I would have.

After an hour of such dismal complaints, I'd had enough.

"Come on, Cat," I told the darkness, "stop feeling sorry for yourself." I realized I was both hungry and thirsty. If I stopped sulking and did something about this, I'd begin to feel happier. This proved to be the case for, standing up, I found that my ankle was much better. Heartened, I picked up my candle and went downstairs in search of company and some food. There would be few people around this late on a Sunday, but I might be able to make it up with Johnny and have supper with him; failing that, perhaps Caleb, the night porter, might have something to eat.

Backstage was silent and very dark. I didn't like it like this: a theater should be full of people and life. Empty, it echoed with ghosts of past performances and dead actors. My candle cast long, misshapen shadows where it caught on the ropes strung like spiderwebs from the roof. I had to be careful as I made my way around scenery waiting in the wings: fragments of castle battlements littered my path, wizened trees grew from the boards in a thicket that caught on my clothes. An enchanter's laboratory, abandoned in one corner, gleamed with glass bottles fastened to wooden shelves and gilt-edged spell books. It rattled as I passed as if it hid a skeleton that was trying to break out of its cupboard.

"Johnny?" I called outside the prompter's room. My voice sounded frail in the yawning darkness. There was no answer. I pushed the door open. A low fire lit the room with a red glare. His office was filled with piles of scripts. A small camp bed, neatly made, stood ready in one corner. Pens, drawing equipment, and paper were bundled underneath it. But there was no Johnny. I closed the door softly.

A noise behind me like the sound of a distant door clicking to caught my ear. I spun around.

"Johnny?"

No answer.

Apart from Johnny and the night porter who manned the door, I did not expect anyone else to be in the theater. Perhaps Johnny had gone in search of me? Perhaps he had also wanted to make up? Even if he didn't, I would have welcomed a further reproof as long as I could have company.

I moved as swiftly as I could in the direction of the noise and found myself outside Mr. Sheridan's office. I paused, trying not to breathe too loudly. Yes, there was definitely someone moving stealthily about inside, but it couldn't be Johnny, not in this office. I could hear the scrape of a chair as it was dragged across the floor. Had Mr. Sheridan come in for something? That was most unusual this late on a Sunday night.

"You'll keep my jewel safe for me, won't you, Cat?"

My promise to Mr. Sheridan came back to me as I stood in the dark corridor outside his office. What if someone was in there right now? What if they had already found the diamond? I had to stop them. Looking around for inspiration, my eyes lighted upon a spear leaning against the wall: I recognized it as the one used in the pageant for "Rule, Britannia". Though blunt, it should be sufficiently menacing to scare off a would-be burglar. But what if it was Mr. Sheridan? I couldn't just go bursting in and threaten him with a spear. There was a chance that he might find it funny; on the other hand, he might decide I'd gone too far. He was very particular as to who entered his office. Taking the spear in my right hand, I gently eased the door open with my left and peeked in. I could see a dark figure, too small for Mr. Sheridan, standing on the chair, searching along the shelves opposite.

"Stop right there!" I shouted, pushing the door open with a bang. My abrupt entrance made the burglar totter on his chair in surprise, and he fell to the floor. I rushed forward, intending to capture the thief by pinning him to the ground with my weapon—he was, after all, not much bigger than me—but he was too quick. He leaped to his feet, seized the end of the spear, and pulled it sharply from my hands, sending me crashing into the table. I squealed with pain as the thief grabbed my arms and bent one up behind me.

"Be quiet!" hissed a familiar voice. "Do you want the porter to find us?"

It was Pedro! I stopped struggling.

"Let go!" I said furiously. He still had my arm bent back.

"Promise not to shout?" he asked, giving it a painful tweak.

I nodded. I couldn't believe it: Pedro was the burglar!

He released me and bent to pick up the spear.

"Thinking of sticking this in me, were you?" he said lightly, touching the blunted end of the spear before leaning it against the desk.

"What are you doing here?" I asked, rubbing my arm. He was avoiding my eyes, pretending to be busy righting the overturned chair.

"I could ask you the same thing," he replied.

"I live here, remember?" I said sarcastically. "You were looking for it, weren't you?"

"What?" he said, now tidying some papers he had pulled from the shelf in his fall.

"Pedro, don't fool with me! You were looking for the diamond."

"So what if I was?" he said with a shrug.

"But that'd be stealing. We promised to look after it!" I protested.

"*You* promised; I didn't."

"But it's still stealing!"

"So what?" said Pedro, looking up at me for the first time, his eyes full of anger. He was glaring at me, not as if he was seeing Cat, the girl he had befriended, but an English girl, a white girl from a nation grown rich on slavery. I didn't like that look. "Don't you think it was wrong that I had everything stolen from me? My family, my home, even my freedom? So what if I just want to have enough money to get away from here? To go somewhere where I can be truly free. A place where people won't see my skin first, but me."

"I see you, Pedro," I said quietly.

He shrugged. "You do perhaps—but maybe that's because you're no better off than me, Cat."

A new thought struck him and he grabbed hold of my forearms, pulling me toward him eagerly. "What about you, Cat? Don't you want to escape all this? If we found that diamond, we wouldn't have to take another beating in our lives. We could repay everyone for the insults we've suffered. When I saw that beast dangling you by your ankle, laughing at you, it reminded me . . ." He stopped and let go of me, turning his back.

"Of what?" I prompted, wondering what he had been going to say.

"Of being a slave, damn you!" he said angrily, as if it were my fault I'd made him remember. "Look, don't you realize that with that diamond you could make Billy Shepherd sorry he ever touched you?"

"No, I couldn't." I shook my head vigorously. "I'd have to run away and hide for the rest of my life if I stole. Anyway, it's different for me. You say your life was stolen from you—and it was—but Mr. Sheridan saved my life. I'd've frozen on the doorstep if he hadn't taken pity on me. I can't repay that by stealing from him."

While I spoke, I could see Pedro locking away the raw pain he had let me glimpse as he remembered his captivity.

"Your problem, Cat, is that you latch on to other people too trustingly." He shoved a ledger back on the shelf as if he were ramming a cannon-ball home. "Do you think Mr. Sheridan cares a damn about you? Of course he doesn't. You're so starved for affection that you think if someone pats you on the head, they must be your friend. Take it from me that pats all too often precede blows. You've got to learn to look after number one."

"Like you, you mean."

"Like me."

"But I do trust my friends. I owe Mr. Sheridan everything."

"It doesn't matter in any case," he said dismissively, giving the room a last inspection to check it appeared undisturbed. "It's not here. I've been through the room three times now and found nothing."

"Three times!" I protested.

"While you were out of the way, burning the

midnight oil on your stories of past adventures, Cat," he said with an ironic grin, "I was thinking of the future."

"But Pedro," I implored him, "promise me you won't risk it again! If you're caught, they'll hang you for certain."

"I promise I won't come here—but only because I'm wasting my time. He must have hidden it elsewhere."

"Pedro! I'll have to tell!" I felt like shaking some sense into him as he stood there so calm, so sure of himself.

"No, you won't." His brown eyes looked defiantly at me.

He was right. My loyalty to Mr. Sheridan did not extend to getting a boy executed. I'd have to rely on persuasion rather than threats.

"Please, Pedro!"

"Don't worry. You don't have to know anything about it. I'll be very discreet." He smiled.

"Argh!" I couldn't bear his smug face anymore. Why did he not listen? How could he hope to get away with so audacious a theft? I grabbed his jacket lapels. "Please . . . don't . . . do . . . this!" I gave him a thump on each word until he caught my fists. He was still grinning at me infuriatingly.

"Sorry, Cat, it's my chance to get out. When someone shows me the exit, I take it. And if you knew what was good for you, you'd take it too. Mr. Sheridan will tire of having you as his pet cat one day and what prospects will you have then? Unless a decent man like Syd takes pity on you and marries you, where will you be in a few years? I'll tell you: you'll be out on the street."

I released his jacket and put my hands over my ears, not wanting to hear this from him.

"You're just saying this to excuse what you're doing," I said bitterly. "But I know it's wrong. I'll be all right. I'll find some way of earning my keep— an honest way."

"You're so naive, Cat."

"At least I'm not a thief."

"I'm no thief, I'm just trying to get what I'm owed!"

"Thief!"

"Coward!"

"Thief!"

"Hey, hey," said a man's voice, "what's all this?" Johnny stepped into the room. "Why're you calling each other names? And what are you doing here in any case?"

I looked at Pedro. The pearl earring he still wore in his ear glittered in the candlelight, but he was staring at the floor, no doubt wondering if I was going to tell on him.

"It's nothing," I said. "We were just arguing about . . . about . . ."

"About today," broke in Pedro when he realized I was not going to betray him. "We were angry about what happened at the boxing."

Johnny looked dubiously at us both. "And you decided to have your argument in Mr. Sheridan's office?" He leaned down and picked up the weapon I had brought with me. "With a spear? It must be more serious than I thought."

We both said nothing. What could we say?

"Well, I'll not mention it to Mr. Sheridan this time, but I expect better from you both in future," Johnny concluded, gesturing to us to leave the room. "Especially you, Miss Royal. After all Mr. Sheridan's done for you, I didn't expect you to repay him by entering his office without his permission. Perhaps his trust in you is misplaced?"

"You don't have to worry about that," said Pedro angrily. "Miss Royal remains his loyal servant—or should I say, slave?" He turned from us both and ran off toward the stage door.

"Johnny, I . . ." I began, though I wasn't sure what I was going to say in my own defense without dropping Pedro into the mire.

"Hadn't you better get to bed?" Johnny said severely, showing no interest in hearing further excuses from me. "You've had a trying day: you need your sleep."

I nodded miserably and headed for my bed, feeling terrible that I had now disappointed him twice today. Would that mean he no longer wanted to be my friend? I could sense his eyes on my back as he watched me mount the rickety stairs to the Sparrow's Nest. When I turned at the head of the staircase to bid him good night, he was already walking to his own room. It was then that I noticed the brace of pistols stuck in his belt. Unlike my spear, they did not look like stage props. They were real.

The next morning, heartily sick of being frowned upon by Johnny, I was determined to find a friendly face. I took the opportunity of an errand to the other theater in Covent Garden to call on Syd. I had come at a bad time—for the squeamish like me, that is—for he was in the process of butchering a particularly large pig. Death had already visited, but there was still much work for the butcher to do in dividing the carcass. Syd's arms were red to the elbows in blood.

"Ah, Cat," Syd said, smiling at me over the pig's snout, his face a lattice of cuts and bruises from the match. The creature grinned affably up at us—a silent third in our tête à tête. "'Ow you feelin'? "'Ow's the ankle?"

"Much better, thanks, Syd," I said hovering by the door, relieved to find that he at least did not bear me a grudge for what happened.

Syd brought his cleaver down with a thwack and threw the head into a bucket, slopping the floor with blood. I hurriedly lifted my skirts out of the way.

"Sorry, Cat. Not used to 'avin' a lady watch me work."

The bloody scene before me took me back to the boxing match.

"Aren't there easier ways of earning a living?" I asked wistfully, leaning on the doorpost to take the weight off my sore leg.

Syd looked hurt. "What's wrong with butcherin'?"

"Nothing," I said quickly and truthfully. It was an honest trade of which no one should be ashamed. "I meant being battered to a pulp in the ring."

"Ah, that." Syd brought the cleaver expertly down on the pig's trotters, shearing them off. "I don't expect a girl to understand, but it's my only way to fame and fortune, Cat. Butcherin' is all right—but I want more."

"Like what?"

"To be champion, of course. Then, perhaps, one day, own a boxin' academy where fine young gents like your Lord Francis will pay me good money to teach 'em to box. Then I could afford a decent place to live, raise a family in comfort, send my sons to good schools." He gave me a quick look from under his lashes. "I'd be on the up and up." He gave two short staccato taps at the curly pig's tail and threw it onto a tray behind him.

I felt uncomfortable hearing him talk about the future; it was safer to bring him back to the here and now. "You'll be careful, won't you, Syd? Be careful about who you get involved with?"

He laughed. "Course, Cat. Don't you worry your pretty little 'ead about me." He put his cleaver down and gave me a serious look. "To tell you the truth, Cat, I'm worried about you. Word is, the Boil's after you for somethink. You stay away from the market for a bit, won't you? Until I've sorted 'im."

I swallowed. "Sorted 'im—I mean, him?"

"Yeah. We're settling it tonight. In the market. "'Is boys against mine."

"Syd!"

Syd smiled and wiped his hands on his apron, pleased to see, I think, that I was concerned for him. "Don't worry, Cat. 'E don't stand a chance. I'll walk you back now, check nothing 'appens to you."

He would not accept a refusal but escorted me like a prisoner under guard across Bow Street.

"Wait a moment," I said as we paused outside the magistrate's house. A new notice bearing a familiar name had gone up on the sign by the runners' office. A crowd had gathered around it and they were talking animatedly. I had to read it.

Syd obligingly stopped. The people at the front of the gathering respectfully made way to allow him to the best position.

"What's it say, Cat?" he asked. He had never learned to read, having contented himself with mastering a few sums, which came in handy for his trade.

"It's a reward notice," I said glumly. "They're offering a hundred pounds for information leading to the arrest of the man known as Captain Sparkler."

Syd clapped his hands. "Gawd, that'd be a nice sum for someone to pick up!"

"You're right there, mate," a bystander replied.

"I wouldn't mind an 'undred pounds—I could buy my own boxin' club for that and forget about the fightin'." He guided me away from the sign. "Won't be long before someone squeals on him, I'd say."

I nodded, while fervently praying he was wrong. One thing was certain: after last night, I would not breathe a word of what I had found out about Johnny to anyone, particularly not to Pedro. With the lure of a hundred pounds, telling Pedro would be like sending Johnny to the gallows myself.

SCENE 2—THE ROOKERIES

I didn't see either Pedro or Johnny for the remainder of that day. Signor Angelini informed me that Pedro had gone to entertain a duke's son for the afternoon. He seemed to be under the impression that this involved playing the violin; I didn't want to disabuse him, but I suspected that it meant that Lord Francis and Pedro were roaming London in disguise again. I had hoped that I could make it up with Pedro and try to persuade him not to take part in the fight planned for that night. But being warned by Syd to stay indoors, I did not think it wise to go in search of the boys.

As for Johnny, he was in the theater, but "busy." A sign had appeared on his door: "Do not disturb," it read in Johnny's elegant curling script. I pressed my ear to the door and, sure enough, I could hear him inside. From the sounds of the scratching pen, I guessed he was drawing. I could well imagine the reason he did not want any callers: seeing a half-finished drawing by Captain Sparkler on his desk would be as good a way of revealing his identity as running through the streets shouting the secret to the heavens. I waited outside for a time, sitting on a large wooden anchor used to dress the stage for the pieces with a nautical theme, but my watch was barren. Giving up, I trailed back to the Sparrow's Nest and asked Mrs. Reid if she had anything for me to do.

"Lord, girl, look at your face!" she exclaimed. "I've not seen you this miserable since Mr. Salter boxed your ears." She threw me a bundle of darning. "See what you can make of that. Small stitches, mind—none of your fishing nets!"

I picked up my needle and sucked the end of some gray wool to thread it. "Where is Mr. Salter?" I asked. "I've not seen him for ages."

"Oh, he's gone," she said, her brow creased into a worried frown. My heart leaped—at last a piece of good news! "Mr. Sheridan was kind enough to send him off to Bristol the day after his play failed. He said he had an errand for him there, but it's been over a week now and we've not heard from him. I thought the change of scene would do him good, but now I'm very worried about him." Mrs. Reid's eyes, grown short-sighted after years of close sewing, now seemed to be staring at nothing. Her glasses slipped from her bony nose and dangled from their ribbon on her chest. As a widow, it was widely known backstage that she had set her cap for Mr. Salter, the most eligible bachelor to appear in Drury Lane for many years. She had a fair bit set by for a rainy day, it was said: what with her money and his pretensions to gentility, it was an advantageous match on both sides. But I couldn't imagine it myself. Anyone marrying that dry old stick of a playwright, even if he was the second cousin to a lord over Norwich way, must need their head examined.

"Perhaps he's not coming back?" I asked hopefully. "Perhaps his cousin has decided to stop him ruining the family reputation with his plays and has offered him employment."

"Don't be silly," said Mrs. Reid waspishly, coming to herself and stabbing her velvet pincushion with a pin. "The Earl of Ranworth does not think anything of the sort. In fact, from what Mr. Salter says, it's the Earl of Ranworth's own son that causes him sleepless nights, not his cousin."

"Oh?" I said, intrigued. This sounded like good material for a story: dissension in high places, wayward sons and worried fathers. It would certainly serve to pass the tedious time of sewing.

Mrs. Reid was flattered by my interest—I knew how to coax her to be indiscreet. She loved passing on gossip and, from the sly expression on her face, I could tell that this was a piece of news she had been sworn not to relate. That made it all the more tempting, of course. She probably excused herself by the thought that I hardly counted.

"Apparently," she said, lowering her voice to a confidential whisper, "the Earl of Ranworth's son has run away. He got himself into some kind of trouble and cleared off without so much as a change of clothes." She pinched her glasses back onto her nose and picked up her needle. "Fell out with his father over plans for his future, Mr. Salter says. He'd be disinherited if it wasn't for the entail."

"The entail?"

"The Ranworth estates are legally tied to the next male heir. The poor Earl of Ranworth has no power over his son."

Lucky son, I thought. He could afford to be rebellious.

"I shouldn't be telling you this," she went on, though from her face, I could tell she was enjoying speaking so freely before me, "but Mr. Sheridan has been helping to find the young man. He sent Mr. Salter, who knows what he looks like, you see, thanks to the family connection, to search the docks at Bristol. There was a rumor that he was heading abroad from there."

I hid a smile, imagining the prim Mr. Salter poking his nose into the rough and ready dealings of Bristol docks. I could understand now why Mrs. Reid was concerned: if Mr. Salter wasn't picked up by the press gang and thrown on board one of His Majesty's ships, he could easily be worked over by a party of drunken sailors. He would stand out as rich pickings for any troublemaker.

"Oh, I'm sure Mr. Salter will be all right," I lied to comfort her. "He'll be back soon, probably bringing the young lord with him, having had a splendid adventure."

"And it might give him something worth writing about," I added under my breath.

She grumbled something in denial of my optimistic words, and we returned to our sewing. I was making a hash of mine as usual, doubly so because of my unsettled mood. I tried to hide the evidence from the eagle eye of Mrs. Reid by covering the worst with my apron. I had enough experience of her temper to know that if she was fretting about her lost beau she might take it out on me with her birch measuring rod. My hands still bore the scars of her last bad day.

It came to me as I sat there that since I had first heard about the diamond, everything had turned strange. It was as if the stone stood between me and all the usual things of my life, fracturing and distorting them from their true shape. I wasn't the only one hiding things under my apron. No one was as they seemed. Mr. Sheridan, who claimed not to have enough money to pay for candles, had a valuable diamond somewhere in the theater, probably not so very far from where I was sitting.

Then there was Johnny. At first glance he seemed an innocent young man making his own way in the world, when in truth he was branded a traitor by the government and was hiding from the law. Not only that, he continued to disguise the fact that he was still drawing his treasonous cartoons by shutting himself away from us all.

And did it bother me that we had a criminal in our midst? I must admit it didn't. I just thought that the government lacked a sense of humor if they took offense at his drawings. Some of the things he told me, like equality for men and women, for black and white, made a lot of sense. As for the "dung heap of history," you may be shocked, Reader, to know that I wasn't too concerned what happened to our monarchy hidden away in their palaces of marble and gold. ~~If the people decided to get rid of the king, good luck to them~~,* it was unlikely to make

*Struck through by the censor.

much difference to me stuck here at the bottom of society. But I couldn't see it happening in my lifetime, not least because we wouldn't want the Froggies to think we were copying them.

And then there was Pedro. He had been deceiving me. Since he had rescued me from the balloon, I'd taken him on trust as a friend and introduced him to my own circle, but now I thought that he'd really only ever been thinking about cheating on me. From the very first day, he had taken advantage of my indiscretion in telling him about the diamond and intended to steal from my patron. The belief that Pedro had used me hurt deeply. You see, Reader, I liked Pedro: he was talented and brave, he had a self-composure that I could never aspire to—he had the bearing of a little king. No wonder Syd and the others called him "Prince." I had wanted to be Pedro's friend and had hoped that he had begun to like me too, but it appeared I had been mistaken. I'd just been a rung on the ladder he was climbing to riches. Now I didn't know whom I could trust.

Except Syd. Yes, I thought with a smile, he was straightforward. If he didn't like something, he told you to your face and that was that. There were no surprises with him. At least, I hoped not. Recently I had begun to fear that maybe he . . . No, I didn't even want to entertain the idea that he had feelings for me. That would make them more real somehow and complicate everything horribly. Syd was Syd. I'd leave it at that.

Monday was a quiet night for the theater. After the play finished, the crowds dispersed quickly and we were ready to close up by ten thirty. I stood at the stage door with Caleb watching Mrs. Siddons, our leading actress, sign autographs for her admirers before she retired for the night. She was a stately lady with a mass of elegantly arranged hair and good taste in gowns. She shared her brother's mesmerizing dark eyes—eyes which were now bent to speak to a young admirer—but on stage she could rivet thousands to their seats by the power of her presence. Under her spell, they groaned when she groaned, wept when she wept. To see her play Lady Macbeth was to experience true horror.

"Fine lady that," muttered Caleb appreciatively. "Famed throughout the land but still remembers me by name and gives me a penny for my smokes now and then."

I murmured my agreement and thought him very lucky. Mrs. Siddons moved in circles far above mine. She rarely spoke to me—perhaps only to thank me for doing some small errand for her—but I idolized her. She was the queen of British theater and I her most loyal subject.

"Here, Caleb, can I have a word?" It was Johnny. He had waited for the crowds of Mrs. Siddons's admirers to disperse before collaring the porter. "Can you find someone to deliver this for me?"

I peered with interest at the long, thin package wrapped and sealed with red wax. It took no great brains to guess that it was the cartoon he had been working on all afternoon. Johnny saw me looking and frowned.

There was no time to dwell on this, for a ragged boy ran into the little courtyard by the stage door, his face the very picture of terror, and bounded straight up to me.

"You Cat?"

"Yes. What is it?" I didn't recognize him—his clothes were hanging on by threads and he was crusted with dirt.

"I's told I'd find you 'ere. You've gotta come wi' me. The African boy's askin' for you. It's bad."

"What? Pedro? What's bad?"

"The fight. 'E's been 'urt—mortal 'urt."

All my anger at Pedro was swept away on hearing the threat to his life. If he was asking for me at this moment, it must mean that I hadn't been completely wrong: Pedro did care for me too. What did a silly argument between us matter when he could be dead by tomorrow morning?

"Where is he?" I asked, grabbing the boy's arm.

"Foller me," he said, running back the way he had come.

"Cat! Where're you going?" called Johnny behind me.

I had no time to explain: he'd try to stop me going and every minute might count. I'd never forgive myself if I arrived too late. *Too late for what?* a voice in my head asked. I didn't want to think about that. I dashed after the boy, flakes of snow stinging my cheeks. The boy did not lead me toward Covent Garden as I had expected. Instead, he raced over Long Acre, heading northwest for the narrow streets of St. Giles, otherwise known as the Rookeries. I hesitated on the curb, but fearing to lose him, darted across the slushy street in pursuit. I knew London too well to choose to go into St. Giles of my own free will. In normal circumstances, I would have given this district a wide berth. The people who lived there, mostly vagrants, thieves, and beggars, were said to strip the possessions of any fool who wandered into their lanes, hair and teeth included. They were a law unto themselves, a patch of wild savagery, a running sore in one of the richest cities in the world.

Plunging into the maze of alleyways, I immediately felt the threatening atmosphere: the houses were so shoddily built they seemed to collapse onto each other across the street, blocking out the sky above. Whispers of smoke seeped out of the crazy chimney pots. The only lights came from the gin shops and taverns, which stank of drink, sweat, and sickness. Even the steady fall of pure white snow was sullied by the time it landed on the cesspool that passed for a roadway in these slums.

"Wait!" I called after the boy. "Where are you taking me?"

The boy paused, shifting from leg to leg nervously as I caught up with him. He too felt happier to be on the move rather than standing still waiting to attract trouble.

"Not much farther," he said, wiping his nose on the back of his hand. He had a feverish look: his cheeks were flushed and his eyes unnaturally bright. "'E's been carried into the King's 'Ead."

He set off again and darted down a side street into an even darker courtyard. The stench of overflowing drains was unbearable, and I had to force myself to follow him. I shuddered as I nearly stepped on a dead rat lying stiff in the roadway. A mangy cat with one eye and half a tail slunk past, disappearing into a crack in the wall of a boarded-up house. The boy ducked into a low doorway with a creaking sign overhead. A crude painting of Charles I, holding his severed head under one arm, swung above the entrance, snow resting like a funeral wreath on the picture. I dashed inside. Expecting to see Pedro lying in a pile of bloody rags, perhaps already dead, I found the taproom empty. There was only a small fire in the grate, a table and bench, an untended barrel of beer.

Once across the threshold, I had a very bad feeling about the place. The feverish boy had disappeared. Every instinct was screaming that, Pedro or no Pedro, it was time to run for it. I turned to leave but at that moment a customer stepped into the King's Head and shut the door firmly behind him, shaking the snow off his hat. Billy Shepherd. My heart sank to my boots. Footsteps came from the back room and Ferret-Features, Pox-Face, and Meatpie Matt lumbered in, all looking mightily pleased with themselves.

"Delighted you could make it, Cat," said Billy with menacing politeness as he gestured for me to take a seat on the bench. I remained standing, snow melting on my shawl and dripping to the floor.

"Where's Pedro?" I asked bleakly. "What've you done with him?"

"I've no idea where Blackie is, Cat," said Billy with a laugh. "'E's probably in Covent Garden waitin' for the fight—the fight they all thought was goin' to 'appen. You see, I 'ad to think up a little distraction so I could get you out of Drury Lane. It was pretty clever, don't you think? You all fell for it 'ook, line, and sinker."

I felt sick. It was a trap. There was no Pedro in his death throes, no big fight in the piazza, just stupid old me stuck with my enemy in a place where anything could happen. And I mean anything: they could murder me here and now and no one in St. Giles would turn a hair. If I wanted to live, this was no time to annoy Billy. I sat down.

"So, 'ow do you like my center of operations?" He gestured around the squalid room. "I'm thinkin' of branchin' out from the market, takin' a piece of the Rookeries under my wing. You're privileged: you're the first outsider to see my 'eadquarters. What'ya think?'

"It's very, er, very nice," I said, my voice shaking slightly.

In fact, it was cold, foul, and damp. I could see why a rat like Billy would be attracted to it.

He smiled at me, displaying his rotten teeth like gravestones in his ugly mouth. He reached forward to brush the snow from my hair. I tried not to flinch. He was testing me, looking for an excuse to hurt me as I knew he so badly wanted to do. I'd insulted him by giving him a nickname; I'd humiliated him in front of his gang; I had twice offended his "honor"; and I was to pay for it.

"Now, Cat, about our little discussion yesterday." He moved to stand behind me out of sight, but I could see Ferret-Features grinning over my head at him, anticipating what was to come. "It didn't quite end 'ow I'd like. You see, I know that you know somethink—somethink that I want to know very much."

This wasn't quite what I expected.

"Oh?" I asked. "What's that?" Perhaps I could bargain my way to safety.

"The diamond." Billy rested his hands on my

shoulders, one finger caressing my neck. "If you tell me where I can find it, I'll let you return 'ome. In fact, even better than that, I'll let you get it for me and I'll buy you a new dress for your trouble." Ferret-Features was now smirking at my street-stained woolen gown. "I can't say fairer than that, can I?"

"Diamond? What diamond?" I spluttered. How had he heard about that?

"Come now, Cat, you're not the only person to 'ang around the stage door. You were seen. We know you know."

"But I don't!" I protested.

There was a grating noise of metal on metal, and I felt a cold blade against my neck.

"Do you know what my family does for a livin', Cat?" he asked casually.

Ferret-Features stared at the knife at my neck like a dog waiting for a bone.

"No," I said, trying not to move.

"We're barbers—'andy with the razor. Now you think about that while you remember where Mr. S. put that diamond."

I was shaking with terror. I really didn't know, but if I told him that he'd probably just cut my throat and have done with me.

"Billy, please!"

"Not convinced yet, Cat? Now, 'ow'd you like it done? Cropped? Or like an Injun Mohican?" There was a sharp jerk on my head, and a lock of red hair fluttered onto the table. Billy caught it up with his left hand and pocketed it.

"A keepsake," he said calmly. "Something for me to remember your pretty curls by. Wot'ya think, Meatpie? Should fetch a decent price at the wig makers, don't ya think? Shame red's not the fashion."

Meatpie laughed dutifully, but unlike Ferret-Features he had the decency to look uncomfortable.

"Please!" I was crying now, tears rolling down my face as I sat rigid, trying not to move, though every instinct in my body was begging to make a dash for the door. "I really don't know where the diamond is. But I'll look for you—I will. I promise."

Billy gave a tug on another strand of hair.

"Sorry, that ain't good enough, Cat. You've always said you know everythink that goes on in that theater, so I bet you know where it is. Anyways, I prefer it like it is now—you 'ere with me with no backup. I think it'll 'elp you make the right decision, 'elp jog your memory. If I let you go, what's to stop you runnin' off and telling your friend Syd about our little chat, eh?"

He was right: that was just what I had been thinking of doing. What would I have given to have Syd by my side at that moment!

"No, I need an answer and I need it now. Then we're goin' to take a little stroll to the theater and you'll 'and it over to me. Agreed?"

What could I do? Make something up? That seemed my best option. At least I'd buy myself some more time.

"Agreed?" Billy said fiercely, giving a painful tug on my hair.

"I, er, I . . .

"Yeah, I'm listenin'."

The door behind us banged open and Billy spun around. As his hand was still grasping my hair, my head was pulled as he turned. Through tear-filled eyes, I saw a man standing framed in the doorway. His black cloak and hat were covered in snow. Both arms were held up in front of him, each hand holding a pistol, one trained on Billy, the other on Meatpie. Meatpie gave a whimper and dived behind the beer barrel.

"In that case, I suggest you listen to me, and listen hard. Put that razor down and move away from the girl," Johnny said. The barrels of the pistols were rock-steady in his hands, both cocked, prepared to fire.

Billy tightened his grip on my hair, dragging me from the bench so I was on my knees in front of him. He brought the blade to my throat. I could feel its sharp edge prick my skin.

"Oo the 'ell are you?" Billy growled.

Johnny gave a flick of the gun barrel, gesturing to Billy to move away from me. His eyes were fixed on my captor, blazing with anger.

"Her backup. Let her go," he said menacingly.

"Or what?" sneered Billy. "I'll cut 'er throat if you take a step nearer. 'Oo said you could come in 'ere and break up our private talk? You don't want 'im 'ere, do ya, Cat?" He used his grip on my hair to shake my head like a marionette.

"You won't find out about the diamond from her," said Johnny coldly. "She knows nothing."

Billy pulled my head back, exposing my throat to the knife.

"So why don't ya tell us then? Tell us, or I'll kill the kitten."

"You won't do that," said Johnny, not even looking at me but keeping his eyes on Billy. Pox-Face made a move on Johnny's left, trying to creep up behind to jump him. "Stay where you are!" ordered Johnny. Pox-Face stood still, eyes fixed on the second gun barrel now pointing at him.

"Oh, won't I?" jeered Billy. "Why not?"

"Because I'll shoot you first."

"You won't do that: you might 'it the girl," said Billy, pressing the blade tight against my throat.

"Take my word for it: I'm a very good shot. I won't miss. Now, what are you going to do?"

There was silence. Then a clatter as Billy dropped the razor on the floor in front of me.

"Very sensible," said Johnny. "Now let her go."

Furious, Billy released his grip on my hair and kicked me away from him, sending me sprawling onto the floor so that I landed on top of the razor. I felt it cut into my arm.

"One more trick like that and I'll blast you to hell," said Johnny fiercely. "Get up, Cat, and come over here."

I scrambled to my feet, cradling my bleeding arm, and stumbled past Johnny out of that hateful place.

"Now understand this," I heard him telling them. "I'm going to escort the young lady home. If I spot so much as a whisker of any of you following us, I'll fire without warning." With a final look at each of them, he ducked out of the room, slamming the door so violently it made the sign creak on its hinges. He then stuffed one of the pistols in his belt, seized my injured arm, and began to run.

"Come on, we must get away from here!" he urged, setting off at a smart pace.

Not needing to be told twice, I ran after him, though hampered by slipping several times on the icy cobbles. Only Johnny's firm grip on my arm stopped me falling to the ground. I was too numb to think of the pain. Pale faces appeared in dark doorways, like ghosts rising from tombs. They watched us pass in eerie silence as the snow fluttered down in frozen tears. Suddenly, a scrawny woman darted forward and made a grab for my shawl. I let it go, leaving it hanging like a tattered flag in her hands.

We turned a corner into a busy thoroughfare of smoke-filled taverns and shabby lodging houses. A drunken Irishman stumbled out of a dark alleyway and into our path.

"Gi' us that!" he shouted at Johnny, trying to pull me away.

I didn't see exactly what Johnny did, but next thing the man was doubled up, hands clenched to his stomach, and we were running out onto St. Giles High Street, and away.

"I can't breathe!" I gasped, my side pierced by a stitch.

"Forget breathing; just run!" Johnny said with an anxious look over his shoulder.

He towed me along after him, back across Long Acre and into Bow Street. Taking a side street to avoid passing the magistrate's house, he did not stop until we reached the stage door. Caleb was on the watch: he threw it open for us and we burst inside, collapsing as soon as we were across the threshold.

"What 'appened to you, sir?" asked Caleb, looking with concern at Johnny's bloodstained hand as my rescuer bent over to regain his breath.

Johnny stared down uncomprehendingly at his palm.

"But I'm not hurt!" He turned to me. I was on all fours, panting and sobbing with relief. "It must be Cat. Let's see."

I raised my left arm to him: a cut, about four inches long, was oozing bright red droplets vivid against the white skin of my inner arm.

Johnny gave a low whistle. "Nasty! An inch lower and that would have got the vein. Here, let me take you to my office and I'll clean it up."

Caleb blanched as he caught sight of the blood dripping down my wrist.

"Will she be all right?" he asked huskily.

"She'll be fine," Johnny assured him. "But keep a sharp eye out tonight, Caleb. The boys who did this might come looking for us. Bar the door and don't let anyone in unless you know them."

"Don't worry," said the old doorman, picking up a stout cudgel he had concealed behind the door curtain. "They won't get past Caleb Braithwaite in a hurry."

"Thanks, my friend," said Johnny.

He then knelt and picked me up. I was so shocked and exhausted by my adventure that I no longer cared what became of me: I just wanted to curl up, fall asleep, and forget all about it. But Johnny had other ideas. There were matters he had to attend to first. He sat me in a chair by his fireside and put a kettle on the fire to boil. Tearing up some clean strips of linen, he set about tending to my wound.

"I'm sorry about that, Catkin. I should have acted faster," he said, shaking his head over the cut.

"You're sorry!" I said in surprise. "You've nothing to be sorry about. It was all my fault: I should never have fallen for their trap."

"They set a trap, did they?" Johnny probed gently as he staunched the wound.

I nodded.

Johnny pressed my hand comfortingly. "I really must know what they said to you. I must know what they know about the diamond."

So he was in on Mr. Sheridan's secret too! It occurred to me then that he might even have been put here to help defend it. I looked up at him to see if I could read the truth in his face. His eyes were no longer cold: they had returned to their old friendly expression, and yet tonight I thought I could sense a new shadow in their depths as if he was particularly sad about something.

"And I need to know why you were with those blackguards in the first place, Cat." He turned to take the boiling kettle from the grate and poured some of the contents into a china bowl. "It wasn't you who told them about the diamond, was it?" he asked levelly as he put several teaspoons of salt into the steaming water.

"No!" I protested. "I never said nothing about the diamond—except to Pedro."

"To Pedro?" Johnny asked, his voice careful as if he was walking on thin ice.

"But it wasn't him, neither!" I added. At least, I hoped he hadn't told them. "Ouch!" Johnny had just dabbed my cut with the salted water.

"Billy Boil told me one of his gang had seen me at the stage door. It must have been the night Mr. Marchmont came."

"Who is Billy Boil?" Johnny looked puzzled.

I smiled weakly. "I mean Billy Shepherd. I'm afraid I gave him that nickname: we aren't the best of friends, as you saw. He was the one with the razor—the one you threatened with the pistols."

"Oh those," said Johnny contemptuously, taking the pistols from his belt and throwing them onto the camp bed still cocked. I ducked, half expecting them to explode. "I didn't have time to load them. If I had, I would have ended that interview much sooner, believe me. No, I was curious as to why you were running off into the night and I took it into my head to follow you."

"The messenger told me Pedro had been hurt."

"Ah. Now I see."

I suddenly realized why Johnny had taken the risk of following me into St. Giles. It hadn't been out of gallantry as I had assumed.

"You didn't trust me, did you? You thought I was going to betray you."

He tied off the bandage around my arm and sat back on his haunches.

"I must admit it did cross my mind. I was going to run for it if I saw you going to the magistrate to tip them off about the new cartoon. Whatever my motive, I am heartily thankful I did follow you. I dread to think what would have happened if I hadn't been on hand."

"I'd be dead and my hair a wig in Pollard's window. I think you can be quite certain of that," I said with a small laugh that turned into a shudder.

Johnny pressed my fingers again. "That would have been a very sad loss to Drury Lane. So, tell me, what did they know about the diamond?"

"Not much," I said with a shrug. "Just that it's hidden in the theater. They thought I could fetch it for them."

He bit his lip and looked away from me to the fire. Bright flames danced on the coals, casting an orange glow over his handsome features. I was beginning to love seeing that face about the theater. He was the only one who called me Catkin in that affectionate way of his, the only one who took the trouble to tell me things.

"I think it's become too dangerous to have the diamond here," he said. "I'll have to tell Sheridan it's got to move."

"Move where?" I asked eagerly.

"Come now, Cat. You don't really want to know that, do you?" he laughed. "Look what danger a little bit of knowledge got you into tonight."

"It was my ignorance, not what I knew, that landed me in trouble," I countered.

"So you would've handed the diamond over to them, would you, if you'd known where it was?" he asked with a strange smile.

"No, of course not. I'd've thought of something before it reached that point."

"I doubt that. Shepherd does not look the type to allow little girls to trick him out of a great prize. But in any case, you need not worry. I meant that the diamond should be put far out of anyone's reach. Sent to America, for example."

"America! So far?" I exclaimed. "What do they want with diamonds in America? I thought there was nothing but Indians and rebels in America."

"That about sums it up," said Johnny with a laugh. "Come now, to bed with you."

He helped me to my feet.

"Thank you, Johnny," I said quietly. I had to say it before I left.

"For what?"

"For saving my life."

He bent down and kissed the top of my head as a father or brother might do. Receiving this tender gesture, I felt an acute sense of loss. I had survived by not thinking too much about what I couldn't have, but tonight I suddenly missed having my own family more than ever. Being with Johnny made me realize what I might have known.

"It was the least I could do," he said, "especially as it was the diamond that put you in danger in the first place."

I was about to put him right on that and explain about the bad blood between Billy and myself, but he ushered me out.

"No more tonight, Cat. We can talk in the morning."

I turned to go but a thought snagged me like a hook.

"Johnny, don't tell anyone about this, will you?" I pleaded.

He shrugged. "I'll have to mention it to Mr. Sheridan—but no one else, I promise. But why?"

"If Pedro hears, he'll tell Syd."

"Syd?"

"The Bow Street Butcher. If he finds out what Billy did to me, it'll be war in Covent Garden. Someone might get hurt, and I wouldn't want that."

"I understand." He paused. "You know, Catkin, you are wiser than you look. Good night."

"Good night, Captain."

SCENE 3—BACKSTAGE

'Are you all right, Cat?'

Pedro found me in the auditorium, replacing the candles in one of the chandeliers. Long Tom had lowered it to be within my reach so I could assist him in the never-ending chore of keeping the theater brightly lit.

"Why do you ask?" I said, not looking at Pedro as I chipped off the drips of wax from the glass reflectors with my nail.

"Are you still cross with me? Don't you want to hear what happened last night?" He sat down on a bench and rubbed his calf muscles like an athlete limbering for a race. He was expected onstage in five minutes for his rehearsal.

I already knew, of course, that nothing had happened in Covent Garden last night, but he was not to know that. A total lack of interest on my part would look suspicious.

"So what happened?" I asked dutifully.

"Nothing. Syd thinks Billy funked it."

"Oh." I spiked a white candle on the prong in an empty bracket.

"I thought you'd be relieved," said Pedro in a disappointed voice. "This means that Billy's surrendered the market to Syd, doesn't it? You'll be able to go out again. He won't dare touch you."

When I closed my eyes, I could still feel the choking pressure of Billy's razor on my throat and touch the stub of hair where he had shaved off a fistful. Pedro's comforting words could not be more ill-founded. I swayed on my feet and reached out for the bench to sit down before I collapsed.

Pedro was alarmed. "Cat? What's the matter? You really don't look well." He now noticed my bandaged forearm. "What did you do to yourself?"

"Nothing," I said, taking a steadying breath, determined not to faint.

"But your arm!"

"It's nothing—just a cut."

Pedro gave me a dubious look but did not pursue the matter. "Well, I know something that will cheer you up. Lord Francis and Lady Elizabeth are coming to the rehearsal today."

I raised my eyebrows quizzically. "In what capacity?"

"Dressed as themselves, of course. Now that you've whetted their appetite for the stage, Mr. Sheridan invited them to bring a party of their friends. They should be here soon."

I looked around quickly, wondering if Johnny was in view: he had to be warned. He would want to keep out of sight of such an invasion in case someone recognized him.

"Come on, Cat," chided Pedro. "Aren't you the least bit pleased?"

"Sorry, Pedro," I said, turning back to him. "Of course I'm pleased." Looking into his deep brown eyes, it was hard to believe at that moment that this was the boy who had cheated on me. He did seem to care. Maybe the diamond-stealing was now all water under the bridge and we could start again?

"Good, for I told Frank that you'd show them around."

"Pedro!"

Pedro leaped to his feet and gave me a bright smile. "Well, I can't, can I? I've got to be onstage." With a final stretch, he bounded away like a gazelle, climbing over the bars to the orchestra pit and up onto the forestage.

Typical! I had just begun to like him again, and he had sprung another surprise on me, using me to entertain his guests. If it weren't for the fact that I liked Lord Francis too, I wouldn't let him get away with it!

I found Johnny in the wings, running through the cues for that night's play with Mr. Bishop. Hovering behind the stage manager, I tried to attract Johnny's attention. This couldn't wait: they could be here at any moment. Finally, my friend looked up and saw me waving at him.

"Mr. Bishop," said Johnny quickly, "I'm sorry to interrupt this, but could we finish this later?"

The rebuff annoyed Mr. Bishop. He was clearly having one of his bad days, but even he found it hard to show offense at Johnny's polite but masterful manner.

"If you must," he said grudgingly. He stuffed his dog-eared copy of the script into a deep jacket pocket. "I'll see how the enchanter's laboratory is coming along. Problem with the hidden compartment—keeps springing open."

He shuffled off, yelling to the carpenter to hurry. It appeared the poor chippie was going to bear the brunt of his anger.

"This better be good, Cat," said Johnny, steering me into the prompter's office. "I have to tread carefully around Bishop. I think he suspects something."

I hurriedly told him about the arrival of the party of young ladies and gentlemen. Striding to and fro in front of the fire, Johnny ran his fingers distractedly through his hair.

"Who do you think will come?" he asked.

I shrugged. "I met a few of their friends at the tea party. Besides Lord Francis and Lady Elizabeth, there was a young lady called Jane, a young gentleman called Charlie, and the Marchmont children."

"The Honorable Charles Hengrave, I imagine," mused Johnny. "I don't know the girl, Jane—probably some poor relation from the country. As for the Marchmonts, I know them all right: horrid little bores, the whole family. I can tolerate the father only because of his political views. As a man, I find him repugnant."

I was surprised by Johnny's intimate knowledge of Lord Francis's circle.

"The Marchmont boy's not like his father," I said quickly. Johnny looked surprised. "What I mean is, he's still horrid, but he doesn't share his father's politics. Lord Francis said he was a supporter of Mr. Pitt and dead against reformers. He certainly didn't like my manuscript—thought it revolutionary stuff, unfit for the delicate ears of his sisters, and all because I wrote about what he considers 'low' subjects."

"Hmm." Johnny fiddled with an inkwell on the mantelpiece, his shoulders in a dejected hunch. "Backstage at Drury Lane is not as safe as I thought—far too public. It's a shame. I wouldn't have minded seeing Lady Elizabeth again." He turned to me. "Is she still as pretty as ever?"

"When did you meet Lady Elizabeth?" I asked, intrigued.

"Oh, here and there," said Johnny lightly, flicking dust from a brass candlestick.

"You're not telling me everything, are you?" A suspicion was beginning to form in my mind, based on a growing awareness that my friend was not as he seemed.

"Of course not." Johnny smiled at me, his eyes twinkling. "But thanks for the warning. I'll lie low in here until the coast is clear. You'll let me know when I can come out of hiding, won't you?"

I nodded. "Of course. And yes," I added slyly before I shut the door behind me, "she still is as pretty as ever."

I met the party of visitors by the main entrance. They had come in two carriages and on horseback. In the lead was Lord Francis with his friend, the Honorable Charles Hengrave, on a pair of fine geldings, accompanied by a footman.

"Here she is!" exclaimed Lord Francis in delight as he bounded up the steps to me, shaking my hand vigorously. "You should've seen her, Charlie! She flattened that bully and saved my skin. She made a splendid boy."

I blushed as Charlie gave me a bow and a grin. It appeared that news of our recent exploits had traveled.

"I hope, Miss Royal, you'll record your adventures for us," Charlie said politely. "I am eager to hear all about it from your pen."

Lord Francis clapped his hand to his head.

"That reminds me!" he cried. "Father was very impressed by your manuscript. He told me to tell you that he'll support your first venture into print when you finish it."

"In that case, she'd better get a move on." This was from Pedro, who had ducked out of the rehearsal to greet his friend. Surrounded by the silk waistcoats and velvet jackets of the young nobles, he looked most out of place in his sailor's costume of blue jacket and white trousers. He was playing and dancing a hornpipe in the musical interlude that night.

Lady Elizabeth arrived on the arm of the young Marchmont. From the pained expression on her normally serene face, she appeared to be doing her best to humor the boy. It was a lost cause: he had come intending to despise everyone and everything. He wrinkled his nose at the tawdry gilt of the auditorium. Drury Lane was in need of renovation and it never looked its best by daylight.

"Poor Lizzie," muttered Lord Francis to Charles Hengrave, "she keeps on trying to be polite to Marzi-pain for Father's sake, failing to comprehend that he's beyond saving."

"Marzi-pain?" I whispered.

"Marzipan—Marzi-pain Marchmont—because of the hair," Lord Francis explained in a low voice.

I still looked puzzled.

"You know, marzipan, that yellowy-white almond stuff you get on cakes?"

He may get it on cakes, but I had never been so lucky. The closest I'd come to confectionery was with my nose pressed against the baker's window.

"Oh, of course," I said, trying to appear perfectly familiar with all details of the confectioner's art.

I hadn't fooled him. "I'm sorry. That was stupid of me. Next time you come to tea, I shall ensure that you sample every sort of marzipan under the sun, Miss Royal. Our French cook is a master."

Marchmont's voice now reached us. Lord Francis grimaced.

"It is not a patch on Covent Garden," he was saying loudly. "Father has a private box there, you know."

He had better pipe down or he might find himself rudely ejected by one of the crew, I thought sourly.

"But, Mr. Marchmont, I'm sure you'll agree that it is not the gaudy wrappings, but the content that counts. The acting here has no rival, with Mr. Kemble, Mrs. Siddons, and Mrs. Jordan to call on," said Lady Elizabeth as she approached us.

Bless her, I thought.

Marchmont sniffed at this statement but said nothing.

Pedro bowed to the ladies. I curtsied.

"I was just telling Miss Royal about Papa's admiration for her manuscript," said Lord Francis loudly. He had evidently not forgotten Marchmont's disapproval of my work and was happy to trump it with a duke's approbation.

Marchmont gave a thin-lipped smile. "Your father has peculiar taste, Lord Francis. I grant that she writes a fair enough hand for a girl of her class, but as for the contents . . ." he left his disapproval hanging in the air. "The drawings, however: thinking about them afterward, I was most intrigued. You surely did not do them yourself, Miss Royal? The style was very distinctive. I could almost swear it was . . . familiar." He looked hard at me, his smile as false as a stage moustache. Had he guessed too much?

Unfortunately, Pedro was oblivious to the sensitivity of the subject.

"No, she didn't. That was Johnny Smith, the prompter," he said. "Cat'll introduce you to him if you're interested. He does really wicked likenesses, really clever."

Not for the first time I could have kicked Pedro for his overeagerness to show off before prospective sponsors. The last thing Johnny needed was for Pedro to go patron-hunting for him.

"Wicked likenesses?" said Marchmont coolly. "I've no doubt of that."

"But he doesn't draw much," I added quickly, trying to warn Pedro with a look. "In fact, it was probably the first time he's put pencil to paper when he drew for me." Pedro looked surprised and was going to dispute this, but I plowed on. "And unfortunately, he's been called away suddenly to . . . to see a sick uncle. He's not here. Not in the building."

I raised my gaze to Marchmont's heavy-lidded eyes. He was now looking at me with a skeptical curl to his lips.

Guiding the young people around Drury Lane was more difficult than I anticipated. The phrase beloved of Mrs. Reid came into my head as I extricated Charles Hengrave and Lord Francis from the basket of the balloon backstage: it was like herding cats. No sooner had I headed off one group from doing something they shouldn't in one department then a new crisis would erupt elsewhere. Hardest to manage was Marchmont.

He seemed determined to open every door and every closet. I could've sworn he was looking for something, and I thought I could guess what it was.

We were approaching the greatest danger: the corridor containing the prompter's office. I had to think of a diversion before he burst in on Johnny.

"Oh, sir," I cried quickly as he approached the door, "you can't go in there."

He turned to give me a bitter smile, scenting his quarry to be nearby.

"Why not, Miss Royal? Mr. Sheridan has given us the passport to roam. He said we were to go anywhere we liked."

"Did he?" I replied, silently cursing my over-generous sponsor. "Well, I'm sure he did not intend the permission to include the ladies' powder room."

Marchmont flushed and removed his hand from the handle as if it had burned him.

"There's no sign," he said hotly.

I shrugged. "Of course not. Those who need it know what it is. If you require the privy, I could ask one of the stagehands to take you."

I enjoyed watching Marchmont's cheeks turn red. "No, no, that won't be necessary," he said, striding purposefully off down the corridor.

Just as I was about to congratulate myself on my cleverness, disaster struck. Lady Elizabeth, waiting for the young gentlemen to leave, whispered aside to me, "I'll call in here for a moment and catch you up."

"No!" I protested, trying to stop her. But it was too late. She had opened the door and stepped inside, closing it swiftly behind her.

"Miss Royal!" called Lord Francis from the scenery lot at the back of the stage. "Miss Royal, tell us again how this balloon thing works."

I stared at the door in agony, expecting Lady Elizabeth to rush out screaming at any moment.

"Leave Lizzie; she'll find us all right," Lord Francis continued.

Not daring to imagine what was happening inside that room, I tore myself away and joined Lord Francis, Miss Jane, and Mr. Charles by the deflated splendors of the balloon. I don't know what they made of my mechanical explanation: I was so distracted that I must have talked utter rubbish.

"What do you think, Charlie?" wondered Lord Francis. "Shall we test it out on old Marzi-pain and leave him up there? It would be doing the world a favor."

Charles Hengrave laughed. "Good idea. You still haven't got your own back on him for snitching to your father about that coach you drove around the Square."

"You're right! How had I forgotten that?"

"Your problem, Frank, is that you're too good-natured to bear a grudge," said his friend approvingly.

"Or too absentminded to remember anything for long," added Miss Jane, with an indulgent smile at her cousin.

Soft footsteps behind me and Lady Elizabeth appeared at my elbow. She looked a little shocked but managed to give me a small smile.

"Unusual powder room, Miss Royal," she said softly. "As I was unable to avail myself of its facilities, perhaps you would be so kind as to guide me to the appropriate chamber?"

"Of course, Lady Elizabeth," I said, feeling a wave of gratitude toward her.

Leaving the rest of the party in the Sparrow's Nest under Sarah Bowers's capable eye, I led Lady Elizabeth to the privy.

When she re-emerged, she took me to one side.

"Do you know who that is, Miss Royal? I assume you do as you were trying to prevent our paths crossing."

I nodded.

"So how did Lord Jonathan Fitzroy come to be here?" she whispered.

"So he is a lord," I said half to myself as her question confirmed my suspicion. Johnny's knowledge of the Avons and their friends had given me a hint that he had moved in higher circles than the one he was currently occupying. I should have put two and two together when I heard Mrs. Reid's story about the Earl of Ranworth and his troublesome son. The rift between Johnny and his father could be explained by the predilection of the son for treasonous cartoons. And why else had Mr. Sheridan dispatched Mr. Salter off to the other end of the country? My patron knew better than to send a fool like that to find someone. He'd been sent out of the way to stop him recognizing his cousin. But Johnny's identity as Captain Sparkler must be preserved as a secret, even from the Avons.

"I think Mr. Sheridan is helping him until a reconciliation can be arranged with his father," I explained. "You won't tell anyone, will you?"

She shook her head, her neat ringlets whispering like silk at her neck.

"No, I've given him my word. He said I could tell my brother if I wished, but no one else. He also said I could trust you." Her cheeks were now blushing. "He said that you'd pass him any messages I might care to send him and you'd bring any word from him to me."

Clearly there was much more to the history of Lord Jonathan and Lady Elizabeth than I knew. As Johnny's friend, I felt it my role to blow his trumpet for him.

"Certainly. I'd like to be of assistance to you both, especially since Johnny saved my life last night."

"He did?" Her eyes glowed with pride to hear of her sweetheart's courage.

"Yes, he saved me from certain death, armed only with a brace of unloaded pistols. I had a razor held to my neck at the time."

Lady Elizabeth frowned and took my arm in her gloved hand. "You're serious, aren't you? Someone did this to you?"

I hadn't meant her to set off on this track. I tried to shrug, but the shock in the eyes of a girl who had only ever known the comfortable life of the affluent made me realize just how far below her I was. My life was a series of buffets and blows, hers a round of tea parties and pretty dresses. I felt ashamed of myself. But, to my surprise, Lady Elizabeth said, "You are the bravest girl I've ever met, Miss Royal. I admire your courage."

I met her gaze and saw that she was not looking at me as the scruffy commoner, but as the heroine of my own tale. As her equal.

"Please call me Cat," I said. "All my friends do."

She smiled. "Yes, I'd like that. And call me Lizzie—that's what Papa and Frank call me at home."

Our friendship sealed, we returned to the Sparrow's Nest to find the rest of the party decked out in a fantastical selection of robes and crowns. Lord Francis had Pedro's turban perched drunkenly on his head, and he was making Sarah howl with laughter as he tried to imitate Pedro's spinning dance.

"Lawd love us," said Sarah. "You'd sure be a treat on the stage you would, sir."

Lord Francis stopped twirling and gave her a wobbly bow.

"Ma'am, may you be blessed a hundred times for your kind words. An actor's life for me, it is!"

"How many dukes do you know who combine their duties with clowning in front of the rabble?" asked Marchmont as he toyed contemptuously with a patched cloak.

"Not enough!" cried Lord Francis, making Miss Jane and Sarah giggle.

"I think I'd better take my brother away, Cat," said Lady Elizabeth, "before he does himself an injury. Thank you for your kind attention this morning."

Her thanks were followed by the warm farewells of the rest of the party—excepting the Marchmonts, of course. Still, I had to remove an ostrich feather that the younger Miss Marchmont had inadvertently slipped inside her reticule, much to the chagrin of her brother. I wondered if he had put it there.

"Well," said Sarah, rocking in the armchair with a pile of mending on her lap, "if all lords were like that Lord Francis, England would be a fine place."

I heartily agreed with her. Unfortunately, there were too many Marzi-pain Marchmonts to make that a reality.

SCENE 4—SNOWBALLS

"So, what's the story behind you and Lady Elizabeth?" I asked Johnny as I sat over the slate of sums he had set me. It was mid-afternoon and the sun was pouring obliquely through the grimy windows of his office, lighting his face with a pale golden glow. What a fine couple he and Lady Elizabeth would make if fortune smiled on them. No longer needing to conceal his activities from me, he was inking in a cartoon he had done about the complicated love life of one of the princes. He looked up at me and brushed a stray strand of dark hair off his face.

"A short story, I'm afraid, Cat. Not enough to satisfy your voracious appetite for information. We met in the autumn at her coming-out ball."

"Her what?"

"Her first venture into society as an adult. They call it coming out. When you see a young lady, you must ask yourself, is she in or is she out?"

"Sounds like cricket," I said glumly, remembering a tedious afternoon I had once spent with Syd's gang when they had played against a rival team from Smithfield. Johnny laughed.

"Not really. It's a kind of code, meaning is she on the marriage market or is she not?"

"And are you bidding for her?" I teased.

"I might've done—had circumstances been different. That was before I fell out with my father. He discovered all this." Johnny gestured at the cartoon lying on the table before him. "Didn't take too kindly to it, staunch royalist that he is. He failed to understand how his son could be a republican at heart."

The earl could be forgiven his confusion. How did the son of an earl end up rejecting the system that so favored him and his kind in exchange for the new ways of France and America? I wondered. Well, the only way to find out was to ask.

"Why are you?"

"Why am I what?"

"A republican."

"Ah." Johnny put his pen down and wiped the ink from his fingers with a rag. "It's all thanks to Mr. Shore, my old tutor. He taught me that all men are equal. Titles are nothing when you place man beside man in the wild. What is important then is character and intelligence. He told me how many so-called savage races around the world live noble lives, free of our corruption, greed, and envy. It's not the man's title but his qualities you should look to."

"Or the woman's."

"Quite so." He acknowledged my correction with a slight bow. "That's why I despise Billy Shepherd as much as I do the prime minister. It has nothing to do with Shepherd's lowly station in life; it's his cruelty and greed that bring him into contempt. And it's why I admire Lady Elizabeth. Her rank is nothing, but her mind and her heart are everything. She's so different from all the other young ladies I've met. When you talk to her, you know she understands you, follows your thoughts through all their fancies and wanderings."

He meant she'd put up with him rambling on about his revolutionary ideas, I thought with a smile, picturing him talking earnestly to her in some corner at her coming-out ball. But he was right: she had the air of someone intelligent and thoughtful. Not to mention her beauty. I could see how he had fallen hopelessly in love with her.

He rolled up the cartoon he had been working on and looked at me thoughtfully, tapping the end of the tube of paper on his chin. "Cat, are you happy to venture outside now? Do you think you are in any danger?"

"Not now. I'm prepared. Not during the day," I replied. I wasn't going to let a steaming pile of dung like Billy Boil stop me getting a breath of fresh air. He wasn't going to make me a prisoner in my own home.

"Then would you mind running this to Mr. Humphrey, the printer in Gerrard Street?"

"Of course." I jumped up eagerly, not least because Johnny appeared to have forgotten that I had an unfinished slate of sums to do.

"Good girl. I've used Caleb too often. What I need is a confidential messenger." He pressed a sixpence into my hand. "Keep a weather eye for danger, Catkin. Stay on the main streets."

"Yes, sir," I said with a grin. I hardly needed the warning, but it was nice to hear that someone cared.

"Oh," he said, as if an afterthought, but I could tell he had been planning to say it all along. "If you bump into Mr. Sheridan, deny all knowledge of this one."

I unrolled it and took a peek at the picture.

"I suppose he wouldn't be too pleased to see you've drawn his best friend in his underwear."

"No, he wouldn't." Johnny smiled grimly. "Sheridan may be my friend—and a good friend in times of trouble—but he hasn't bought my conscience. I serve no party but the truth."

"And," I added, "it's a good way of throwing people off the scent. Who would look for Captain Sparkler under Mr. Sheridan's wing when this is printed?"

"You are a sharp one, Cat. What are we going to do with you?"

"But mightn't he throw you out for insulting his friend?" I asked.

"He might," said Johnny with a shrug as he ushered me out of the room, "but that's a chance I am prepared to take. Hurry now. The deadline's already passed. Mr. Humphrey's waiting to let his etchers loose on it."

Pausing this time to wrap up warmly, I emerged onto Russell Street to find the world had changed. A steady fall of snow had covered the street with a purifying shroud, hiding the mud and mire that lay just beneath. London was muffled, the snow quelling the evil and violence for a few brief hours, lifting spirits for a holiday of innocence and beauty. I knew it would be all too brief an interval. The white blanket would be quickly sullied by the passage of heavy boots, hooves, and wheels. When night fell, the benign-seeming snow would become a menace to those with no roof over their heads, freezing to death the vagrants sheltering in doorways. But for the moment, I wanted to enjoy the spectacle.

Slipping my way to the market, I found Syd's boys engaged in a furious snowball fight, Pedro among them. The snow-covered houses looked like iced cakes in the confectioner's window: each sugar-frosted rooftop and window ledge good enough to eat.

"Here, catch!" Nick cried as he sent a large ball in my direction. I parried it with the tube of paper I carried, then cursed, remembering the value of the contents.

"Not fair!" I called over. "I'm on an errand. I'll get you when I come back!"

Nick laughed and Pedro sent another snowball sailing toward me. I did not duck in time and it hit the side of my cheek, leaving icy water dripping down my neck.

"You wait!" I cried, but Pedro and Nick scampered away, turning their attention to other targets.

Once out of Covent Garden, my holiday mood faded. An uneasy feeling crept over me; I felt as if I was being followed. It may have just been a shadow in my imagination cast by the events of the previous night but I could not help but look over my shoulder several times. Everyone was muffled up against the cold. It was hard to tell if I was being shadowed. I thought I saw the same gray scarf twice, but when I looked again, it had gone. The posters offering a reward for information leading to the apprehension of Captain Sparkler flapped on the brick walls of many a street corner, as if trying to snag my attention. I saw one lying in the gutter, ripped in half. Someone had scrawled on it "Down with kings!" leading doubtless to its disposal in the sewer by an angry royalist. Was Johnny really in danger of being hanged, drawn, and quartered? This was a barbaric punishment not seen in our modern enlightened times, where the felon was cut down from the noose before he was dead and disemboweled before his own living eyes. They wouldn't do it now, surely? Not to Johnny! But then, I reminded myself with a shudder, you could still see the heads of the rebels of 1745 on the spikes at the entrance to London Bridge—stuck up there like black, boiled sweetmeats for the crows. We had entered a new and fearful age: the revolution in France had made the rich fear for themselves. As for the poor, some sought the rights granted to our French cousins; others, it must be admitted, did not want the Froggies to show us how to live. Which would win out? I wondered. The rights of man or John Bull? Since meeting Johnny, I had only just woken up to understand that the answer to this would decide my future too.

Beset by dark imaginings of Johnny passing through these same streets on his way to the scaffold, I was relieved when I finally reached Gerrard Street. Set in a well-to-do area, home to a mixture of comfortable lodging houses and shops, Gerrard Street did not let my grim fantasy survive long. It was the kind of place I would like to live in one day if I had enough money, a place where I need not fear dark alleyways and thugs like Billy Shepherd, where there would be neighbors and friends looking out for you. I found Mr. Humphrey's easily: it was marked by a gaggle of onlookers outside the window ogling the latest productions of the press on display. Sharp-nosed ladies jostled with fleshy-cheeked men, all craning their necks to be up to date with the latest political gossip without having to fork out any money to do so. A ragged boy slipped between their legs, no doubt relieving them of the coins they had been so reluctant to spend.

The bell clattered above the door as I entered.

"Is Mr. Humphrey here?" I enquired of a handsome woman with rosy cheeks behind the counter.

"My brother's out, I'm afraid, miss. Can I help?"

I hesitated. Johnny had told me to put his work into the hands of William Humphrey alone.

"Will he be long?"

She shook her head and pointed me to a high stool by the counter.

"No. If you'd like to wait, you may sit there."

I sat in my corner watching Miss Humphrey deal with the steady flow of customers. It soon became apparent she did more than just serve at the counter: she was well versed in all aspects of the business and had her own firm views on what to sell to her customers.

"No, you won't like those," she said confidently to one elderly gentleman in a clerical hat. "At least,

Mrs. Buchet will disapprove, if I know her. How about this new batch by Mr. Gillray?"

"Ah, Miss Humphrey, I swear you can read my mind sometimes," said the elderly gentleman, handing over some coins. "I'll tell my wife you recommended them."

The doorbell clanged again as he left, announcing a new customer.

"Can I help you, sir?" asked Miss Humphrey affably.

"Perhaps. I'm looking for the most recent cartoon by Captain Sparkler—the one with the chamber pot."

What terrible luck! It was Marzi-pain Marchmont, the boy who had been so eager to pry into Johnny's affairs. I hid the roll of paper in my skirts and kept my head down.

"Indeed I know it, sir. But unfortunately, we've sold out and are expecting a reprint. My brother should be back soon with the new stock. Would you care to wait? This young lady is already waiting for him. I'm sure he won't be long now."

Marchmont glanced carelessly in my direction, then, seeing who it was, he stopped and turned back.

"Miss Royal! Well, this is a most unexpected pleasure," he said with a smile of suppressed triumph. He gave a shallow bow. "Quite a coincidence."

I rose to curtsy and the roll of paper clattered to the floor. I bent to pick it up but he was quicker.

"Allow me," he said, scooping it from the floor. He held it out to me. "A little something of your own or by your *friend*, I wonder?"

I took it back and shoved it out of sight.

"It's nothing," I said quickly.

"I very much doubt that," he said, meeting my eyes. His gaze was unnerving: he seemed to be staring straight through me, trying to extract the truth like a surgeon removing a gallstone. I shivered.

"So, what brings you here?" I asked to change the subject.

"I live near here—just a few doors away." I quickly abandoned my wish to live in Gerrard Street. "And you?"

Damn! He'd turned the tables again.

"I'm on an errand. For Mr. Kemble."

Miss Humphrey had innocently been listening in on our conversation.

"You're from Drury Lane, my dear? Would you mind very much taking something back for me? I've got a parcel here for the theater." She reached under the counter and pulled out a small package. I could see even upside down that it was addressed to Jonathan Smith, Esq. My hand shot out to relieve her of it before Marchmont could note it, and I tucked it away in my apron pocket.

"Of course," I said. "On second thought, I'd better run. Can you see your brother gets this?" I handed over the rolled cartoon. It seemed better to flee before Mr. Humphrey returned in case anything more incriminating was said in Marchmont's hearing.

"That I will," she said, smiling at us both. "Take care now: it's getting dark."

Marchmont and I both turned to look out of the window: indeed, it was already very gray and some of the houses had candles in their windows, making the twilight seem even gloomier by contrast.

"Miss Royal, I cannot allow you to cross half of London unescorted at this time of day. Allow me to accompany you. I'll get our man, James, to come with us. He's waiting just outside."

"Now, isn't that handsome of the young gentleman!" said Miss Humphrey, beaming at him.

"No, really, Mr. Marchmont. That's quite unnecessary," I began.

"No, no, I insist." He took my arm and propelled me to the door. "I think it is time we had a few words in private," he said in a lower tone.

James, a burly footman armed with a stout cudgel, was indeed waiting for his master outside.

"James, change of plan," said Marchmont briskly. "We're to walk this young lady back to Drury Lane."

"Right you are, sir," said the footman, not showing much interest in me or the destination. It seemed that he was used to his master's brusque ways.

"Now, Miss Royal, about those drawings," said Marchmont as we dodged our way across St. Martin's Lane, his arm firmly clamped on mine. "You do know that there is a reward promised for information leading to the capture of Captain Sparkler?"

"Really?" I said in what I hoped was an unruffled tone.

"A girl like you could do with a few guineas, I dare say."

I said nothing. He knew nothing about girls like me.

"In my opinion, it's not the reward that should tempt a person, it's the satisfaction of putting out of business one of the most wicked traitors this country has ever known."

"You won't do that by buying his cartoons," I replied, hopping over a pile of manure that I noted with pleasure Marchmont was too preoccupied to avoid.

"Dammit!" he cursed on noticing. "That purchase was research. I have a theory, but I needed a specimen of the man's work. I wouldn't touch the stuff otherwise, believe me. I'd also like another look at your manuscript, if you would be so obliging."

I knew what he suspected but he had also revealed that he didn't have the proof. No way was I going to give it to him. I said nothing.

"Miss Royal, you are no fool. You know why I'm so interested in your circle. If one of your fellows, some self-taught scribbler with pretensions to higher things, has taken it into his head to insult his betters in this low fashion, it's your duty to stop it going any further. We're living in dangerous times. Just look at France!" Marchmont's eyes were blazing with a mad enthusiasm; he thumped his fist in his other hand to give emphasis to his words. "Heads will roll if this is not stopped!"

"And what about the Englishman's right to free speech?" I asked, growing more and more alarmed at the boy's high-handed tone toward me. Who was he to talk about my friends and me in this style? He had worked himself up so much that he was scaring me with his passion on the subject. I was rather glad to have the neutral presence of James within call.

"Free speech? Pah! Englishmen who attack the very institutions that give us our freedom resign their right to claim this."

"Your father doesn't think this—or so Lord Francis said," I hurriedly covered my mistake, remembering I should claim no acquaintance with that gentleman.

"My father! I despise him." He must have seen my shocked expression—I'd never heard a son speak so ill of his father before. "I assure you the feeling is mutual. All my father cares about is his own political advancement. He sees Captain Sparkler as serving his cause."

"And you? What's your cause?"

We were approaching the market, and I was beginning to feel safer now that we were on my home turf.

"I'm amazed you have to ask, Miss Royal. King and country, of course!"

"And nothing to do with spiting your father?"

He bent toward me. "Once someone can prove where Captain Sparkler is skulking," he hissed, "expect a visit from the magistrate. It's not far from there to the lockup in Bow Street—but someone may find that that short walk is his last. And as for those protecting him, they should also expect to feel the heavy displeasure of the law."

He was right. I hadn't thought about the penalty that would be incurred by those of us who knew who Johnny really was if we were caught hiding him. Not that this changed anything of course—I knew where my loyalties lay.

"I'll bear that in mind," I said lightly.

Flump! A snowball sailed out of the twilight and hit Marchmont on the side of the face.

"What the devil!" he exclaimed.

"Come on, Cat, come and get me!" jeered Pedro. A snowball flew in my direction, but I ducked in time and it hit James squarely in the chest.

"The little beggar!" laughed James, stooping to grab a handful of snow to retaliate.

Another snowball hit Marchmont, this time full in the face so that his flat nose and watery eyes were crusted with ice. He looked at me furiously for an explanation.

I shrugged. "Just some friends, sir, having fun, if you know what that is." I dodged behind James, leaving the big footman open to two more hits. James was laughing uproariously, sending back missiles with great gusto. I aimed carefully at Pedro as he poked his head out from behind a grocer's stall and scored a hit with my first attempt. It was then that I noticed the sooty figure beside him who seemed to be sending all his throws in the direction of Marchmont. I hit Lord Francis with my second attempt.

All this while, Marchmont had been standing paralyzed with cold fury, not heeding the many snowballs that had splattered upon him.

"James, stop that!" he barked.

"Right, sir," said James, sneaking a final throw at Nick when his master's back was turned. The footman gave me a wink, but his face immediately became impassive when Marchmont next faced us.

"I bid you good night, Miss Royal," Marchmont sneered. "As you are among *friends*, I need take no further concern for your safety."

"You are very kind, sir," I said politely, though we both knew I meant exactly the opposite. He was not kind: he was insufferably interfering, bent only on bringing destruction upon one of his fellow men. I bobbed a curtsy and ran over to Syd's gang, arms held up to ward off the snowballs they were most ungallantly sending in my direction now that I had emerged from the protection of James.

"Enough!" I shouted. "Unfair!" I reached Pedro, scooped up the remnants of the last snowball to hit me, and stuffed it down the back of his neck. Pedro gave a squeal.

"Now who's unfair?" he protested.

"Do you think he recognized me?" asked Lord Francis as he watched Marchmont's small upright figure fast disappearing westward.

"Not a chance," I assured him. "Good shot!"

He grinned. "He deserved every one of them, believe me. By the by, what were you doing with him? I didn't think you two were friends."

"We're not," I said shortly.

My mind was racing as I spoke. There were too many enemies lined up to get Johnny. First, there was his father trying to find him; second, the government men were after Captain Sparkler; third, Marchmont was pursuing him because of some personal grudge to do with revenge on his father. And from the evidence of Johnny's new cartoon, he was far from being a friend to his own cause, as he seemed intent on seeking martyrdom by angering yet more people, including his current protector, almost as if he no longer cared for his own safety. He was like a man sawing off the very branch he was sitting on. Well, if Johnny had become careless about his fate, then I had to help him, but I couldn't do it on my own. I felt pretty sure of Lord Francis and Lady Elizabeth. The only problem was Pedro. Was he trustworthy or would the lure of the reward prove too much? It was best if he was left out of this.

"Lord Francis . . . ?" I began.

"Frank—it's Frank, Cat."

"Frank, would you and your sister spare me a few minutes? There's something I need your help with."

Lord Francis looked surprised. "But I already told you my father's interested in supporting your work."

"It's not that," I said, blushing that he had immediately leaped to the conclusion that I was after a handout. "No, it's about your sister's friend. It's urgent. He's in danger."

I saw that Lord Francis understood what I meant. But Pedro was naturally intrigued.

"What's going on, Cat? Which friend's this?" he asked scanning our faces.

Lord Francis did not enlighten him. "You'd better come home with me now, Cat. Our father will be out and Mother's still in the country. I should be able to smuggle you in unobserved."

"Thank you. Pedro, could you let Johnny know I delivered his parcel safely for him?"

"Absolutely not, Cat. I'm coming with you. You can't wander the streets on your own when it's getting dark," said Pedro firmly.

"I'm not on my own; I'm with Frank."

"And what good will he be in a scrape? You need someone who knows their way around." Pedro looked at me with a glint of anger in his eyes at my rebuff. I could tell that the bad feelings between us aroused by our recent confrontation in Mr. Sheridan's office were rearing their ugly head again.

"No, I don't need your help, Pedro," I repeated.

"But Cat, Pedro's right: a young lady should not wander the streets on her own, and you will need someone to escort you home," said Lord Francis, oblivious to the undercurrents passing between Pedro and me.

This was all going wrong. The last thing I wanted was for Pedro to hear about Johnny's real identity. They were both as bad as Marchmont, using the excuse of my sex to force unwanted company on me. "I'm not a parcel to be handed between you," I protested.

"Typical Cat! Too proud for her own good," said Pedro as if I wasn't there. "Of course I have to come; she knows it really."

"Good," said Lord Francis, "because I won't be able to slip out again to bring her home."

"Will you two stop it!" I snapped at them, stamping my foot in anger. "I was finding my way around London on my own before you" (I turned to the duke's son) "were breeched and when you" (I glared at Pedro) "were still baking under your hot African sun. I can look after myself."

Pedro and Lord Francis smiled in understanding at each other, driving me further into a fury.

"Stop treating me like an empty-headed fool! I can decide what's best myself!"

"Well, Cat, let us say that I have invited Pedro as my guest. If you still want to come, you will just have to put up with his company," said Lord Francis, with a wink at Pedro.

I was now sorely tempted to give up the whole idea of appealing to Lord Francis and Lady Elizabeth for help. Perhaps I should just go back to the theater and tell Johnny to make a run for it. But what was he to do for money to fund his escape? On balance, I realized that I trusted Johnny less to look after himself than I mistrusted Pedro.

"I still wish to come," I replied sullenly.

"In that case, you won't object if I ask you to accompany my friend back to the theater then, Cat?"

I shook my head. Having lost the more important battle of keeping Pedro out of the secret, I was not going to kick up a fuss about the journey home.

"Shall we go?" The chimney sweep lord offered me his arm, and we headed west for Grosvenor Square.

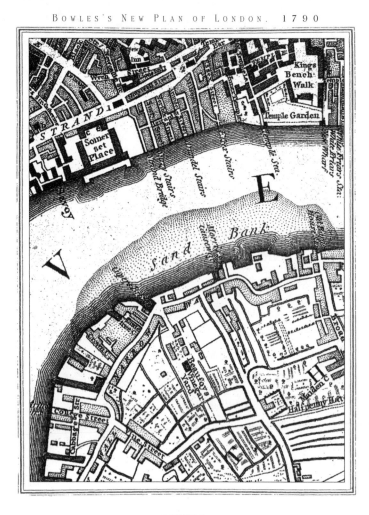

Act IV - In which Pedro is shown the ropes and reveals where his loyalties lie . . .

ACT IV

SCENE 1—FRIENDS

The back entrance to the Duke of Avon's London residence smelled heavily of horse. The stables in the mews were close, and from the slushy trails in the snow, it appeared that the horses were frequently employed.

"Wait a moment," said Lord Francis, disappearing into a stall. "I'll just get changed."

Pedro and I shivered by the pump in the backyard, trying to look inconspicuous. Snow still fell. Pedro's short black hair was frosted with flakes. He looked more than ever like an exotic bird out of place in cold, wintry London. He noticed me looking.

"What's the matter?" he asked. "Why are you staring at me like that?"

"I was just thinking how strange it is that you're here."

"I wasn't going to let you come on your own."

"No, not here here, I mean here in London."

He shrugged. "Is it that strange? All sorts of queer folk wash up here. London sucks us in and spits us out to sink or swim as we can."

It was time to test him out, before Lord Francis came back.

"You know what we said about the diamond?"

Pedro suddenly looked shifty. His eyes left my face to gaze at the icy pump handle. "What about it?"

"I understand you need money, Pedro, but you'd not do anything to get it, would you? There are some things you wouldn't do?"

"Many things. What do you take me for, Cat?"

"You wouldn't send a man to his death, would you?" I asked.

"Not unless he deserved it. What's this to do with the diamond?"

"Nothing. It's just that there's something other than a diamond hidden in Drury Lane at the moment."

Lord Francis reappeared from the stable dressed in his usual smart clothes, though his face and hands were still an unlordly sooty shade. He flipped a coin to the stable boy, who followed with his old garments.

"Put them away for me, Jenkins," he said.

"Right you are, sir," said Jenkins with a toothy grin.

"And now, the final step in my transformation!" Then, despite the freezing conditions, Lord Francis put his head under the spout, pumped the handle twice, and gave himself a hurried wash. He emerged dripping but returned to his normal color. "Let's get in before I catch my death of cold," he panted.

We slid our way over the cobbles to the rear entrance. Lord Francis held us back just as we reached the step. "Now understand, most of the servants can be trusted, but watch out for the French cook and my tutor. Both would see me beaten severely for being out without permission. I have to time my excursions for when they are otherwise engaged."

We nodded and crept in after him. To our right, in what I presumed was the kitchen, I could hear the sound of clattering pans and swearing.

"*Mon dieu!* Zat sauce iz not fit for a *cochon*, a pig!"

There was a loud slap and then a cry from an unfortunate maid.

"Good!" said Lord Francis in a whisper. "Monsieur Lavoisière is too busy with dinner to notice us."

Barely had he said these fateful words than an apparition in a white floppy hat and apron burst from the door on our right. With well-honed reactions, Lord Francis hauled Pedro and me into a room off the corridor on the left. From the rows of copper pans gleaming on the walls, I guessed we were in the scullery. For the first time since I had met him, Lord Francis looked scared. Heavy footsteps approached. I shrank behind a large washtub; Pedro and Lord Francis took refuge behind the door.

"Where iz zat blancmange?" shrieked the cook. "If you 'ave not finished it, Pierre, I will 'ave your guts for my garters!"

"Here it is, sir!" said another voice outside, speaking with the military precision of a lieutenant reporting to his commanding officer. Pierre appeared to be rather more fortunate than the maid: his dessert passed muster and, with only a few grumbles, Monsieur Lavoisière retreated into his den.

"Quick!" said Lord Francis. "Let's get out of here."

As quietly as we could, we ran down the corridor, mounted a flight of stone steps, and pushed through a green baize door into the hall. Once on the marble paving, Lord Francis heaved a sigh of relief.

"Safe!" he exclaimed. "Let's find Lizzie." He charged up the stairs shouting for his sister. The footman who had opened the door to us on our first visit intercepted him on the landing.

"I think you will find Lady Elizabeth in the library, sir," he said. "And Mr. Herbert said to tell you that he wanted to see you on your return."

Lord Francis grimaced. "I've not come in yet, Joseph."

"Indeed you haven't, sir. But when you do decide to come in, can I take it that my message will be delivered promptly?"

"As soon as I set foot across the threshold," he confirmed with a conspiratorial wink.

"Very good, sir."

The footman clearly had a healthy loyalty to his young master.

"Mr. Herbert is your tutor?" I asked.

Lord Francis nodded. "I've been trying to stave off going to boarding school. Mama's on my side but I rather think my days at home are numbered. Shame, just when I was beginning really to enjoy myself!" He looked at Pedro regretfully. His expeditions on the streets had evidently made a deep impression. "But I'm determined not to go until I've got your friend Syd to teach me a few moves. Should put me in good stead at school. Scare off the bullies."

"There are bullies even in schools for your sort?" I asked. I had thought that these were only to be found on the streets where my kind lived. Surely rich children were too refined for bullying? Didn't they spend all day speaking to each other in Latin and dining off china plates?

"You'd better believe it!" said Lord Francis. "Schools are a breeding ground for bullies. I could tell you a few tales of my father's old school that would make your hair curl. Not that either of you need it," he joked. "Here, Cat, what happened to you?" He'd noticed that one of my locks was missing.

"Nothing," I said quickly, feeling sick again at the reminder of my brush with Billy. I put my hand up to my forehead defensively, but that only revealed my cut arm.

Pedro had also noticed. "There's something you're not telling us, isn't there, Cat?" he asked astutely. "You've not been yourself today. You seem . . . you seem frightened."

"Is that you, Frank?" Lady Elizabeth stepped out onto the landing, a book held in one hand, her finger marking the page. "I thought I heard voices." Her face broke into a smile when she saw us all standing there. "Oh, I'm so pleased! You've brought me some visitors. Quick! In here. Mr. Herbert's on the warpath, but he'll never think to look for you in the library."

"Course not! What would I be doing in there? It's only bluestockings like you that find this a congenial place to sit before dinner," said Lord Francis.

Lady Elizabeth ushered us into the most beautiful room I had ever seen. Two high windows on one wall looked out on the darkening square. Candles flickered on the many small tables set between comfortable armchairs and sofas. A large desk, with silver inkpot, blotter, a fresh supply of paper, and wax, waited invitingly on the far side of the hearth. How I would have loved to sit at it and write! But the most impressive things about the room were the shelves upon shelves of books, all neatly arranged and lavishly bound. One could have been set loose in here and not need to emerge for years, thanks to all the fascinating reading matter on hand. I envied Lord Francis and Lady Elizabeth this privilege above the many others they enjoyed.

"Now, what is this about?" asked Lady Elizabeth, inviting me to take a seat on the silk-covered sofa. I hesitated, worrying that my grubby skirt might stain it, and I sat down on a wooden stepladder instead.

"I'm not sure," said Lord Francis, taking a final listen on the landing before closing the door. "Cat needs to talk to us. It's about Lord Jonathan Fitzroy."

Lady Elizabeth's face went red.

"Lord Jonathan Fitzroy?" asked Pedro.

"Johnny," I explained reluctantly. "He's not what he seems."

"So I see," said Pedro slowly, digesting this latest news. "A lord? He's the most unlordly lord— with the possible exception of Frank here—that I've ever met."

"You don't know the half of it," I said. "But first you must promise me, all of you, that even if you decide you cannot help Johnny and me—Lord Jonathan, I mean—what I tell you will go no further than us four. You must promise not to betray him, even if this means passing up the opportunity to earn a lot of money." I looked directly at Pedro, who was slowly beginning to understand what I had been hinting at earlier.

"Of course I won't," he said indignantly.

Still far from certain that I could take him at his word, I knew I had to proceed if I were to get the help we so urgently needed.

"Johnny has another name—a name that you all have heard before. He's also Captain Sparkler."

I was watching Pedro closely as I spoke and thought I saw a strange gleam light up in his eye. This worried me: what was Pedro thinking? He now knew that Johnny belonged to the privileged classes—he might even be from one of the many families grown rich on sugar and tobacco at the expense of thousands of slaves' lives in the West Indies. Did this weaken any personal loyalty Pedro might feel toward him? Would the temptation to sell him out prove too strong? After all, no one had cared about the feelings of Pedro and his family when they were sold. Why should he care now?

The duke's children were easier to read. From the steady expression of Lady Elizabeth I could tell Johnny's identity did not come as a shock to her; to Lord Francis the news was almost welcome.

"Fancy that! Lord Jonathan Fitzroy turning out to be the captain! I never knew he was so clever—not just a stuffed shirt then, like most of Lizzie's suitors."

"Hush!" said Lady Elizabeth as Pedro now looked at her with renewed interest. I wondered with a sinking heart what scheme he was concocting with these pieces of private information.

"But I think your friend Marchmont suspects something," I continued, trying not to let Pedro distract me from my purpose. "Not about Lord Jonathan, of course, but he suspects that the captain is hidden in Drury Lane. The net is closing in. Johnny'll have to find somewhere else to stay."

"And you need our help to find him somewhere? What does Lord Jonathan think?" asked Lady Elizabeth.

I dropped my head and examined my grubby fingers. "I have to admit he doesn't know I'm asking you. I have only just found out about Marchmont."

"He'll be cross with you," said Lady Elizabeth. "He's very proud, you know."

"But it's too much for him to handle on his own," I replied. "He's taking too many risks. He doesn't see the danger—or doesn't care. And it's not just him, it's the diamond as well."

"Diamond? You mean there really is a diamond?" asked Lord Francis excitedly. "It's not just something you made up for your story?"

I nodded, my eyes again on Pedro, who was keeping suspiciously quiet. "It's quite possible that the Shepherd gang'll try to get it, and that puts Johnny in double danger."

"What's Johnny got to do with Billy Boil?" asked Pedro shrewdly. He seemed very interested to hear that Billy had got wind of the diamond.

I was trying to think up an explanation that avoided divulging the events of last night, but Lady Elizabeth was too quick.

"Lord Jonathan saved Cat from those ruffians," she replied, remembering the praise I had given her sweetheart.

"He did what?" exclaimed Lord Francis. "This gets better and better!"

I was now compelled to tell the whole story, but only after I had again sworn them to secrecy. A stunned silence followed my brief but brutal narrative.

"So it's not only Johnny in danger. You are too," said Lord Francis, looking at me with concern.

"Maybe," I said dismissively. "But Billy's not interested in me, he's interested in the diamond and Johnny's protecting it for Mr. Sheridan—perhaps in exchange for having a place to hide. I'm not sure."

"Hmm," said Lady Elizabeth. "There's something not quite right about this. Where would Mr. Sheridan get a diamond from and why hide it?"

"The second part's easy: he's probably hiding it from his creditors," said Lord Francis. "It's well known that it's only because he's a member of Parliament that he's not arrested for debt. If they got wind that he had some money for once, they'd be down on him like a pack of crows."

"And he's best mates with the Prince of Wales, isn't he?" asked Pedro. "If anyone is dripping diamonds in this country, it'll be royalty. Maybe it was a gift."

"Maybe," said Lady Elizabeth skeptically. "I just don't see it though."

"But the long and the short of it is that Johnny's in danger," I continued. "He's got to get out and the sooner the better. He'll need help to do so. He'll need you and—" I felt embarrassed to say it "—and your resources."

He would have to leave London—go abroad even—and I had no gold to buy him a ticket out of England. If his father had disowned him, he needed rich friends to help him—friends like the children of a duke, not a pauper like me.

"Of course," agreed Lord Francis, "but it won't be easy, even for us, Cat. My pocket money hardly stretches to a passage to a safe country."

"I suppose I could pawn some of my jewels," suggested Lady Elizabeth. "That is, if someone would take them to the broker for me. Papa would be furious if he found out I'd gone."

"You are an angel, sis," said Lord Francis. "I'll take them for you."

Pedro wrinkled his nose in disdain. "Not a good idea: any self-respecting pawnbroker would fleece you and send you packing with half their value. Let me do it."

"No, I'll take them. I've an idea where to go," I said quickly. Who knew where Pedro would be this time tomorrow if entrusted with a small fortune in jewels?

Pedro frowned but did not object.

"If Cat raises the money for us, I'll find out how to get safe passage out of the country," said Lord Francis.

"Good idea. Johnny must get away as soon as possible," I said. "They might come looking for him at any moment. And when he does leave, he may be recognized, so we should prepare a disguise for him."

"Leave that to me," volunteered Lady Elizabeth. "I'll think of something so that even his own mother won't recognize him."

The clock on the mantelpiece began to strike a melodious six. Two mechanical dancers emerged from a door set in the face, approached each other, and began to twirl around. I was just thinking how pretty it was when another thought came to me.

"Pedro, aren't you supposed to be doing the hornpipe tonight?"

He looked thunderstruck. It was not like him to let a professional commitment escape his attention. "You're right! We've got to run!"

"Wait. I'll get the jewels," said Lady Elizabeth. She disappeared upstairs and returned a few minutes later with a small package wrapped in a silk handkerchief, which she thrust into my hand. "Look after them, Cat, won't you? I would like to redeem them in time. Some of them are special to me."

We arrived back at Drury Lane at half past the hour. The play had already started, but Pedro was just in time for his musical interlude. He had barely ripped off his livery and donned his costume before he was summoned onstage. I could see Johnny looking mightily relieved as Pedro bounded onto the boards.

"Safely delivered?" Johnny asked me under his breath.

I nodded, but my eye was caught by Pedro dancing in the footlights. The cartoon might now be in safe hands but I realized that Pedro had been delivered onstage far from complete.

"Violin!" I hissed under my breath to Johnny. "Pedro's forgotten his violin!" After the first dance, he was supposed to do the same steps again while playing.

"Fetch it then!" whispered Johnny urgently. "I'll think of something."

I ran to the green room and found the violin. Grabbing it, I darted back toward the wings, dodging through the press of performers, accidentally treading on Miss Stageldoir's toes, and receiving a cuff to the back of my head in retaliation.

I arrived at Johnny's side to find he had thought of something, but it was a "something" that made my heart leap into my throat.

"Here!" he said. "Put these on." He thrust an old spangled Harlequin costume at me.

"No, you!" I hissed.

"Don't be funny! I'm supposed to be in hiding, remember? But you, you can run on, do a twirl or something, and give him the violin. The crowd will think it's all part of the act. They love a clown."

"You're joking," I said hollowly as he pulled the baggy costume over my head.

"I'm not. Go! You're on!"

With that, Johnny clapped a black beaked mask over my face and gave me a firm shove in the shoulder blades. I staggered onto the stage. Pedro had just come to the end of the first fast and furious rendition of the hornpipe and was taking a bow. He had not yet realized he was missing a vital ingredient for the next part of his act. A few people in the boxes began to titter, seeing a confused Harlequin dithering by the side of the stage. I had no choice now: I had to do something other than stand here like a fool. Clutching the violin and bow under one arm, I took a short run and turned my one-handed cartwheel. I'd never performed it before others and was gratified to find it brought a wave of applause from the audience. I landed neatly at Pedro's side and presented him with the violin. Pedro looked shocked for a brief second, then recovered himself. He began to mime, making it clear to the audience that I had brought a challenge to do the dance again while playing. I nodded vigorously.

"Go on, Prince!" shouted someone in the audience.

"You can do it!" called another.

Pedro gave me a deep bow, accepting the challenge. I was about to run off, but he gestured to me to sit on the anchor that dressed the stage. I was surprised: I had thought that Pedro Hawkins was only interested in having the stage to himself. As it would have looked strange if I had refused, I sat down. All these years of living in the theater, I'd never been on the boards with a full audience in front of me. I felt heady with excitement.

Pedro composed himself to play. Signor Angelini raised his baton and signaled for his protégé to start. Pedro then began the most extraordinary dance I had ever seen. With legs stamping as in an Irish jig, upper body still, he began to play a hornpipe. Sitting so close to him, I could see the beads of sweat flying from his brow, but all the time he kept an impassive expression on his face. From a distance, it would look as if he was having to make no effort. The audience began to clap in time to the music. He went faster and faster. I thought that it must be impossible for him to carry on playing without losing step or fluffing a note, but no. It was almost as if he had found freedom in the dance and would take flight if it did not end soon. I could see him do it: he'd fly out of the theater, out of the smoke of London, into the blue sky and home to his land of hot sun and friendly faces. But before his wings had a chance to sprout, he brought the hornpipe to an end with a flourish.

The applause was immense. It rolled toward the stage like a barrage of thunder. Pedro bowed three times, perspiration dripping off the end of his nose and falling onto the boards. He then turned to me.

"How about it, Cat? Run off with a cartwheel together?"

He was testing me, I thought, paying me back for my earlier doubts about him and seeing if I could repeat my performance. I nodded, accepting the challenge.

He took my hand. "Go!"

We ran toward the wings in step.

"Now!" he shouted, dropping my hand. With perfect timing, we cartwheeled off the stage, landing neatly by Johnny's seat.

"Well, well, well!" Johnny said, laughing as he slipped the mask off my face. "Who would've guessed you could do that? If you're not careful, Mr. Kemble will give you the part. Cat the clown. Has rather a ring to it, don't you think?"

Pedro slapped me on the back. "You saved my skin out there, Cat. I owe you one."

"Don't worry, I'm not likely to let you forget," I said with a wry smile.

SCENE 2—PAWNBROKER

E arly the next morning, I slipped out of the theater and headed down toward the Strand and the pawnbroker's shop that many of the actors and musicians used. I'd been there before for Peter Dodsley, the first violin. When he had been going through a particularly lean patch, he had pawned his watch on a Saturday and redeemed it after being paid on a Monday. He'd explained at the time that as he spent most of Sunday resting in bed, he did not need to know the time, but he did need a few creature comforts, such as a bottle of fine French wine. I had always thought this a poor way of managing his money, but he was by no means the only one to use the services of the broker.

As I arrived outside the shop, who should come up behind me but Jonas Miller, the hog-grubber clerk who was more usually to be seen causing trouble in the pit.

"Out of my way, girl," he said rudely, pushing me aside. He was in a fearful hurry to get into the shop. I wondered why. I probably would have followed him in to find out even if I had not had an errand myself.

Pushing the door open, I entered the darkened room. It had the secretive atmosphere of a Catholic confessional: little cubicles separated the customers from each other so they could admit their monetary failings in privacy. Behind an iron grille, Mr. Vaughan and his assistants heard their clients' troubles and offered a temporary cure. The items put up for pawn were displayed in locked cases, tempting their owners with a knowing twinkle and glitter to claim them back—if they had the money, that is, and they rarely did. Among the snuffboxes and rings, I noticed with a shudder of disgust that someone had even pawned their porcelain false teeth: it was hard to imagine what depths of despair had pushed them to that extreme. The teeth grinned back at me from their red velvet cushion in a smile like the rictus of death.

"Ah, Mr. Miller, I have your silver inkstand waiting for you," said Mr. Vaughan loudly. Perhaps he had not noticed someone else coming in, for he was speaking more openly than usual. "Have you the money?"

"That's all I have." Jonas pushed a bag of coins over to him.

Mr. Vaughan pulled the bag under the grille and carefully counted out the silver and coppers. "Hmm, not enough, sir, not enough," he said with a regretful shake of his head.

Jonas ran his fingers through his dirty hair in desperation.

"Look, I've got to have it back. There'll be hell to pay if I don't. You see, it's . . . it's not exactly mine."

Mr. Vaughan frowned. "I don't deal in stolen goods, sir," he said sharply, hand hovering over a bell to summon his assistant.

"No, no, you misunderstand me," said Jonas. "It's borrowed . . . from a friend."

A friend? All my eye! That was nonsense. I recognized that inkwell: it was the one from

Jonas's desk in the lawyer's office where he worked. I'd seen it hundreds of times when I'd passed by his window. Jonas was now fingering his pocket watch nervously.

"Perhaps we could come to some arrangement, Mr. Vaughan," he pleaded, placing his watch on the counter.

I did not see the conclusion to this transaction, for Mr. Vaughan's assistant, a pale youth with a high forehead like the dome of St. Paul's, glided out of the back room.

"Yes, miss, can I help you?" he asked, spying me waiting on the hard bench.

Jonas turned around and his eyes widened with consternation. I could tell that the presence of someone who knew him was most unwelcome. Come to think of it, I'd prefer not to be seen by anyone I knew either. I hurried over to the vacant cubicle and pushed the package of jewels under the grille.

"How much can you offer me for these?" I asked in a low voice.

With a bored expression, the assistant unfolded the handkerchief. The boredom stopped there: on to the counter fell a jumble of glittering gemstones and gold chains. His eyes lit up.

"Are these real, miss?"

"Of course."

Giving me a skeptical look, he screwed a jeweler's eyeglass into his socket and began to examine each piece. One by one he gave a little nod and put the item reverently aside. Finally, he put down the eyeglass and gave me a searching stare as if willing me to reveal where I had come by such riches.

"Mr. Vaughan, Mr. Vaughan, I need your advice on something!" he called to his employer.

Mr. Vaughan was still arguing with Jonas Miller.

"A moment, sir," he told Jonas and moved across to the patch of grille in front of me.

"All real?" he asked his assistant.

"The genuine article, sir."

Mr. Vaughan pawed the jewels lovingly. I could see he hungered to have them in his possession, if only for a short time, but he was worried how I came by them.

"I'm here on behalf of a lady," I explained as he surveyed me. "I'm her confidential agent in this transaction."

"Hmm. I can offer you five pounds for them," he said.

As an opening bid it was laughable. We both knew it.

"Fifty," I said firmly.

He smiled. "What do you take me for, miss? A charity?"

"Then I'll take my jewels elsewhere."

"Thirty," he snapped.

"Forty-five."

"Forty."

"Done." Forty was not a bad amount. Far more than any of my friends could hope to earn in a year. But the sum was still far short of the true value of the jewels: if Lady Elizabeth failed to redeem them, Mr. Vaughan would make a handsome profit.

Mr. Vaughan drew out his cashbox and counted out a weighty sack of guineas. He pushed a paper receipt under the grille.

"Tell your 'lady' that she has six months to redeem them from me. After that time, I'm at liberty to sell them."

"I understand."

I pocketed the bag of gold and receipt and turned to go. Jonas Miller was standing at the door waiting for me.

"Here, Cat, lend us some of that, will you?" he asked, with what he evidently thought was an ingratiating smile on his face. "It's all up with me if you don't help."

I shook my head. "Sorry, it's not my money. I can't lend it to you."

His smile vanished. "They weren't your jewels neither, were they, Cat? Have you been a naughty girl?" He took a step toward me. "I'll wager that you wouldn't want someone to tell the Bow Street runners about that!"

"It's none of your business," I said angrily, pushing past him. "Just because you filch from your employer doesn't mean to say everyone else does."

I slammed the door behind me and ran as fast as I could back to the theater. Jonas's threats did not bother me—I knew he was a creeper and a cheat. Lady Elizabeth could be summoned in my defense if he did go blabbing, but if Jonas was going to make trouble with the magistrate's men, it made it more important than ever to get Johnny out of Drury Lane as quickly as possible.

"You did what?"

Johnny was pounding to and fro on the hearthrug, the bag of coins glittering on the table between us. Reader, as you may guess, it wasn't going well.

"I told you. I happened to mention to Lady Elizabeth that you needed help and—"

"Do you realize what you've done?" he cut across me. "You've humiliated me, Cat. You and your friends, acting as if you can snatch me from the frying pan, but instead you're just dropping me into the fire! Did it not occur to you that I might be quite capable of making my own arrangements? I've lost everything, choosing the path I've taken— my family, my rank, even the woman I love—but I thought I had my self-respect intact!"

He wasn't going to pull the wool over my eyes with this bluster; he needed our help.

"So, Johnny, what plans had you made?" I asked coolly.

"I was going to America," he said, stopping to slump dejectedly on the mantelpiece.

"With the diamond?" I asked.

He gave a bitter smile. "That's the plan."

"And how were you to afford it? Unless Mr. Sheridan cashes in this diamond—which I doubt he'd do even for you—you'll need money for your ticket. He doesn't have any, from what I've heard."

"No," conceded Johnny, "Sheridan is short on ready money, that's true."

"And you, do you have any?"

"Only several hundred thousands—but all in my father's pocket, I'm afraid." He sighed. "I thought perhaps Marchmont might help."

"You're all abroad there, Johnny; he won't. I know their sort: penny-pinching lice hunters who wouldn't cross the road to help their grandmother. They're only happy so long as they stand to gain themselves."

"You're probably right, Cat." Johnny looked defeated, depressed by the weight of anxiety that had descended on him since he was first charged with treason. He was just beginning to find out what most of us already knew: what it was like to have no money.

"So," I said, gesturing to the guineas I had brought back with me, "why not take this?"

"Because it's hers, of course!" I must have looked puzzled, for he continued, "You're too young to understand, Cat, about . . . about love. How could I look her in the face again if I take advantage of her in this way?"

I couldn't believe the man: he was being a downright fool, too scrupulous for his own good.

"Believe me, she'd prefer to look you in the face as you wave good-bye from the deck of a ship, holding a ticket that she's paid for, than watch you go blue in the face as the noose tightens. When you die of a hempen fever, it'll be no comfort to her then to know that you owe her nothing."

He shook his head, still unconvinced. Though many years my senior, he was no better than an infant, completely oblivious to the hard truth of his situation. He made me feel so much older and wiser than him. He couldn't afford to indulge his romantic notions of honor and pride. If he did, he'd die. I tried another tack.

"You know, Johnny, I think it's you who doesn't understand love. Love is not forced; it gives without expecting anything in return. It drops like the gentle rain from heaven—"

"Upon the place beneath," said Johnny, finishing the quotation I had adapted for the occasion. "I know, I know."

"So why can't you allow her to give you this? You're denying her the right to put her love into action if you spurn it."

"But—"

"I'm certain you'd give everything in your power to help someone you love. You're not treating her as your equal if you reject her assistance."

I had finally found an argument that hit home.

"My equal?" he said.

"Yes, your equal. You mustn't treat her like some china doll that you admire but are afraid to allow off the shelf. She's a sensible person: she knows what she's doing. Anyway, it's too late: I've pawned the jewels and Lord Francis is sorting out your passage. You're outvoted on this, four to one."

Johnny laughed. "I regret I taught you about democracy, Cat. It's come back to haunt me."

"You won't regret it when you reach New York. Have you thought what you might do when you get there?"

Johnny sat down beside me, signaling that he had given in to the inevitable and would let us help him.

"I thought I'd start a community, a place where men and women can live together, dividing their time between honest physical labor and intellectual pursuits—an ideal republic."

"It sounds a load of moonshine to me. What do you know about hard work? Do you know how long it takes to scrub a floor or clean a shirt, let alone plow a field?"

Johnny looked awkward: he knew he was on dubious ground when he, the nobleman, talked to me, the commoner, about the simple life. "No, but I can dream."

"Carry on dreaming," I said briskly. Clearly, someone had to look after him, or he was heading for a fall. "But in the meantime why don't you plan for something more substantial than that? Do something you know you know well, like drawing, for example. There must be opportunities for an artist like you even in so uncivilized a place as America."

"Well, I do have a contact who has set up a newspaper in Philadelphia." He laughed. "Listen to me. Taking career advice from a—how old are you?"

I shrugged. "I don't know."

"From a young lady then," he said with a wink, pocketing the guineas.

That afternoon Mrs. Reid sent me to dust the offices. I had just finished Mr. Kemble's and had made a start on Mr. Sheridan's when the owner came in with a gentleman I did not recognize. They did not see me, for I was crouched behind the desk—if the truth be known, wondering if I could find the infamous diamond and take a peek at it before it went to America with Johnny. From Mr.

Sheridan's tone, I could tell that he was trying to get his companion away from the theater as quickly as possible.

"Look, Ranworth, why not come to the club and talk about it?"

Ranworth? I peered over the desk and saw the back of a portly, white-haired gentleman dressed in a claret-colored jacket and shiny black boots. That must be Johnny's father. Thank goodness Johnny was locked in his room for the afternoon checking over the proofs of his latest cartoon. He had better stay there. Someone had to warn him. But the men were standing between me and the door.

"Is there really no news of my son?" said the Earl of Ranworth, refusing to budge. I had the impression Mr. Sheridan had been avoiding answering his questions, and so the earl had come to the theater to corner him. "I'm ashamed of the pup, I admit, but I do have the feelings of the father. I would like to know that he is alive and well. These wanted posters everywhere make my blood run cold! Just imagine what a scandal there'd be if they knew who Captain Sparkler really was!"

"Quite so," said Mr. Sheridan, patting the old man's arm. "But they won't find out, will they? Who would suspect such a thing? I'm sure the young rascal has come to no harm."

"And Salter, you say, has drawn a blank in Bristol?"

"Completely. I've asked him to enquire at Plymouth and Portsmouth. I expect news very soon."

So Mr. Salter was safe and still on his wild goose chase, I noted.

The Earl of Ranworth took a handkerchief from his pocket and mopped his brow. With the weary movements of a man exhausted by worry, he slumped into the chair facing the desk. Seeing there was no shifting the man, Mr. Sheridan came to the far side to take a seat.

He stopped, finding me at his feet. "Cat! What on earth are you doing here?"

The earl jumped up from his seat, a look of consternation on his face.

"Dusting, sir," I said, holding up my cloth as evidence.

"Hmm," Mr. Sheridan said skeptically. "You always seem to be cropping up in the most inconvenient places, don't you?"

There was a bold knock on the open door. We all looked around. In the corridor stood a man wearing a blue coat with brass buttons and a leather hat, armed with a cutlass, pistol, and truncheon: unmistakably a Bow Street runner.

"Sorry to trouble you, sir," he said deferentially to Mr. Sheridan, "but I'm following up a report that there may be a wanted man on the premises."

The Earl of Ranworth looked up abruptly and gave Mr. Sheridan an astonished stare. He was no fool. At least for him, the penny seemed to have dropped. Mr. Sheridan gave him a quelling look.

"Indeed, Constable . . .?" Mr. Sheridan said lightly.

"Lennox, sir."

"Constable Lennox. And what is this to me?"

"Well, sir," said the runner awkwardly, "the old man on the door said I had to ask your permission before I can carry out a thorough search."

"You have no warrant from the magistrate then?"

"No." The runner coughed. "I, er, I thought the report, an anonymous letter, was not sufficient grounds to disturb him."

I bet the letter came from the greasy paw of Marzi-pain Marchmont! I called him as many colorful names as I could think of under my breath.

Mr. Sheridan strode across the room. "But you thought it grounds enough to make havoc in my theater?"

"I intended nothing of the sort, sir! I—"

"You are already interrupting the work of my maid here. Run along, Cat; I'm sure there is something *very important* you should be doing." Mr. Sheridan shooed me out the door. As he knew I would, I sprinted as fast as I could to Johnny's office. Ignoring the sign, I burst in upon him, the surprise making him spill ink across the picture he was working on.

"For heaven's sake, Cat, look what you've done!" he exclaimed in exasperation.

"Forget that!" I said, stuffing a cap on his head and hauling him from the table. "A constable's here—so's your father."

"My father brought the runners for me?" he said incredulously, getting quite the wrong end of the stick.

"No, you fool, they came separately. But you'd better run for it."

Johnny made a grab for his drawing things.

"Leave them—I'll deal with that. You can't get caught with these on you."

"Where can I go?" he asked wildly, pulling his jacket on.

"Go to the butcher's in Bow Street. Ask for Syd. Tell him you're my friend. I'll send a message when it's all clear."

"Bow Street? But that's nearer danger!"

"Exactly—the last place they'll look for you. Now hurry!" I pushed Johnny out of the door and watched him bolt off down the corridor, colliding with Mr. Bishop halfway.

"What's got into him?" Mr. Bishop asked me in confusion.

"Urgent errand. Uncle on the point of death, asking for him," I invented.

Mr. Bishop shook his head sadly. "Reminds me of my old girl. Didn't get there in time, but she was asking for me after the baby was born. Never did see the child. . . ."

"Sorry, Mr. Bishop," I interrupted him, not having time for family reminiscences, "I've got to tidy up in here for Johnny."

"That's right, Cat, you do what you can to make him comfortable." With that, Mr. Bishop plodded away, his mind fortunately on the wife he had lost many years ago rather than on the strange behavior of the prompt.

I shut the door and began to sweep away the evidence of Johnny's employment. Roughs of his cartoons littered the floor, and I threw them higgledy-piggledy into the grate. Voices could be heard in the corridor outside.

"Why here first, constable? What's my prompter to do with this business?"

"Nothing, I hope, sir. It's just that my informant said he'd been here himself and suggested I start with Mr. Smith."

They were upon me. I grabbed the proof Johnny had been working on and stuffed it into my bodice. The door opened.

"What are you doing here, girl?" asked the runner suspiciously when he saw me kneeling by the burning grate.

I got up. "Just laying the fire, sir," I said, bobbing a curtsy.

"As I told you," said Mr. Sheridan coldly, "my staff have their jobs to do."

The runner, however, was no half-wit. He strode over to the fire and pulled out a singed piece of paper. Faintly, you could make out the bulbous nose of a cartoon head.

"And what's this?" he said severely to me. "Why were you lighting the fire with this, girl? Has someone been drawing?"

"Yes, sir," I answered nervously, twisting my apron in my hands. I could see Mr. Sheridan waving urgently behind the runner's back to stop me saying any more, but I knew what I was doing. "I'm afraid it's me, sir. I've been taking drawing lessons, you see, sir, b-but I'm not very good yet and—"

He cut through my stammered explanation with a flick of the paper. "Drawing lessons? What's a maid doing taking drawing lessons?" he exclaimed.

I turned to Mr. Sheridan. Now was the time for me to rival Mrs. Siddons with my acting ability. I had to be convincingly abject with my apology.

"I'm so sorry, sir," I said, wiping the corner of my eye with my apron. "I've been sneaking in here to practice." From my workbox over at the foot of Johnny's bed, I pulled out the drawing of Caesar I had done and held it up as proof. "Mr. Smith's half-blind, as you know, so he can't see what I'm up to. You can dock the cost of the paper from my wages, sir, if you like, but, please, please, don't turn me away for it."

Wages? Wages would be a fine thing! I never got anything but board and lodging. Mr. Sheridan eyed me closely. I could see laughter twinkling in his eyes but he was managing to look suitably stern.

"And who is this meant to be, young woman?" he asked.

"A portrait of Julius Caesar, sir." Sniff, artful wipe of the eye with my apron. "I made a mess of the nose."

"There, Constable Lennox—hardly topical political satire," said Mr. Sheridan, rounding on the runner. "Had you better not move on and look for someone whose targets are a little more up to date, by about eighteen hundred years?" Mr. Sheridan rolled up my picture and tucked it in his pocket.

"Right you are, sir," said the runner sheepishly. He could at least regain some dignity by turning on the only victim present. "As for you, miss, you keep your hands off your master's things or I'll be having words with you down at the courthouse."

I bent my head, trying to look suitably cowed.

"That's enough, man. I'll deal with my own staff, thank you," said Mr. Sheridan sharply.

He led the constable out of the room, but the Earl of Ranworth lingered. He was staring at some papers covered in Johnny's handwriting that I had not had time to burn. He gave the desk a caress with his fingertips, then came over to me.

"Thank you, my dear," he said hoarsely. "You did well." He pressed a sovereign into my hand. "And when you see my son, tell him . . . tell him the old man misses him, won't you?"

SCENE 3—ATTACK

Johnny crept back in after darkness fell and hid himself away in his office. I found him sitting on his bed, his belongings rolled up into a small bundle at his feet, all traces of his work obliterated.

"Here, I managed to save this," I said, producing the proof from my bodice.

Johnny did not even look at it but got to his feet and threw it into the glowing heart of the fire. The paper caught flame and began to curl up, writhing like a spirit in torment as the black touch of fire consumed it.

"Enough," Johnny said grimly. "Captain Sparkler is dead. Johnny Smith is bound for pastures new."

"You're really going then?" I asked, sitting in the place he had vacated. I stared down at the meager bundle—not much to show for an earl's son. "But I thought that . . . well, it seemed to me that your father was ready to have you back. He was sad. He misses you."

Johnny sighed. "And I miss him. But he has agreed with Sheridan that the best thing now is for me to go abroad for a few years, until this Captain Sparkler business dies down. He thinks the passage of time will mellow my firebrand views." Johnny gave a bark of laughter. "He thinks I'll be ready then to take up my duties and responsibilities."

"So you intend to go to America at once?"

"If I can arrange safe passage."

"Perhaps Lord Francis will have found out something useful," I said, half-hoping for a reprieve to give Johnny time to change his mind. He sounded as if he could be convinced. Though I sympathized with his principles, it still seemed madness to me for him to turn his back on the life of luxury that was his if he remained and accepted his birthright. I wasn't sure that I'd stand firm if I was facing such a choice.

"But what can Lord Francis do?" asked Johnny. He was obviously inclined to look on the gloomy side of everything tonight.

"You'd be surprised. Lord Francis knows far more about London than you'd expect, thanks to the peculiar education he has been receiving of late."

That raised a halfhearted smile. "So it would seem, Cat. You've led him far astray from the usual path of duke's sons. I doubt his father would approve if he knew, but I think it a very good thing." Johnny dug into his breast pocket and took out the money I had given him earlier. "Here, take this back. I won't be needing it. Tell her that I send my heartfelt thanks, but the Ranworth estate is covering the costs of my removal from these shores."

I took it. "Just that?" The message didn't live up to my expectations as to what was fitting between two lovers about to say farewell to each other for many years. That certainly wasn't how it was done on the stage. Clearly, Johnny needed a bit of tutoring in the sweetheart department.

"What more is there to say?"

"Shouldn't you at least ask her to wait for you? Tell her you'll gaze upon her picture every day at a certain hour so that she can do the same? Send her a token, a lock of hair perhaps, for her to wear in a locket over her heart? Assure her of your unchanging love?"

He shook his head sadly. "One of the things you'll learn as you get older is that we all change, Cat. I wouldn't ask a girl of sixteen to wait for me: it would not be fair. Who knows what we both might be feeling and thinking in a few years' time? What kind of home could I offer her?"

He was a hopeless pupil for Cupid. His spirits were too low to rise to the occasion. I couldn't blame him: he was leaving all the people he loved, setting off to live among strangers, abandoning the old certainties of his life. Added to that, he would be facing the novelty of earning his own keep for the first time. I imagined that, for all his radical, equalizing notions, this must be a fairly terrifying prospect for a gentleman raised in privilege. It was one thing to preach, another to practice. Mind you, he had a head start on most of us if only he knew it.

"You shouldn't worry too much, Johnny. You'll get on famously once you make a beginning. You possess an extraordinary talent. I'm sure you'll be able to offer Lady Elizabeth a good home when you've made a name for yourself over there." I thought he still stood in need of a little more worldly advice, so I lowered my voice. "And you know you could always pawn the diamond if things get tight. Mr. Sheridan will never know. It could set you up in your own business until you earn enough to redeem it."

"That would be more difficult than you suppose." He walked over to his desk and got out the two pistols to add to his bundle.

"Why? If Mr. Sheridan wants it back, it'll take months for the message to reach you in America. You'll have plenty of time. It wouldn't be like stealing."

That made him laugh. "No, that's not what I mean. The diamond isn't the kind of thing you can pawn." He picked up some pens, checking the nibs before slipping them inside his jacket pocket.

"Why not?"

"Well, because it's not exactly a diamond."

What did he mean? I could tell from the way he was behaving he was concealing something from me. My gaze was drawn to the pen he was examining; it glittered like a jewel in his fingers . . . Then it hit me. I had been a fool. Of course! Johnny was Captain Sparkler. *He* was the hidden jewel!

"*You're* the diamond, aren't you, Johnny? There never was a real one, when Mr. Sheridan was talking about you to Marchmont—that was the night you arrived." I shook my head in disbelief—it had taken me so long to see what appeared so obvious now. It was my imagination that had created the jewel—a fantasy that Mr. Sheridan had thought useful to continue in order to divert me from the real treasure.

Johnny sat down on the bed beside me and took my hand. "I wondered when you would guess, Catkin. There have been many times when I wanted to tell you. I realized that you needed to know the truth when it got you into trouble with the Shepherd gang, but it seemed hard to undo the lie once it had got lodged in your head."

"I've been so blind."

"Don't blame yourself. We encouraged it— Sheridan and I. We didn't know if we could trust you at first. And the price of our lack of trust in you was an injury to your arm and a very frightening night in the Rookeries. At least when I'm gone, you'll no longer be bothered by my enemies."

"But I don't want you to go, Johnny," I blurted out. "I'd prefer to spend my life defending you against all those who are after you than never see you again! Stay here. I'll look after you."

He ruffled my hair affectionately. "In your heart of hearts, you know you can't do that, Catkin. You can't keep me safe, even in Drury Lane. Anyway, I'm sure we'll see each other again, either here or in America. It may take a few years, but it will happen. Perhaps then you'll be a world-famous writer on a tour of England's former colonies and I'll have to queue for your autograph. You'll see this shabby old man in front of you holding out your best seller, and he'll remind you of someone you once knew."

I didn't like this picture very much. "No, that's not how it'll be. I'll turn up in Philadelphia and they'll be holding an exhibition in your honor: the man who changed the course of history—the man who brought the crowned heads of Europe to their knees! You'll drive past me in a coach and four and all the crowd will cheer. Next thing you'll be elected president!"

I had been intending to cheer him up, but my words had the opposite effect.

"Hardly. I don't think a renegade lord will suit the taste of Americans. They like homegrown heroes." He sighed, looking down at his ink-stained fingernails. "I don't fit in anywhere, Catkin—not in my father's house, not here, not in America."

His melancholy mood was infectious; I felt quite low when I returned to the Sparrow's Nest to hide the money under my pillow. I did not undress immediately, but sat by the window looking out at the stars and thinking of Johnny's remark about us all changing with time. Despite what he said, I didn't need to grow up to learn that there were few constants in life. Those who cared for me never stayed around for very long—my mother, my father, the old prompter who taught me so much, and now Johnny. Even this, my little refuge at the top of the theater, would not last forever. We all had to move on eventually.

A crash on the stairs below made me jump out of my skin.

"Shut up, Meatpie!" I heard someone hiss. "She'll 'ear you."

Billy's gang had broken in. They were coming for me! Quickly, I threw open the window, swearing under my breath as it rattled, and clambered out onto the roof. This was a bolt-hole I retreated to when Mrs. Reid was after me for some misdemeanor or other, but I had never used it on so cold a night, or when the leadings were so treacherously icy.

The door to the Sparrow's Nest banged open and, from my vantage point crouched beneath the window, I could hear boots thumping across the floor.

"She's not 'ere," said Meatpie, tipping up the old couch I slept on.

"But what's this?" said Pox-Face gleefully as forty pounds worth of guineas rolled across the floor. I cursed them as I heard them scrabble to collect the money. "I didn't know the pussycat was so rich."

"Ha, ha, ha! She's not now," said Meatpie with his stupid slow laugh.

They continued to upend chests of clothes and overturn racks of costumes in their hunt for me.

"'Ere, Kitty-Kitty!" crowed Pox-Face. "Come to Daddy. We've someone 'oo wants you!"

I crouched low on the ledge, shivering, praying that they would not think to look out of the window.

"It's no good. She's not 'ere," said Meatpie at last.

"But at least the pistol-man didn't get away," said Pox-Face. "Billy won't be too cross about losing the minnow now 'e's caught the fish. Let's get over there before the fun starts."

Footsteps retreated down the stairs. I paused, hardly daring to breathe. Silence. I got up slowly, taking care not to lose my footing. They'd come for the diamond. They'd got Johnny and were going to try to make him tell them where the nonexistent stone was. But what could I do? Run for help? Who to? Mr. Sheridan? He lived too far away. The law?

But the runners would arrest Johnny rather than help him. Syd's gang? Yes, Syd was my best hope.

I climbed back into the room. It looked as if a hurricane had swept through it. Mrs. Reid was not going to be pleased. I crept to the door and listened. Nothing. In stockinged feet I padded down the wooden stairs, remembering to jump over the one second from the bottom that always creaked loudly. I could hear my heart thumping, my breath hissing between my teeth, and now the murmur of distant voices. They sounded as if they were coming from Johnny's room. I had to pass his office to get to the stage door. Keeping to the shadows, I made my way past the green room and toward the hubbub. I could see several people crowded by the entrance to Johnny's office. One turned—Pox-Face—and I ducked behind the anchor propped up in the corridor. I waited a few moments and then poked my head out. They were all intent on the scene in the room. I slid along the wall, wishing I were not wearing skirts that whispered with every step I took. I was right behind Meatpie now and could smell his sweat of excitement. He leaned over to say something to Pox-Face, revealing Johnny trussed up on his back on the bed. Billy was sitting on the desk, twirling the pistols in his hands. Ferret-Features was ransacking every drawer and chest in the place. Even Johnny's little bundle had been ripped open and strewn across the floor.

"No shot?" said Billy calmly, admiring the guns. "So I could've skinned the cat then? Fortunately, it's never too late. 'Er time will come."

"Makes you feel big, does it, Shepherd, threatening a girl?" spat Johnny.

If I could've, I would've told him not to rile Billy. The consequences were felt immediately. Billy struck his prisoner across the cheek with the handle of one of the pistols. He then turned to Meatpie.

"Take 'im onto the stage. I can feel one of my greatest performances about to begin as I beat the whereabouts of that diamond out of 'im. There ain't room to swing a cat in 'ere—though perhaps we can try that later when she turns up, eh?" he sniggered.

The gang laughed sycophantically. I shuddered.

They were coming out. I had to hide. But poor Johnny—I couldn't leave him to this! First things first: I had to get myself out of sight. I would be no use to Johnny if Billy had the chance to carry out any of his threats against me. Trying not to make noise, I ran down the corridor and onto the scenery lot at the back of the stage. There, stacked against the wall, was the enchanter's laboratory Mr. Bishop's carpenter had been fixing. I clambered onto the set and groped in the dark for the catch to release the hidden compartment. There! A small hole, not much bigger than Mrs. Reid's sewing cabinet, opened before me, in the wooden fireplace to the left of the cauldron. I slid the door closed, but as I did so, one of the glass bottles fell from its shelf and smashed on the floor.

"Did you 'ear that?" said Ferret-Features, running onto the stage.

"It came from over there," said Billy. "Check it out."

"Could it be that old man from the door?" asked Pox-Face.

"Nah, 'e's out cold. I tied 'im up," said Ferret-Features.

Lanterns flared in the dark as Pox and Ferret searched for the source of the disturbance. I could hear a dragging noise and, through the crack in the compartment, saw Meatpie pulling Johnny out of the wings. Billy was standing center stage, torch raised above his head, looking up at row upon row of empty seating. Above his head the basket of the balloon from that evening's farce swung gently in the draft. He gave a deep sigh of satisfaction.

"You know, boys, I always wanted to be on stage, and now's me chance."

Footsteps approached my hiding place; the enchanter's laboratory rattled as Pox-Face jumped onto it.

"Billy, over 'ere!" he shouted, only feet from my position. "Broken glass all over the shop."

"It could've been the wind," suggested Ferret-Features feebly.

"What wind, you dung brain?" snapped Billy. "No, I smell a rat—or should I say Cat? Find 'er!"

Pox-Face began to look through the scenery leaning up against the back wall. Ferret-Features, displaying more intelligence than I had expected, started to thump on the hollow walls of the battlements and buildings. I murmured a quick prayer that the carpenter had managed to fix the fault with the compartment: the last thing I needed was for it to spring open now.

Thump, thump, thump! Ferret was right by me. Crash, smash, crash! Bottle after bottle fell from the shelf, exploding as they hit the floor. They made so much noise that he missed the strange echo as he rapped on the door of the compartment.

"Nothink, Billy," Ferret called over to his leader. "If she was 'ere, she must 'ave done a runner."

"Leave it then. Let's get on with the show."

Ferret-Features and Pox-Face moved to the front of the stage, taking their lanterns with them. Now was my chance to slip away.

"So, Pistol-Man," Billy was saying. I could see him holding Johnny by the hair. "Are you goin' to give me the pleasure of a long and painful beatin' or are you goin' to tell me now where the diamond's 'idden?"

"Diamond? What diamond?" replied Johnny fiercely. "There is no diamond."

Billy let go of Johnny's hair. He took a step back and laced his fingers together, bending them backward so they cracked like pistol shots.

"Good. I 'oped you'd say that."

I turned my eyes away but could tell by the sickening sound of knuckle on bone that the beating had begun.

I could delay no longer: I had to get help. I slipped out of my hiding place and tiptoed to the stage door without attracting the attention of any of Billy's gang. On the threshold, cudgel clutched in his hand, lay Caleb. I knelt down beside him, feeling for signs of life. He was still breathing—but out cold.

Suddenly, I heard a noise behind me. A hand clapped me on my shoulder. I twisted around and bit hard into it, giving rise to a sharp exclamation behind me.

"Dammit, Cat!" hissed Pedro, shaking his hand in agony. "Why did you do that? What's going on? Why's Caleb on the floor?"

I had too much to tell him to berate him for frightening me like that. I decided the bite would be punishment enough.

"Billy's gang's here. They've got Johnny. They're trying to make him talk—to make him tell them where the diamond is." I didn't have time to explain that the diamond had been a figment of my imagination, for an alarming thought had just struck me. I looked over Pedro's shoulder into the dark corridor. What was he doing here? He wasn't in league with Billy and his gang, was he? I moved away from him. "Why are you here? Is Syd with you, or any of the others?" I asked suspiciously.

"No, I've come from Frank. He's sorted out a passage for Johnny—if we can get him out of here."

My suspicions subsided a little, but I was left with the unpleasant truth that we were still only two against four.

"Shall we go for Syd?" I asked.

Pedro hovered indecisively. There was a shout from the stage and the snap of something breaking—I prayed it wasn't Johnny's legs.

"No time," said Pedro, his hand shaking slightly as he helped me to my feet. He looked as terrified as I felt. "Any ideas?"

I thought for a moment. Was he trying to trap me? There was a cry of pain from the stage. I couldn't afford to think like this. I had to help Johnny, and to do this I needed to trust Pedro. Surely on my home ground I should be able to beat those pea-brained thugs? At least, with Pedro's help it should be possible.

"One, but it's going to be tricky." I told him what I had in mind.

He smiled, his white teeth gleaming in the shadows of his face. "Brilliant—just show me the ropes."

After rapid instruction in backstage management, Pedro said he was ready.

"Remember, do nothing till you see them in their places. The white cross, remember," I whispered urgently as we wormed our way to the wings, keeping out of sight of the forestage. "You won't let me down, will you?"

"Of course not. Good luck!" he hissed, giving my arm a squeeze. I took a deep breath, more nervous than any actress on her debut, and walked onto the stage, my life now depending on a boy I had spent the past few days suspecting of treachery.

"Oi, Billy! I've been looking for you," I called out boldly.

My sudden appearance came as such a surprise that all five of them were momentarily arrested in their actions. Johnny, of course, had no choice: he was sagging in the ropes that bound him. Blood trickled from his nose and his left eye was puffy. He was barely conscious. Billy was poised above him, his fist raised. The three lieutenants were standing around them: Meatpie with his arms folded; Ferret hovering at his leader's shoulder for the best view; Pox feeling the edge of his knife thoughtfully— hoping no doubt for a go at the victim. Billy lowered his fist.

"Cat!" groaned Johnny in despair. I suppose his one solace had been the thought that I had escaped.

"Well, well, if it ain't my little pussycat," said Billy, pushing his sleeves up to reveal his lean, muscular forearms. "I was lookin' for you too. I knew you were about the place somewhere." He gave Meatpie a nod, and the pudding boy started forward to seize me.

I held up my arms to ward him off. "Whoa! There's no need for that between friends, surely?" I said, hoping my voice would not betray my fear. "I only wanted to tell you that I've done what I promised. I got the diamond for you."

Billy waved Meatpie off and beckoned me forward.

"Bring it here then, like a good little girl," he said with his rotten grin.

"Ah. You see, Billy, I'm no flat. This good little girl doesn't trust big bad boys like you," I said archly, hands on my hips, still keeping my distance. "How could I know you'd keep your side of the bargain? So, naturally, I put it somewhere for safekeeping."

In no mood for playing, Billy strode over and seized my elbow. In an attempt to make my movements as natural as possible, I pulled away from him, trying to lead him farther upstage to the white cross chalked on the floor. The boys formed up behind us, right on target. Why wasn't Pedro making his move?

"What bargain?" Billy asked with a dangerous edge to his voice. "You'll find that you're in no position to bargain with me."

"But what about my dress?" I asked with a petulant pout as I tried to resist turning to look into the wings where Pedro was supposed to be waiting. "You promised! You can't have one of your girls going about dressed like a scarecrow, can you?"

Billy thought he understood me now. He gave a knowing smile and eased his grip. Changing tack, he put his arm around my shoulders, which was far worse than his previous menacings.

"One of my girls, eh? You've seen the light then, Cat?" He squeezed me to him. He smelled like the Fleet ditch. "Well, if you give me the diamond, I'll let you in me gang and buy you a dress—a silk one. Anythink else?" My eyes slid to

Johnny, who was watching me in horror. He must have guessed I was up to something but he thought I had miscalculated badly. I hoped he was wrong. But what was Pedro doing?

"What about your friend 'ere?" asked Billy. He was testing me for weakness, I could tell.

"Oh, he's no friend of mine," I bluffed with a shrug. "He was planning to dump me and go to America, that one."

"Good girl," said Billy, slapping me on the back. "I'm pleased you said that 'cause it wouldn't've done to let 'im go now 'e knows we've got the stone. Come on then, give it to me."

"I can't—not yet," I added hurriedly. "I pawned it." I dug in my pocket and held out the receipt from Mr. Vaughan.

Billy squinted at it. "This says jools—gold and stuff, Cat. I can't see no diamond."

"I put it in with some other things I'd lifted," I explained. "To make it less obvious. Mr. Vaughan and I have a little understanding."

"I'm impressed, Cat! I'd 'eard 'e was straight. Well, what are we waitin' for? Let's go and get it.

I'm sure 'e won't mind openin' up for so special a customer."

"Probably not," I shrugged, "but I need my forty pounds back first." I put the receipt into my pocket.

"Forty pounds? What forty pounds?" Billy looked angry again. His grip now became painful.

"Ask Meatpie and Pox-Face," I said coolly.

Billy turned on his followers. "Is this true? 'Ave you got the money?"

"Well, Billy, it's like this," said Pox-Face digging into his pockets. "We were goin' to tell you, weren't we, Meatpie?"

"Were we?" said Meatpie dully.

"Give me that!" hissed Billy, snatching the coins from them. "I'll deal with you two later."

He began to count the gold.

"Here, Billy," I said with what I hoped was a winning smile, "let me help you."

I lifted the lantern up, moving a few paces forward as I pretended to stagger under its weight. He smiled indulgently at my girlish feebleness but moved toward me to take advantage of the light, feet now planted plumb in the center of the white chalk cross.

As Billy hit his mark, Pedro released the balloon and pulled the lever to drop the trap center stage. The floor gave way under Billy. With a curse, he made a grab for the nearest thing to hand (yours truly), pulling me over the edge with him. Flinging the lantern aside, I just managed to take hold of the edge of the trap. With a jolt, his grip on my dress gave way and he fell into the black hole, taking half my skirt. Usually put to use for Satan's sudden descents to hell, the trapdoor had sent a new devil to the underworld.

Meanwhile, the balloon had plummeted to the ground, crushing Meatpie, Pox-Face, and Ferret-Features like beetles beneath a giant's boot.

Pedro darted onto the stage and hauled me out of the hole. Below I could hear Billy cursing. He had not broken his neck then. Shame.

"Quick, we don't have long," said Pedro, hurrying to untie Johnny. Once free, Johnny slumped, limp as a rag doll, unable to get to his feet.

The boys under the basket were beginning to stir. I could see Meatpie's foot twitching. I took one side of Johnny, Pedro supporting him on the other.

"I thought you'd never pull that damned lever!" I swore as we heaved Johnny up.

"But you told me to wait until they were all lined up!" Pedro protested.

"I'd've settled for three out of four—I thought Billy was never going to move into range and I was running out of ideas."

"You? Out of ideas? I don't believe it!" said Pedro with a grin.

I smiled back into the eyes of my friend.

"Where to now?" I panted as we dragged Johnny to the door. He was so heavy, it was clear we could not keep this up for long.

"Have you got any money on you?" asked Pedro.

"Yes," I gasped. I had the Earl of Ranworth's sovereign still in my pocket.

"We'll take a cab—get him to Grosvenor Square. It's the safest place."

Pedro left us at the corner of Russell Street and ran off to find a hackney carriage. It was late and the street was quiet. The only person about was a man loitering in a doorway opposite. I did not like the look of him. Sooner than I hoped, I heard the clatter of hooves and wheels behind me.

"Let's see your money, girl," said the jarvey from his driving seat on top of the cab, skeptical that either Pedro or I could afford the luxury of a ride across town. I held up my sovereign. He gave me an appraising look. "All right," he said finally. "In you get."

Pedro and I heaved Johnny into the cab.

"What's wrong with him?" laughed the jarvey. "Too much to drink?"

Punch-drunk, I might've said, but I didn't want to share this information with the coachman.

"I'll double the fare if you get us to Grosvenor Square in ten minutes. Stop for nothing and no one," I called up.

"Right you are, miss," said the jarvey, cracking his whip. "Brownie and I'll show you the meaning of speed."

The carriage pulled away with a clatter of hooves. As it did so, I heard a yell behind us.

"Stop!" bellowed Billy after us. "Stop that cab!"

But the jarvey had his orders and with a shrill whistle urged his horse to a faster trot. I craned my head out of the window to see if Billy was gaining on us but I need not have worried: he could only manage a hobble as far as the end of Russell Street and he soon gave up. I gave him a cheery wave.

"I'll get you, Cat!" he shouted. "You're dead!"

"You forget, Billy," I called back. "Cats have nine lives!"

I sat back on the seat to give my companions a delighted smile, but I found them looking at me somberly.

"What's up?" I asked.

"Nine lives?" croaked Johnny, his hand clutching his ribs. "You seem to be running through your portion rather fast."

"He's right, Cat," said Pedro. "You shouldn't bait Billy Shepherd."

"As if I had a choice in the matter!" I exclaimed. "To hear you two, anyone would think that I enjoyed it!"

"And didn't you?" probed Johnny with a pained smile as the cab went into a pothole. "Didn't you enjoy outwitting him?"

"Just a little, a very little," I admitted, unable to keep a huge grin from my face.

Act V - In which our heroine has an arresting experience . . .

ACT V

SCENE 1—DRESSES

Johnny managed to walk from the cab into the mews behind Grosvenor Square without assistance. We led him into the unlocked stable Lord Francis used as a changing room and dropped him onto the straw. In the next stall, a horse stamped its feet. From the quarters above the stables came the loud voices of the grooms, punctuated by the occasional thump of a game of shove ha'penny.

"What now?" I asked Pedro, peering through a barred window at the house. It was brightly illuminated: it seemed as though the family was still awake.

"One of us needs to go in and find Frank and Lady Elizabeth," said Pedro. We looked at each other, remembering the fierce French cook and the hordes of servants we had seen on our last visit. It would be a miracle if either of us got in unseen.

Someone pulled a curtain on the third floor—a girl's hand.

"Do you think that's her bedroom?" I asked, nudging Pedro.

He nodded. "Makes sense."

"I'll go then," I said.

"No, let me," said Pedro.

"You can't. It's got to be me. Think what'll happen if they find you creeping round a lady's bedroom at this time of night! You stay and look after Johnny."

Pedro gave in, recognizing the sense of what I was saying. If he were caught, he'd be lucky if they spared his life and only packed him off to a slave plantation in the West Indies; I might escape with a thrashing.

I ran across the cobbles and slid in through the back door to the kitchens. The place was once again alive with activity: from the clatter of pans and splash of water in the scullery I guessed that the plates from some fancy dinner were being washed. No refuge there this time, then. I crept as far as the open kitchen door and peered in. The chef was sitting with his feet up on the table swilling a glass of red wine, humming to himself. I stole past and ran as quietly as I could up the stairs to the green baize door Lord Francis had taken us through.

I stopped. I could hear the confused babble of many voices and a door opening and closing. It appeared I had arrived just as the duke's guests had taken it into their heads to depart. Pushing the door open a crack, I saw a large party of gentlemen fetching their cloaks from the two footmen on duty. There was Mr. Sheridan reaching for his hat and cane and, yes, there was Marchmont senior accompanied by the Earl of Ranworth. If only Mr. Sheridan would look in my direction. How I could do with his assistance! I wished I could tell him how much danger his "diamond" was in! But to break from my hiding place would be to reveal my unauthorized presence in the house and attract far too many questions from the host. I watched despondently as Mr. Sheridan resolutely looked the other way, bade the duke goodnight, and left.

So, no way up those stairs while the duke was still about. I backed down the steps to the corridor and paused for thought. Where were the back stairs? I wondered. There had to be some for the servants to pass unseen about the house. As if in answer to my question, a maid emerged from the scullery carrying a jug of steaming water. I hid behind a row of aprons hanging from pegs along a wall. The maid walked straight past me and took a passageway on the left. I crept after her. She then took a sharp right and disappeared. I followed, discovering that she had indeed led me to the stairs. I had to be quick: this narrow flight offered no hiding places. I'd have to be up and off them before she headed back down.

She carried her burden up three flights, pausing only to straighten her cap when she reached a landing. She then knocked on the door of the room closest to the stair and entered.

"Put it over there, please, Mary." It was Lady Elizabeth! Feeling a wave of relief, I remembered to dart behind a linen chest just in time.

Mary's feet could be heard getting farther away as she went down the stairs. I had a final look up and down the corridor—all clear.

Tap, tap! I knocked softly on Lady Elizabeth's door.

"Come!" she called.

I opened the door and saw her reflection in the dressing-table mirror. She looked beautiful, like a mermaid rising out of a silver pool: her hair was strewn with pearls and her silk dress was the color of bluebells.

"Cat!" she exclaimed, dropping her brush onto the table with a clatter. "Whatever has happened to you?"

I caught a glimpse of myself in the glass. My hair was in a hopeless tumble, and half my skirt was missing, displaying grubby white petticoats beneath.

"Ah," I said gesturing to my dress ruefully. "I had a merry meeting with my friend Billy Boil."

She got up, moved swiftly across the thick rose-colored carpet, and pulled me inside the room. She took a quick look at the silent corridor before she closed the door and turned the key.

"Oh, Cat, are you all right?" she said. "Have a seat. Tell me what happened."

"Forget about that, Lady Elizabeth—"

She held her finger to my lips. "Lizzie, Cat. Remember!"

"Lizzie, then. What I've come to tell you, Lizzie, is that Johnny's here. He didn't come off quite so well in his encounter with our friend, so we've brought him here. He's in the stable with Pedro."

Lady Elizabeth now ran to the window and peered out into the yard.

"Is he all right?" she asked anxiously.

I nodded.

"He'll be safe there for the moment," she told me. "It's quiet now. It is very fortunate you did not arrive half an hour earlier: we had all the carriages lined up in the yard. They've only just gone around to the front of the house."

"Will you help us?" I asked anxiously.

"Of course. Stay where you are. Don't answer the door unless you hear four taps. I'll fetch Frank." She picked up a candle from her dressing table. "Father sent him to bed an hour ago, but if I know him he'll be spying on the guests as they leave, giving their carriages marks out of ten or some such fancy of his."

She slipped out and I locked the door behind her. It would not do for a maid to find me in here alone. I sat at the dressing table and stared at myself in the mirror. I did not have the luxury of my own glass at home, though there were plenty in the dressing rooms for the actors. A solemn face looked back out at me. My red curls were matted with dirt. My freckled nose was smudged, my bodice torn where the skirt had parted from it at the waist, my hands red raw with marks of hard work and blows. Compared with the vision with white skin and chestnut locks that had just sat there, I was a complete troll. It was a depressing comparison.

Four taps on the door. I quickly opened it to find myself almost knocked down by the arrival of Lord Francis.

"Cat!" he exclaimed, giving me a relieved hug before remembering himself and giving me a formal bow at arm's length. "Lizzie's told me what happened. I'm so pleased to see you in one piece. When our gang gets to hear about this, Shepherd'll wish he had never been born!"

Our gang? Since when had Lord Francis been enrolled among Syd's followers? But I had forgotten—he was a boy, wasn't he? That was sufficient to earn Syd's approbation.

"Now, you sit down and let Lizzie look after you. I'll fetch the others," he said, taking charge.

To be honest, it was a relief to relinquish responsibility for seeing Johnny to safety. This was Lord Francis's home: it was right that he should deal with the ticklish matter of smuggling a wanted man inside it. He led me back to the dressing table, gave me a pat on the arm, and left.

Minutes later Lady Elizabeth returned. She slopped some hot water into a porcelain bowl decorated with pink roses and carried it over to me.

"Here, you can clean yourself up with this," she said, passing me a linen towel.

It was worse somehow with her standing there watching me. I went hot with embarrassment, feeling common and dirty. A girl like me should not be sullying her bedchamber with my presence. I was distressed to find a tear had trickled out of the corner of my eye and dripped in the bowl in front of me.

"What's the matter, Cat?" Lady Elizabeth asked, coming to kneel beside me.

"I'm not fit to be here," I said despairingly, dropping the linen cloth into the now gray water. "I should go."

"Nonsense," she said, getting up and going to a closet on the far side of the room. "You won't feel like that when you've put this on tomorrow. I've grown out of it but it should fit you." On the bed she laid the loveliest emerald silk dress that I had ever seen. "Green never was my color, but it will suit you.'

"I can't take it," I protested.

"Of course you can," she said, smiling. "Now, you get yourself into bed. You must be exhausted."

"Bed?"

I looked around the room. The only bed I could see was Lady Elizabeth's four-poster, hung with muslin curtains and covered with a white satin counterpane.

"My bed, of course," said Lady Elizabeth. "There's plenty of room for both of us. You get in; I'll just go and check on the boys to see they have arrived safely."

She left, closing the door softly behind her. I stood irresolute for a moment in the middle of the carpet and then made my decision. I was used to sleeping on the unyielding surface of the old couch in the Sparrow's Nest. I had no need of the luxuries Lady Elizabeth had so kindly offered me. Finding a spare blanket in the chest under the window, I curled up on the floor behind the screen and, despite my determination to stay awake to hear her news when she returned, I must have dropped off to sleep.

I was woken the next morning by hushed voices at the door to the chamber.

"No, Mary, I really do not require your assistance to dress this morning, but I would like you to prepare a bath for me next door."

The door clicked to, and a bare foot appeared around the corner of the screen.

"I am sorry to have woken you, Cat. I had to send her away or she would have discovered you. Did you sleep well?"

I nodded, noticing for the first time that my cheek was cushioned on a feather pillow. I sat up and stretched.

"I thought you had gone when I came back," laughed Lady Elizabeth. "You did give me a fright."

"Johnny and Pedro—are they safe?" I asked anxiously, throwing off my blanket.

"Yes, quite safe. Pedro went back to his master's house once Johnny was smuggled into Francis's room. He wanted to find out how it all ended at the theater last night. He said he'd come back and tell us this morning."

That was good. There would be an uproar when Caleb was discovered and Johnny and I were found to be gone. I hoped the old man was all right, but I dreaded to think what construction would be put on the whole affair. Would they be worried for me or blame me? Probably the latter if Mrs. Reid had anything to do with it.

"I did wonder if you would like a bath," Lady Elizabeth asked delicately. "I've arranged for one to be put in the dressing room next door and will propose that Lord Jonathan take a dip, but I thought I'd give you first refusal."

A bath? What a luxury! I could not remember the last time I had had one, as normally I had to make do with a basin of hot water once a day.

"That would be wonderful."

"Good. Then would you be so kind as to help me into my clothes and I will go and tell Francis what I've planned."

Dressing a lady was a far more complicated affair than I had imagined. I did my job as lady's maid very inexpertly, buttoning garments and lacing stays. Not surprisingly, Lady Elizabeth would not let me near her hair but dressed it herself in the mirror. She took a final look, straightening her rumpled skirt.

"That'll have to do. When you're ready, go through there." She pointed to a door in the corner of the room. "The bath should be waiting for you. I'll make sure Mary is out of the way, but remember to lock yourself in."

I gave her a few minutes to fulfill her promise about the maid, then quietly opened the door into the dressing room. The window was veiled with a curtain, filtering the morning light. In the center of the wooden floor stood the very same bath I had seen down in the scullery only a few days ago. It was now filled to the brim with steaming water. A pile of linen towels stood waiting on an ebony rack. To me, so unused to such an excess of comforts, it was like stepping into the heart of a temple dedicated to cleanliness, the steam rising like incense to the gods of soap and water. I locked both doors as instructed and stripped to my skin. I knew it was immodest of me to take a bath without keeping on my shift but I had only one and besides, who was there to note my behavior? Then the wonderful moment of truth came: I stepped in and sub-merged myself completely under the water.

I allowed myself some fifteen minutes of indulgence and then toweled off quickly. The bath water looked far less enticing now that it was filled with soap bubbles, but Johnny would just have to put up with it. I assumed that as a lord, he had the frequent pleasure of taking a plunge, so today it was just his hard luck that I got there first.

Lady Elizabeth was waiting for me when I came back into her bedroom wrapped in a large white towel, clutching my pitiful bundle of clothes.

"I'll go and tell Lord Jonathan he can go in now. I've put some clothes for you behind the screen," she informed me.

She had laid out a complete change of clothes: a bright white shift, petticoats, and the emerald green dress I had refused the night before. This morning my rejection of her bounty evaporated like mist under the newly risen sun, and to honor my scrubbed state, I succumbed to temptation, putting on each garment with due reverence. But the greatest wonder were the silk stockings: they slid up my legs so that I hardly knew they were there, so different from the scratchy woolen stockings I normally wore.

"Shall I help you do up the back of your dress?"

Lady Elizabeth had returned.

"Please." I emerged from behind the screen and displayed my new finery for her approval, arms held wide.

"I told you it would suit you," she said, guiding me to the dressing table. "As I have forced you to be my maid this morning, it is now my turn to do you the same service."

I definitely got the better part of the bargain. Lady Elizabeth brushed and fastened up my damp hair to look like something from a fashion plate. I had never seen myself so smart. I looked almost like a highborn lady.

"Now I will need your help with Lord Jonathan," she said, giving my curls a final tweak. "He will be here in a moment."

"Help? What kind of help?" My playtime was over, and I was businesslike once more, remembering we were far from safe.

"With the disguise." Lady Elizabeth moved to the closet on the far side of the room and pulled out a pile of clothes she had prepared. "Frank has secured a berth for Lord Jonathan on a ship leaving for America. It will sail as soon as the wind is favorable. He's arranging to bring around the carriage so that we can take Lord Jonathan to the docks this morning. He can hide on board until the packet sails. All that remains is to ensure that he is not recognized on the way there."

She threw the clothes onto the bed. I could now see that they consisted of a large red velvet gown, stays, a shift, and other items of female apparel. A black wig crouched among them like a cat curled up before the fire.

"You're going to dress him as a woman?" I asked, wondering if I was allowed to giggle.

"Of course," she said with a smile. "What better disguise could there be? I did promise to dress him so that even his own mother would not recognize him. Though my mother might, for it is one of her gowns I've borrowed."

"Does Johnny know yet?"

She shook her head.

At that moment, there was a tap on the dressing room door.

"Come!" said Lady Elizabeth.

Johnny stepped into the room wrapped in a dressing gown, admittedly looking far better than he had last night, but nothing surely could disguise that puffy black eye and cut lip?

"What are you smiling at?" he asked, looking from one of us to the other.

"Nothing," Lady Elizabeth said brightly. "Now, go behind the screen and put on the things I give you."

Obediently, he did as he was bidden. I had never heard Johnny swear before a lady, but that changed when the shift was handed over the top of the screen.

"Dammit, what's all this?" he spluttered in outrage.

"Your disguise," said Lady Elizabeth calmly. "Now stop making a fuss and get yourself dressed."

"I can't wear this!" he exclaimed, jiggling the stays over the top of the screen. "It's bad enough that I've been beaten black and blue around my ribs without squeezing into this infernal contraption."

"Stop complaining," she told him in a firm, no-nonsense voice. "Half the population wears them all the time: I'm only asking you to put it on for a few hours."

The grumbles ceased and Johnny finally emerged wearing the dress. In my opinion, the disguise was not convincing: he looked like a man in a gown. Anyone would see at a glance that he was an impostor.

Lady Elizabeth, however, was not down-hearted. She hadn't finished with him yet.

"Sit by the glass here," she ordered.

Johnny shuffled over, tripping on his skirts.

"Pull the strings tighter, Cat," she said, gesturing to the laces dangling from the back of his dress. "Then do up the buttons."

As instructed I began to pull.

"Wait a moment," she said. Diving into a drawer in the tallboy by the screen, she pulled out a pair of woolen stockings.

"I think you can guess where to put these," she said, blushing scarlet as she handed them to Johnny. With a few furtive gropes down the front of his dress, he suddenly began to take on a much more womanly form.

"Ow!" Johnny cried as I resumed pulling on the strings. "I don't know how you ladies stand for all this."

"Neither do I," agreed Lady Elizabeth, now approaching his face with a large powder puff. "Pure madness."

As I buttoned Johnny's dress up at the back, Lady Elizabeth placed the wig on his head, adorning it with a lace cap and bonnet.

"There!" She stepped back, hands on hips.

The transformation was uncanny. Gone was handsome Johnny; in his place was an ugly matron with her face plastered in white powder.

"As long as he doesn't move or speak, we might get away with this," I mused.

"I'll ring for some breakfast," said Lady Elizabeth enthusiastically. "We'll try it out on one of the servants. I'll tell them you are my dressmaker come for a fitting."

In response to the summons, a maid appeared at the door.

"Jenny, is Papa in the breakfast room?"

Jenny nodded.

"Can you tell him that I can't come down as the dressmaker has arrived? I'll take my breakfast up here."

Jenny's eyes slid to Johnny, who was busying himself with a sewing bag Lady Elizabeth had thrust in his hands a moment before. Lady Elizabeth took her to the door and said in an undertone, "I would be most obliged if you would not stare at the lady's eye, Jenny. Her husband is a nasty piece of work—he beats her. She has been in floods of tears this morning telling me about it."

Jenny's face now registered pity for the unfortunate seamstress.

"Of course, your ladyship."

"In fact, would you bring up some tea for us all—to help settle her nerves?"

Jenny bobbed a curtsy and left.

"What do you think?" asked Johnny anxiously. It was most unnerving to hear his deep voice issuing from the bonnet. "Was she fooled?"

"I think so," said Lady Elizabeth, taking a seat by the window. "Women are always the hardest to deceive, but if she had thought you were a man, she would have run from the room screaming."

After breakfast, Lord Francis came to announce the arrival of the carriage. He could not resist

smirking at Johnny and was cuffed by the seamstress for his rudeness.

"Sorry, ma'am," he said, giving Johnny a deep
bow. "I won't do it again."

"And I won't give you the opportunity again,"
growled Johnny, picking up his skirts and following
Lady Elizabeth down the corridor with a sturdy
stride.

"We had better be quick!" warned Lord
Francis. "Papa was still reading the newspaper when
I left the table, but he could be out at any moment."

We descended to the foyer without incident and
were almost at the front entrance when a door to
our left opened and the Duke of Avon strode out,
newspaper tucked under his arm. "CAPTAIN
SPARKLER STILL AT LARGE!" read the headline.

"Morning, Lizzie!" he said, kissing his daughter
on the cheek. "Off out so early?"

"Yes, Papa. I have to return some calls.
Frightful bore, but there you are."

The duke's eyes turned to Johnny.

"Ah, this is my seamstress, Papa," she filled
in quickly.

"Not the one that keeps sending in such scandalously high bills, I hope? Madame what's-her-name?"

"Madame Martine," said Lady Elizabeth as the duke gave the seamstress a hard stare.

"Is she good?" he asked turning back to his daughter.

"The best."

"Well, in that case, I suppose she's worth the money. *Enchanté, madame,*" he said gallantly, bowing and kissing Johnny's gloved hand.

"*Merci, monsieur,*" said "Madame Martine" in flawless, if somewhat gruff, French.

The duke now looked at me.

"Miss Royal, isn't it? What are you doing here? I didn't know you were in the house."

"Cat—I mean Miss Royal—came early on my request. We are paying calls together. All my friends want to meet her," said Lady Elizabeth.

The duke now took in my new finery and a small frown appeared on his brow. My cheeks reddened.

"Hmm," he said disapprovingly. "I'd like to have a word with you when you return, Lizzie. There's something we must discuss."

The duke dismissed us with a nod and retreated into the breakfast room. I could guess what he wanted to talk to his daughter about: he was going to warn her against introducing girls like me into her intimate circle. I had a very dubious position in society, and my company would do nothing to enhance her reputation.

Lady Elizabeth led the way down the steps to the carriage. Hanging on the back, next to the stable boy Jenkins, was Pedro. He jumped down and opened the door for us. Lord Francis handed each of us in and climbed in last.

The coachman had already raised his whip to lick the horses into a trot when there was a respectful cough at the streetside door.

"Your lordship, might I have a word?"

All of us turned to look at the speaker. I saw to my horror that it was Constable Lennox, the Bow Street runner who had checked in at Drury Lane yesterday. He was now standing by the side of the carriage watching us closely. I lowered my head to hunt for something in my reticule. Johnny put a handkerchief to his eye as if wiping away a tear.

"Yes, Constable?" said Lord Francis in a surprisingly crisp tone. I had never heard him sound so lordly before. "Call back later and I will see you then. I have an engagement this morning that I must not break."

"I understand, sir, but I wonder if I might be so bold as to have a look at your carriage? I received a report from one of our informants that two fugitives fled to your house last night in the company of a third person. That person was followed back here this morning. I've already searched the stables but found nothing. That leaves me to conclude that they might be secreted somewhere in this carriage."

"Are you serious, sir?" said Lady Elizabeth, sounding suitably concerned. "How terrible! Lady Catherine, can you imagine it?" She turned to me, her eyes wide. Though surprised to find myself so rapidly ennobled, I gave a shudder by way of agreement. "Of course you must look, Constable. Shall we alight so that you can examine the carriage thoroughly? Countess, would you mind?" This latter remark was directed to Johnny, who was now applying smelling salts to his nose, as if overcome by fright.

"I'd be much obliged, my lady," said the runner.

Johnny, Lady Elizabeth, and I dismounted from the carriage and waited on the pavement while Lord Francis supervised the officer, who began checking under the seats.

"Nothing," the runner said at length when he had exhausted all possibilities. "Though, if you don't mind, my lord, I'd like to question your black servant."

"My servant? What has he to do with it?" said Lord Francis imperiously. "Haven't you wasted enough of our time today, my man?"

The runner looked awkward. "It's just that my informant saw a black boy here last night and followed the same boy here this morning."

"Are you sure it is the same boy? Gustavus did indeed go on an errand for me but I can swear that he was with me last night. Your informant must be wrong."

"True, he might," said the runner, scratching his chin. "And you say this boy, Gustavus, was with you last night?"

"Yes, wasn't that so, Jenkins?" Lord Francis called over to the stable boy.

"Yes, my lord," lied Jenkins cheerfully.

"In that case, I must apologize for intruding. Ladies." The runner gave us a bow and held the carriage door open.

"Not at all, sir," said Lady Elizabeth graciously. "You were just doing your duty." Constable Lennox glowed with pride and bowed again.

As I got in, I felt the runner's gaze fix on me. I could tell he found something about me familiar.

"We'd better get out of here," I whispered urgently to Lord Francis, "before he remembers where he saw me."

Lord Francis nodded and thumped the roof of the carriage.

"Drive on!" he called.

The carriage surged into motion, throwing us back into our well-padded seats. Looking out of the window as we turned out of Grosvenor Square,

I saw the runner suddenly clap his hand to his forehead and start off in pursuit. But even Bow Street runners could not outstrip a carriage pulled by four stallions. He was soon left behind.

"That was close," I said slumping back with relief. "He remembered me—but too late."

"And as for the countess here—he didn't have a clue," said Lord Francis, turning to Johnny. "But may I say, Countess, you do look quite ravishing this morning."

The countess gave the young lord a hearty thump for his impertinence as Lady Elizabeth and I dissolved into laughter.

SCENE 2—THE THAMES

T he carriage took us through the narrow streets of the city to the docks beyond the Tower of London. The sky was iron gray behind the white turrets of the fortress, a sign that more snow was on its way. As I watched, a raven launched itself from the battlements of the White Tower and circled over the roofs of red brick buildings crowded up against the outer walls. Disturbed by some unseen menace, a flock of gulls abandoned their scavenging on the muddy shoreline, spiraled up, and then headed eastward over Traitor's Gate. After the brief pleasure at our escape, a grim mood stole over me: even the birds sensed the threat that hung over us like an executioner's ax.

As we left the Tower behind and rattled through Wapping, Lord Francis leaned over his sister to point out Johnny's ship moored in the stretch of water known as the Pool.

"There she is: the fastest little merchant vessel in the business!" Lord Francis said cheerfully. "Or so Jenkins's second cousin swears. He's a customs man so he should know."

The ship was hard to spot, being but three masts amid a forest. Like the most intricate Brussels lace, the rigging stretched from stem to stern on each boat. From this distance it looked as if some gigantic kitten had got in the yarn bag and made a hopeless tangle. It was hard to imagine how any vessel could escape that knot.

"But even the fastest ship needs a favorable wind," said Johnny, looking anxiously up at the weather vane on top of St. Katherine's Church. It was stuck resolutely pointing east. "Pursuit has been too hot on my heels of late. I'd appreciate a cool west wind to blow me out to the estuary and put some sea miles between me and my enemies."

"I may have many gifts, Lord Jonathan," said Lord Francis, punching his friend in his bodice, "but controling the wind is not one of them." Johnny cuffed him back and laughed. I wondered how they could both be so lighthearted in view of the dangers that surrounded us. My stomach was sick with anxiety.

"I've spoken to the captain," continued Lord Francis. "He's an American, a friend of liberty—you can trust him not to give you up to Mr. Pitt's bloodhounds. We'll put you in a lighter and have you on board the *Potomac* in a jiffy."

The carriage jolted through an icy puddle and turned toward the riverside. Having never been to this part of London before, I craned my head out of the window. The buildings—every other one a tavern, as far as I could tell—were crowded together in a heap as if all London's leftovers had been dumped here higgledy-piggledy. Even stranger were the faces of the people. Among the sailors, I spotted a group of pigtailed Chinese in a tavern window intent on a game played with small white tiles; a curly-haired African dressed in rags shivered by a coil of rope; on a street corner, a turbaned Indian used sinuous hand gestures to negotiate with a fur-hatted Russian who chopped at the air like a woodcutter with an ax. Three smart girls trotted by, their cheeks rouged scarlet, dressed in brand-new red woolen shawls. They held their heads high as they showed off the gifts given them by their sailor sweethearts. The African shuffled out of their way but they paid him no attention.

"Here's the landing place," said Lord Francis as the carriage slowed. He opened the door and jumped down onto the muddy ground. "Wait there, ladies, Pedro and I will look for a boat to carry our cargo."

Johnny made to get up but I grabbed on to the back of his skirts and pulled him down.

"Sit still. People are watching," I whispered. "What'll the coachman think if he sees you striding off after the boys?"

Reluctantly, Johnny returned to his seat but he could not keep from the window, anxiously watching for any signs of trouble.

"That's not very ladylike," Lady Elizabeth warned him as she set him the example of how to sit demurely in a carriage, her hands folded in her lap, her back straight.

"Francis is only a boy!" muttered Johnny. "I feel responsible. What if something happens to him and Pedro?"

"He'll be fine," I reassured him. "He's far less likely to run into difficulties if we do as we're told and stay here."

Lord Francis and Pedro returned a few minutes later with a burly waterman at their elbow. Even in this frosty weather the boatman's arms were bare, displaying his muscled limbs honed by many hours of rowing on the tricky tides of the Thames. His gray-flecked hair straggled like limp seaweed down his back.

"As the lady any luggage?" growled the waterman as Lord Francis handed us out of the carriage.

"No," said Lord Francis curtly. Then, realizing how strange this sounded, he added, "It's being sent on later."

The waterman, however, was not interested in us or our concerns. He spat on the pavement, turned on his heel, and led the way down to the landing stage. Suddenly, after the confines of the maze of alleyways, there it was: the Thames, stretched out before us, free of the buildings that had obscured its full extent from our sight. The tide was rising, the brown waters swallowing up the mudflats, erasing the bird prints and footmarks of the scavengers. The river was buzzing with life: along its banks small boats were coming and going from all directions, crowded with people. Now I had a clear view of the ships anchored out in the Pool, and I was intrigued by the variety of shapes and sizes before me. The sharp prows and sleek lines of the smaller ships promised speed. The blunter prows of the big-bellied merchant vessels, the ones that carried priceless cargoes from the Indies of porcelain and gold, silks and spices, suggested a stately rise and fall, coupled with stubborn resistance to the storms that blew them around the Cape. Even as we watched, another Indiaman, its wooden sides painted in bold, battered colors of gilt and red, sailed in on the tide and glided to a berth on the southern bank, its white sails furling like a butterfly closing its wings after flight. I wondered what treasures it contained— perhaps some real diamonds or silks like that of my new dress?

A splash to our left—out of one of the buildings overhanging the river someone had thrown the contents of a chamber pot. The riverside smelled rank, but now I perceived that the tide bore with it a fresher smell—the smell of the windswept spaces of the estuary and the open sea. The stones of the landing stage glittered with fish scales in the weak morning light. A flake of snow drifted in the air like a dandelion seed before melting on contact with the ground.

The waterman jumped down into his boat and held up a hand to assist "the countess."

"Well," said Johnny in a low voice as he turned to us, "this is it then. This is good-bye. How can I ever thank you all enough?"

"You can't, my friend," said Pedro with a grin. "You are eternally in our debt."

Johnny seized Pedro's hand and shook it. "I can't think of four people to whom I would rather owe so much. I hope to see you again, Pedro— perhaps when you come to America with your own show."

"Perhaps," said Pedro with a pleased shrug.

"And you, Lord Francis, take a bit of advice from an old woman and stay out of trouble!" Johnny clasped the boy's arm in his firm grip.

"Old woman, you worry too much," said Lord Francis, twisting Johnny's hand up to his lips and kissing it. Johnny shook him off with a laugh.

"Lady Elizabeth." Johnny turned hesitantly to his sweetheart. "Lizzie . . ."

She said nothing, keeping her gaze steady on his face. I saw a tear glisten at the corner of her eye, but she managed a brave smile.

"What can I say?" he murmured. "You know my wishes, my hopes. . . ."

She nodded. "I know. Good-bye. Write very soon."

"I will. Look after my heart for me, won't you? I'm leaving it in your keeping."

"And you take care of mine too, Johnny."

He squeezed her hand and with great reluctance let it go.

"And now my Catkin." He turned to me, free of the shyness that had hampered his farewell to Lady Elizabeth, and folded me in a brotherly hug. "I worry about you, Catkin. I won't be happy unless you write frequently to let me know how you are. Remember, if ever you need a friend—a home even—there'll be one for you in Philadelphia."

I returned the hug.

"Thank you. I will remember."

Johnny released me and jumped nimbly down into the boat, much to the surprise of the waterman, who had patiently been waiting to assist "the lady."

"To the *Potomac!*" called Lord Francis, flicking the man a coin.

The boatman touched his cap and picked up the oars. The four of us stood shoulder to shoulder, waving at the bonneted figure of Johnny, until the boat dipped out of sight behind the first of the moored vessels.

Lord Francis and Lady Elizabeth set us down in Bow Street to avoid the spectacle of arriving at the stage door in a carriage. As my foot touched the ground, what was waiting for me at Drury Lane came back like the rush of an incoming tide.

"What did everyone make of the break-in?" I asked Pedro. "And how's Caleb?"

"He's recovering—though he's complaining of a thumping headache," said Pedro, scanning the street with quick, furtive movements to be sure we were unobserved. "When they heard about the attack by Billy's boys, they were worried for you, of course," he added, taking my arm as we slid down Russell Street. "Mrs. Reid was relieved when I told her you'd fled to a friend's house for the night. But cheer up, Cat: I've got some good news for you."

"Yes?" A chill breeze cut through my new finery, reminding me of the virtues of woolen stockings.

"They caught Billy. The night patrol got him soon after we made our exit. You won't have to worry about him anymore."

"Really?"

"Yes, really."

"But that's wonderful." A great weight lifted from my shoulders, and I felt as if I had actually grown an inch or two: not only had we got Johnny safely away, but my enemy was no longer able to reach me. With any luck he'd be for the drop—or at the very least transportation to the other side of the world.

We turned into the little courtyard by the stage door. Seeing my home ahead, I broke into an eager run.

"Come on!" I called to Pedro. "Let's celebrate with a hot drink in the Sparrow's Nest."

"Not so fast, miss."

A hand landed on my shoulder, pulling me to a sudden stop.

"Let go of her!" protested Pedro, rushing to my assistance, but the man pushed him away.

"If you don't want me to arrest you too, Blackie, I suggest you keep away."

"Arrest me?" I turned to stare up at my captor in astonishment. It was Constable Lennox, the Bow Street runner who had come to Grosvenor Square—the same one who had searched Johnny's office. "But what've I done?"

"You know best, miss. I'm arresting you on suspicion of theft."

"Theft? What theft?"

"Oh, don't come over the innocent with me, young woman. We know you are the leader of a gang of thieves preying on the theatergoers. I have my informant—your accomplice—already under lock and key. He's told us all about it. He's been very cooperative."

"But I haven't . . . I'm not . . ." I spluttered helplessly, looking to Pedro for some way out of this nightmarish turn of events.

"You can explain all that down at the station, miss," said the runner pompously, increasing his grip and beginning to march me away.

"Pedro!" I shouted over my shoulder. "Fetch Lizzie!"

"Don't worry, Cat, I will!" Pedro called back, overtaking us as he ran off to Grosvenor Square.

"You've been having a rare old time, haven't you, young woman?" said the constable, giving me a shake as he nodded down at my fine clothes. "First you pop up as a maid, then as a lady going about in a fine carriage. That's what I can't abide: little vicious tricksters who take the softhearted for a ride, rob them, and run off laughing. Well, my girl, it's just as well we caught you young and can put an end to your criminal activities. Nip evil in the bud is my motto."

I let him ramble on. My mind was in a whirl. It was not hard to guess his informant. Billy Boil would be singing like a blackbird to get himself let off. But surely the mistake would all be cleared up once Lady Elizabeth vouched for me? I comforted myself with the thought that I was certain to be allowed back home before the day was out. As long as Johnny was kept out of it, all would be well. I was mindful that, with the wind in the east, he would not yet have sailed and was still within reach of the law.

The runner took me through a side door of Bow Street Magistrate's Court into the sparsely furnished office used by the patrol.

"Sit there," he said, pointing to a wooden bench. "Don't try nothing clever or it'll be the worse for you. We don't normally put nippers like you in irons, but that can change. The clerk will take down your particulars." He nodded over to an old man who was hunched over a writing desk. "Real little vixen this one, Amos. Head of a gang of thieves at her age, would you believe it!"

Amos peered at me shortsightedly over the top of the desk, quill in hand. His thin white hair shone like a halo around his balding crown.

"Ah, a little Moll Flanders in the making, eh what!" he said. "Hard to credit it when you see them so young. They look so innocent."

"Maybe, but this one's heart is as rotten as a six-month-old egg," said the runner, straightening his uniform in the glass-paneled door leading into the court.

"No, it's not!" I could no longer contain my indignation. To hear him speak I was the most hardened of criminals.

"Name?" said Amos, cutting across my protest.

"Catherine Royal," I muttered, blushing despite myself as two runners marched through the office and gave me a curious look. I must appear very out of place, dressed like a lady but being treated like the lowest of the low.

"Residence?"

"Theater Royal, Drury Lane."

Amos raised his eyebrows. "Really?"

I nodded.

"Parents' names?"

"Don't know."

"You're an orphan?"

"I suppose so."

"Guardian then?"

"No one." I was feeling increasingly desperate, as his questions drove home the fact that I had no close family to defend me.

"No parents, no guardian. So, to whom do you belong, child? I suppose I could put down 'abandoned' or 'vagrant' maybe," he mused, sucking the end of his quill.

"I'm no vagrant," I said hotly. "I belong to Mr. Sheridan's household." That's if he did not disown me for ending up in so disgraceful a situation.

Amos gave me another of his bleary looks and scratched Mr. Sheridan's name down on my record.

"Charge?"

"Theft," interjected the runner.

"With a value of how much?"

"Jewels with a value in excess of forty pounds."

"Ah! A capital crime then," said the clerk with a weary shake of his head. "Another one for the hangman."

I thought I was going to be sick. This was like some nightmare! Surely I would wake up any moment and find it was all a dream?

The runner came over to me. "Turn out your pockets, miss."

I got up unsteadily and emptied every last penny and scrap of paper I had in my possession on the counter. The runner poked the pile with distaste and fished out the crumpled pawnbroker's ticket.

"I thought as much. I was told you'd have the proof upon you."

"But I never pawned anything stolen!" I exclaimed staring at my signature on the piece of paper he was waving before me.

"No? I've been watching you since yesterday, my girl. Not long after our first meeting in Drury Lane, I had a witness here who had come to answer questions about a missing inkwell. He was very eager to be obliging and volunteered the information that he saw *you* giving a very large amount of jewelry to a broker two days ago—jewelry that you admitted to him was not yours," the runner said triumphantly. "So how did you come by it if you did not steal it? Did it drop from the sky into your lap or did you find it lying in the road? No, no, miss; your best hope now is to admit everything and pray that the magistrate is in a merciful mood. If you talk, he might think a spell in the new penal colony in Botany Bay punishment enough. If he's not feeling so lenient and you refuse to admit your wrongdoing, it'll be the noose for you or my name's King George."

Amos began to laugh like a pair of wheezy bellows at his colleague's wit. "That it certainly is not, Constable."

Constable Lennox gave him a tolerant smile. "Have you finished, Amos? Can I lock her up now?"

"All done," confirmed Amos, tucking the quill behind his ear.

"Follow me, miss," said the runner, taking a key from a chain at his belt and going over to a heavy iron door behind the clerk's counter.

I had no choice. I followed him and for the first time in my life found myself in jail. Never in my darkest dreams had I imagined I would end up here.

SCENE 3—JAIL

The constable led me down a narrow flight of stairs to the brick-lined basement of the magistrate's house. Once used for storing fine wines, the cellars had been converted into holding cells for unfortunates like me. The only daylight came in through gratings set in the pavement above. You could see the flicker of shadows of the people passing by, oblivious to the captives below their feet. My resolve to keep a brave front in face of adversity was crumbling and I wished I had someone whose shoulder I could weep on and be comforted. I wished I had a mother. I felt very young and very alone.

Before I had a chance to break down, the constable opened the door to the cell. There, sitting against the wall on the far side, was Billy Boil. No way was I going to let him see me cry.

"'Ello, Cat! I thought I'd be seeing you sooner or later," said Billy. "Welcome to my mansion." He threw out a grubby arm to point out the delights of his new abode.

The cell, about ten feet square, smelled worse than the foulest privy. Moldering straw covered the brick floor. A single bucket for the use of the prisoners stood in one corner—I did not look too closely, but it appeared to be full. Gray cobwebs festooned the flaking mortar, home to some disturbingly large spiders, and four rough-hewn benches flanked the walls. Billy was the only occupant for the present, except for the rat that had just scuttled out of sight.

"Glad to see you've found somewhere to your taste, Billy," I said, making light of the horror.

He laughed and stretched out on the bench, taking a bite from a wrinkled apple he held in his fist.

"You can jest, Cat," he mumbled through a mouthful of pulp, "but don't forget: you're in 'ere too. What does that say for your taste?"

"It says that it was tragically bad taste ever to have anything to do with you, you lying ball of cat sick. It's your lies that've brought me here."

"Now, now, that's enough," said the runner, pushing me into the cell. "I'd advise you, miss, to keep a civil tongue in your head, or it'll be the worse for you."

"You're not leaving me in here alone with him?" I asked desperately, grabbing hold of the runner's jacket.

He shook me off. "Naturally. There's only one holding cell and you're looking at it. If you're lucky, you won't be in here long—just a day or two."

"A day or two!"

"Until the magistrate can spare the time to hear your case. Then you'll be moved to a proper prison, of course."

"But if you leave me here with him, he'll kill me!"

"Ha!" barked Constable Lennox. "Serves you right, don't it? You should've thought of that before you got mixed up in this game."

With that, he shut the door behind him and turned the key. I moved to the bench on the opposite side of the room from Billy and sat down, head bowed, hands in my lap, wondering when my enemy would make his move. There was silence for a few moments, punctuated only by the sound of him chewing on his apple. Finally, he spoke.

"May I say, Pussycat, that you're looking remarkably swell today. I'd almost take you for a fine lady. Pity there's only me and the rats to appreciate it."

I said nothing but stared at my hands resting in the green silk of my lap.

"It's good to 'ave some company. Shame your pistol friend couldn't make it. Run off with the diamond and left you in the lurch, 'as 'e? You should've stuck with me, girl. None of this would've 'appened if you'd done that. But don't you fret, Kitten: if we blame the 'ole thing on 'im, we might just squeak out of this one. You tell the beak where 'e is and we're laughin'."

He took another bite of apple and crunched it loudly.

"Want some?"

He held out the half-eaten apple to me. I shook my head. I'd let nothing he had touched pass my lips.

"Fine. Suit yourself. But you'll find them a bit short on the old commons 'ere, Cat—not like those flash 'ouses in Grosvenor Square I 'ear you've been frequentin'. Is that where you got those togs?"

I said nothing.

"Gawd, Cat! It's gonna be a long night if you don't keep me company. We're both in the same boat now, both facing the drop. Can't you at least talk to me?" He took a final bite of the apple and threw the core into the corner, where vermin could be heard fighting over it. "I've been 'ere since the early 'ours, and I can tell you that it's not nice—no, not nice at all. Won't you need someone to run to when the rats start nibbling at your lace, eh?"

I looked up at him. He was grinning at me, enjoying every moment of my distress.

"You'd be the last person I'd run to, Billy. I'd go to the rats for help first."

His grimace broadened.

"That's what I like about you, Cat: your sense of 'umor. We'd've made a great team. Perhaps there's still time: if we stand by each other, we might get out of this mess. And when we do that, where'd you go? The respectable folk at the theater won't want you back. You could come with me and 'elp me set up my little business in the Rookeries. I've got some ideas—big ideas."

"I'm surprised you have any ideas at all."

He let this pass. "Ah, that's where you're wrong. That place is ripe for the pickin'. I'll start with askin' the innkeepers for a small consideration for protectin' their establishments. Move on to ownin' a few places myself. I'd give a fair price for goods people might come by 'inadvertently' like. 'Ave some boys—and girls—workin' for me. You'd be a real 'elp, Cat, knowin' what you do about the 'igh end of the thievin' line. You'd make a capital fence. You could run the girls, if you like, if you give me a percentage of your take."

His picture of our "future" together was laughable. I had to say something.

"Billy, you've got me all wrong: I've never stolen anything in my life."

He gave me a wink. "'Course you ain't, Cat. Nor've I. We're as innocent as a pair of newborn babes, ain't we? Or that'll be our story."

I almost smiled: he was like some persistent suitor, not taking "no" for an answer. He didn't know that I had Lady Elizabeth rushing across town to come to my defense even as we spoke.

"Forget it, Billy. When your heels are swinging in the wind, I'll be free as a bird. You can forget the Rookeries: you're going to pay for what you did last night and I'll be in the front row cheering the executioner on."

"Pay, will I?" said Billy menacingly. He sat up, his boots thumping on the ground with a dull thud. "You may pretend to be Miss Goody Two Shoes, but don't forget, I know you and your game. If I'm for the nipping-jig, you'll be swinging up there with me. I'll make sure I take you."

"Dream on, Boil!" I replied, though I had felt a shiver down my spine as he spoke. "I've got powerful friends. I'll be out of here."

"Not before I've knocked some sense into you!" He sprang to his feet, kicking a mug of beer over as he did so. The sour liquid seeped into the straw. "Face it, Cat, no respectable friend is goin' to 'elp you now you're in 'ere. We're beyond the reach of all that's nice and polite. You've got to rely on yourself now." He ground his fist into his palm in frustration at my obstinacy. "Look, if we stick together, tell the same story, we're both free; if you split, I'm dead meat—and I'm not 'avin' that!" He made a lurch toward me. I cowered on my bench, face screwed up, having all too good a reason to fear his fists. But no blows fell. I opened my eyes and saw that he couldn't reach me: like a guard dog on a chain, his ankle had been manacled to a bolt in the floor. The ridiculous sight of an irate Billy trying to make a grab for me set me off into a peal of hysterical laughter.

The laughter quickly turned into hiccupping sobs. Billy glowered at me and retreated to his side of the room. He slipped a knife from his boot and began to pick at the bolt on the crumbling brick floor. My hysterical fit stopped as suddenly as it had come when the cold realization dawned that he would—given time—be able to work himself free.

Scrape, scrape, rattle went the knife on the manacle.

Neither of us spoke.

"Catherine Royal?"

The runner had returned and was standing by the door, a lantern in his hand. I sat up with a start, having dropped off into an uneasy slumber.

"Yes?" I said blearily.

"You're to come with me."

I got to my feet eagerly. Billy's eyes were on me, the knife concealed in the sleeve of his jacket. So had Lady Elizabeth finally arrived? I wondered. I had expected her to be here much sooner, and terrible doubts had begun to undermine my confidence in her, but at least she'd arrived before Billy had had a chance to work himself free of his bonds.

The runner led me back up the narrow stairs and into the office above. But we were not stopping there: he took my arm and led me through a pair of glass-paneled doors and down a corridor carpeted in a rich dark woolen cloth. We were clearly getting closer to the inner sanctum of the magistrate. The runner paused before a door with a polished brass handle and knocked.

"Come!" came a man's deep voice.

Constable Lennox opened the door to reveal a study lit by two high windows overlooking a pleasant garden at the rear of the house. The walls were lined with books; papers lay scattered in comfortable confusion on the desk and every available surface. In contrast to the chilly cellar the room was very warm, thanks to a fire roaring high in the grate, and in other circumstances it would have struck me as pleasant.

Though I took in all these details, my attention was mainly occupied by the people in the room, who had all turned to watch me enter. An unfamiliar bewigged elderly gentleman dressed in black with a snowy white stock at his neck sat behind a desk, fingers laced together as he surveyed me. On the edge of a chair in front of him perched Lady Elizabeth. Her face was drained of color and tear-stained. She looked quite wretched to see me in this state. By her side stood Lord Francis. His face was pale also, but it was the paleness brought on by the effort of suppressing great anger. On the far side of the room, looking out of the window at the garden, stood Marzi-pain Marchmont. He turned on my entry and gave me a triumphant smile. I now began to have some inkling of what was happening. Next to Marchmont stood the duke. His eyes were directed at me with blazing anger, and I felt their force almost as if he had actually lashed out at me. Marchmont whispered something to the duke, who then nodded as if his worst fears had been confirmed.

"Here's the prisoner, sir," said the constable, standing behind me with his arms folded as if I was some dangerous beast that he was here to guard.

The magistrate cleared his throat. "You are Catherine Royal, also known to the criminal fraternity as 'The Cat'?"

"It's just Cat—and that's to friends, not to criminals," I said quickly.

The magistrate surveyed me with disapproval. "Answer my questions with yes or no, girl. I don't want to hear any long speeches from you. Is that understood?'

"Yes, sir," I said meekly, my eyes straying to Lady Elizabeth for some clue as to what was happening here. I had half hoped for profuse apologies and instant release. This did not now appear to be in the cards.

The magistrate turned to the duke and Marchmont.

"Is this the girl—the impostor—you saw this morning in your house, your grace?"

The duke gave a curt nod. "Yes. I took careful note as the boy here—" he nodded to Marchmont "—had warned me only yesterday of the undue influence she seemed to have over my children. And I will swear that those are my daughter's clothes she is wearing—I recognize them. She must have stolen those as well as the jewels."

"She didn't steal them!" burst out Lord Francis, unable to restrain himself any longer. "Father, you are a fool to listen to the poison that that toad's been whispering in your ear! Lizzie gave them to her, as we've told you already ten thousand times, sir!"

"Silence!" barked the duke, glaring at his son. "I will not have anyone, least of all my own son, call me a fool!"

"Then stop acting like one!" snapped Lord Francis unwisely.

"I warned you," said the duke, his voice menacing, "before we came here, that you are to say no more on this subject. I am shocked—shocked and grieved to find out that a son of mine has allowed his sister to fall into the clutches of so artful a creature. I expected better from you. This means school, sir, school!"

"I don't care if you send me to school, Father, as long as you listen to the truth for once!"

"Insolent boy!" cried the duke, raising his hand as if to box Lord Francis's ears but at the last moment letting it drop.

Marchmont was grinning, enjoying Lord Francis's discomfort. I wished I were close enough to slap him.

"But, Papa," said Lady Elizabeth, laying a gentle hand on her father's sleeve, "it is true—I did give her those things."

The duke patted his daughter's arm tenderly.

"I know you're just saying this in a misguided attempt to help the girl, Lizzie. You would not willingly have pawned the jewels your mother and I gave you on your coming out—I know how dear they are to you. What earthly reason could you have to do this? You want for nothing, need nothing. I've always seen to that."

Lady Elizabeth turned agonized eyes to me. I could guess what she was thinking: if she mentioned Johnny now, before the magistrate, then he would be joining me in the holding cells with little or no chance of escape. Who knows what the law would make of our attempt to help a wanted man? We were all bound to silence until his ship sailed.

"Papa, you've always been very generous to me, but I didn't want to tell you that . . . that . . ." Lady Elizabeth floundered.

"That she needed money to pay my gambling debts," said Lord Francis quickly.

The duke wheeled around to his son.

"Gambling debts? This is the first I've heard of debts! When did this happen?"

"At the boxing last Sunday—the match between the Bow Street Butcher and the Camden

Crusher," he said, the details rolling fluently from his tongue.

The duke flushed red, realizing that his son's illness had been feigned. He had escaped a morally improving dose of church for a surfeit of pleasure at the ring.

"And how did you get to a boxing match, sir? Who took you?" he asked coldly.

"Pedro, the African violinist, took me. Cat was against it and didn't want me with them."

"This girl went to a boxing match?" said the duke, looking at me incredulously. I suppose it did seem very unlikely, dressed as I was in lace and silk with my hair in ribbons. "Did you, girl? Is my son telling the truth?"

I nodded as it seemed I must if the gambling story were to be corroborated.

"She was dressed as a boy, of course," said Lord Francis, wrongly thinking that this would make it more excusable in his father's eyes.

"Dressed as a boy?" The duke's blue eyes blazed beneath his beetling white brows.

I nodded again.

"And I suppose she trapped you into gambling, didn't she?" said the duke to his son.

"No, no, that was entirely my fault. She was against that as well. Later, Lizzie offered to help me out by pawning the jewels. Cat volunteered to take them to the broker."

"Hmm." The duke looked from his son to me. "It would be just like Lizzie to let you impose on her, Francis. You should be heartily ashamed of yourself for abusing your sister's trust."

Lord Francis hung his head, hoping this reprimand was a sign that his father was swallowing the story.

"But you didn't see a penny of it, did you, you young fool?" Lord Francis opened his mouth to protest, but the duke silenced him with a warning finger. "Admit it: you were let down. You chose your agent badly, didn't you? The girl went off with the money and gave it to that Shepherd boy."

"A very bad character, that," interjected the magistrate. "He was caught with the whole forty pounds on him, your grace. The girl had the pawnbroker's ticket in her pocket when we picked her up. It seems an open and shut case of theft by deception—possibly extortion as well when we add in the clothes." He peered down his nose at me as if I was something unsavory the dog had dug up. "That dress must be worth ten pounds at least, I'd say. Faced with such a breathtakingly audacious crime, I don't think I can even take into account the tender age of the offender. I doubt I'll recommend mercy when she comes for sentencing."

Marchmont appeared delighted by the news.

"And, sir, if I may add," he said, driving a further nail into my coffin, "I have cause to think she has been consorting with criminals of an even worse kind—traitors, no less—protecting them, no doubt in exchange for money."

We had to get him off the subject of Johnny. I could find no words to speak in my own defense as the realization hit me that neither the duke nor the magistrate believed in my good character, and both were determined to see me punished for sins I had not committed. I was going nowhere but back to the holding cell; from there to the dock; from the dock to . . . I did not even want to think about that.

"But, Papa, she's not like that! Mr. Marchmont is wrong. You don't understand," pleaded Lady Elizabeth.

"Ah, Lizzie, Lizzie!" said the duke with a sad shake of his head. "Perhaps this whole experience will be a good lesson for you. You've been brought up so narrowly by your mother and me that you were not prepared when you came across your first experience of the depravity of men's hearts. You saw an innocent-looking girl needing your help; I see a bloodsucking leech who has latched on to you and has taken advantage of your unsuspecting nature. If young Marchmont here had not alerted me to the danger, who knows what other liberties she would have taken?"

His insults were too much.

"I'm not a leech!" I protested. "You can have the dress back—I don't care. I never stole that money. It was taken from me before I could give it back to Lady Elizabeth."

"I warned you, young woman," said the magistrate portentously, "save your speeches for the trial. I only allowed you up here on the request of the duke so that he could confront his children with your crimes. I think we've heard quite enough. You can take her back down."

The runner put a heavy hand on my shoulder.

"Cat!" exclaimed Lady Elizabeth, breaking free of her father and dashing across to me to grab my wrist. "I swear it'll be all right. I'll make sure it is."

"Don't touch her!" barked the duke. "You don't know what kind of pests and diseases she might be harboring. I don't want to lose my precious rose to a jail fever." He stepped between Lady Elizabeth and me so that my head butted against his embroidered waistcoat.

Lord Francis scrambled roughly past Marchmont and around the desk to intercept me at the door.

"Is there anything you need, Cat? Other than to get out of here, of course?" he asked with an attempt at a brave smile.

My voice broke into a sob as the runner began to drag me away. I tried to school my lips to respond in kind, but my heart was breaking.

"Ask Pedro to bring some of my things from the theater—if they'll let him," I said in a strangled voice. "But get me out of here quickly, please! I'm in a cell with Billy Shepherd, and I don't think . . . I don't think I'm going to last long."

"Dammit, Cat, we'll get you out—I promise you! Even if it's the last thing I do!" called out Lord Francis as I was led away to my cell.

SCENE 4—CHAMPAGNE

Reader, I can safely say that my first night in jail was the worst experience of my life so far. The green silk dress no longer felt luxuriously soft against my skin; it had become a torment, eating into me with the acid touch of shame. I wanted to rip it off and even would have if I had had something else to put on. I did not dare sleep a wink, for though Billy gave up on working on his chains around midnight and was snoring loudly stretched out on his bench, I was afraid that if I dropped off to sleep, I would wake to find his knife at my throat—or not wake at all. Added to this, I was cold, hungry, and just plain uncomfortable. I sat for many hours hugging my knees, willing myself to stay alert, listening to the sound of the carriages and wagons rumbling past outside, the scratch of tiny clawed feet rooting in the straw. Somewhere in the darkness a steady drip, drip, drip marked the passing moments.

I found myself wondering if I would ever see the light of day again. Just how firmly set against me was the duke? Would his children be believed once Johnny sailed and they could tell the whole truth, or would he think this just another invention to save my neck? And even if by some happy chance I was freed, what then? As Billy said, unless I was released without a stain on my character, no respectable place would want me back. Mr. Sheridan would perhaps believe my story, but even he might be persuaded to doubt me. After all, my conduct over the past few days, eavesdropping and popping up where he least wanted me to be, would hardly endear me to him. Mr. Sheridan had not felt able to trust me with the secret of the diamond. I would understand if he now preferred to see the back of me.

My dark thoughts were interrupted in the small hours of the morning by a soft metallic tapping noise. I started, wondering for a disconcerted moment if Billy had begun work on his fetters again, but then realized that the sound came from the grating in the ceiling—the only entry for light and air to the cellar beneath.

"Cat!" came a soft hiss. "Cat!"

I leaped to my feet and moved as quietly across the room as I could so as not to wake my cellmate. Rats scattered from my path, squeaking in alarm. Billy gave a murmur. I stopped. He then rolled over onto his back and resumed snoring even louder than before.

"Cat!" came the voice again, now more urgent.

I reached the grating and stood directly below it, looking up into the darkness.

"Who is it?" I whispered.

"It's me, Pedro!" said my friend, rather too loudly.

I could have wept to hear his voice.

"Ssh!" I cautioned. "Billy's here—asleep for the moment, but he could wake up."

Pedro lowered his voice. "I've got Syd and Frank with me—they're keeping watch. We couldn't get to you before now. The night patrol's just gone in for some refreshment. We've only got a few minutes, I'd guess."

"I'm so pleased you came." I didn't need to tell him how awful it was. Pedro had been on the lower decks of a slave ship. He'd know only too well and would have seen worse.

"I've got some food. Frank took it from home. I'll slip it between the bars. I've got something to drink too, but I can't get the bottle through," Pedro said.

"Wait!" I said. "I've got a mug." I ran to fetch the cup of water I'd been given with my crust for supper. I tipped the remains into the slop bucket and held it up. Pedro uncorked a bottle and carefully began to pour the contents between the bars. I had to stretch on my tiptoes to reach up and I wobbled slightly at one point. The liquid splashed on the side of the cup and cascaded down onto my upturned face.

"What is it? I gasped as the sweet mixture splashed into my eyes and mouth. I wiped it away.

"Champagne," said Pedro.

"Champagne!"

"It's all Frank could steal from home, Cat."

"I must be the first prisoner at His Majesty's Pleasure to sup on champagne!" I said, managing my first smile since I had arrived down here.

"Cat, you're a marvel." In the faint moonlight, I could see Pedro's eyes twinkling. "Here's the food." He pushed a flat parcel between the bars.

"What's this?" I joked, stuffing it into my pocket for later consumption. "Smoked salmon and syllabub?"

"No," answered Pedro with perfect seriousness. "Game pie, roast beef, and apple and almond tart. Leftovers from some fancy dinner party, Frank says. It might be a bit jumbled up—sorry about that—but I had to squash it to get it through."

We were both silent for a moment, Pedro staring down, me looking up.

"Oh, Cat . . ." he began. I could tell he was going to commiserate with me but I couldn't bear that. It was all I could do to keep from breaking down as it was.

"How's the wind? Has Johnny sailed?" I asked quickly.

"No." Pedro looked nervously over his shoulder, presumably to where the others were waiting. Our time was running out. "And we've agreed that tomorrow we'll let Johnny know what's happened and tell the duke the whole story."

"You can't do that!" I said, aghast. "They'll catch him."

"But we all know that Johnny wouldn't want us to leave you down here on his account. The only way the duke can be brought to believe his children is if Johnny can be produced. The duke's already packing Frank off to school tomorrow—our chances to change his mind are fast running out."

"But the duke will tell the magistrate, then Johnny'll be down here charged with treason!"

"We know," said Pedro grimly, "but in case you haven't noticed you're facing a capital charge too. We think that there's more chance of a rich man with powerful friends, like Johnny, being let off by an English jury for insulting the king, than for an orphan like you, charged with theft by a peer of the realm. Let's face it, Cat, you're as good as dead if this goes any further."

"But— !"

"There are no buts. You're outvoted on this— four to one. Five to one if Johnny were here."

"Four? Who's the fourth?"

"Syd. We've told him the whole story. He said that if they don't let you go he'll break you out himself and finish Billy off while he's at it, but we've persuaded him to hold off for the moment."

"Tell him thanks, but he's not to get into any trouble for me," I said, though heartened to find I still had friends on my side.

Pedro looked over his shoulder. I too heard a sharp whistle.

"That's it. I've got to go. But you're all right, aren't you, Cat? Billy's not giving you any trouble?"

"I'm fine," I lied. What was the point in telling the truth? It would only upset them. "But Pedro, don't tell Johnny just yet. Let's see if we can think of something else. I don't want his death on my conscience."

Pedro gave my outstretched fingers a gentle squeeze. "And we don't want yours on ours! No promises, Cat. Good-bye!"

And with that he sprang to his feet and dashed off into the darkness.

His departure was rapidly followed by the tramp, tramp, tramp of the night patrol resuming their duties.

I returned to my bench and set my mug carefully down beside me. With great care I opened the package of food and spread it on my lap. So there I sat on a hard seat with my back against the slimy wall of the cell, staring down on a terrible irony. On my skirt was the finest supper I had ever seen, even though, as Pedro had warned, it was somewhat mangled in its journey across town. And I had champagne to wash it down—a drink I had never tasted before. Well, it was either look at the food until the rats stole it from under my nose, or eat and have done with ironies. I ate—and enjoyed it. But there was one unanticipated side effect: the wine sent me into an overpowering sleep. Murderous cellmate or no, the bubbles of champagne could not be resisted.

"Morning, Cat."

I was rudely woken by an apple core bouncing on my forehead. I sat up with a start.

"Still 'ere then with poor old Billy, I see. Might be thinking my offer weren't so bad after all, eh?"

I looked across the cell and saw Billy grinning like an evil goblin in a fairy tale.

"You don't look so fine this morning, girl. You'd better get out of 'ere before you ruin that there new dress of yours."

I looked down. The silk was now dirty and stained with the champagne that had spilled on it last night. My once-white silk stockings were gray and had a large hole on one knee. My hair straggled over my shoulders, the once-neat ringlets ruined by a night on the bench.

"So where are your fine friends? Forgotten about their pussycat, 'ave they?"

No they haven't, I thought to myself, determined not to let Billy wear me down with his jibes. After all, I had supped on fine meats and sparkling wine.

"Good morning, Mr. Shepherd," I said, stretching and yawning as if just waking from a deep sleep on a goose feather mattress. I was feeling strangely light-headed, as if buoyed up still on the bubbles of the champagne. "I see the weather is set fair today."

Billy half-turned to look up at the grating but then caught himself.

"You've cracked, ain't you, Cat? Poor girl: one night behind bars, and you've lost it."

"No, *au contraire, mon ami*, I have never been more in my right mind. I was just reflecting on the pleasure a good supper can give an empty belly."

"A good supper? You call a crust of bread and a mug of scummy water a good supper? They must 'ave been meaner at the theater than I thought."

I picked up my mug, which still had an inch of pale golden liquid at its bottom, and raised it to my companion.

"Your good health, sir," I toasted him and downed it with a gulp, then gave a small, contented burp.

"Mad! Quite mad!" exclaimed Billy, rubbing his hand across his forehead, half in admiration, half in doubt.

The rattle of keys at the door made us both look up. Constable Lennox appeared in the entrance.

"Miss Royal. Come with me."

My heart leaped into my throat as I wondered what this summons signified. Surely it was too early for the magistrate to be sitting? I would have thought he would be sipping hot chocolate in his powdering gown, not choosing to deal with the London riffraff like me. Or—I swallowed hard—had they caught Johnny? But I had no choice in the matter: I had to follow.

Billy must have been wondering the same thing. My premature departure did not suit him at all: he'd not yet had time to persuade me to lie to save us both.

"Where's she goin'?" he asked the runner urgently, again rushing to the length of his chain like a zealous guard dog.

The runner did not deign to give an answer, but shut the door on him.

"This way, miss."

He did not place his hand on my shoulder as he had done on my last outing from the cell but walked ahead, shining a lantern so that we would not miss our step. Anxious but intrigued, I followed him up the stairs and into an office. There, standing in front of the desk occupied by the clerk Amos, was a gentleman in a claret-colored jacket and black boots. He turned to face me: it was the Earl of Ranworth, Johnny's father.

"Is this the child, my lord?" asked the runner respectfully, ushering me forward.

"Indeed it is," said the earl. He was staring as if stunned to see me there, though apparently he had asked for me to be brought to him.

"And you say you know for a fact that she gave forty pounds to your son on behalf of the duke's daughter, which he returned to this child on the evening of the day before yesterday, after receiving money from you?"

"That is exactly right. So, you see, Constable, the girl would not have had time to return the money to its original owner as no doubt she intended to do."

"So how did it end up in the hands of Billy Shepherd?" the runner asked, looking at me doubtfully.

"I suggest you ask her. Has anyone thought to listen to what she has to say about the whole matter?"

Constable Lennox coughed uncomfortably. "Well, sir, I can't say that . . ."

"Ask her then, man!"

The runner turned to me. "You heard the gentleman," he said roughly. "What's your story?"

"Billy's boys broke in to steal . . . to steal something they thought was in the theater," I began quickly. "Two of them—I don't know their real names—found the money under my pillow and took it. I told Billy and he took it off them later to count it."

"So he wasn't one of the thieves who stole it from you?"

I reluctantly shook my head, but the truth was I couldn't incriminate Billy without explaining more about Johnny and the beating.

"There you are, Constable," said the earl loudly, putting an arm around my shoulders. "You've got the wrong people. It's those two boys you should be after, not this little girl. Tell the man what they were like, child, and I'm sure that'll be the end of the whole business."

"Now wait a minute, my lord," stuttered the runner. "I can't just let her go. I need proof. Where's this son of yours? What's he to do with it? I'll need to speak to him."

"You can't, sir. He sailed this morning on the tide."

"Where to? When will he be back?"

The Earl of Ranworth drew himself up to his full patrician height and glared at the runner. He reminded me forcibly of Johnny in one of his more frightening moods, such as when he had confronted Billy's gang with empty pistols.

"I don't know, man," he said irritably. "He's gone and that's that. You can't keep an innocent child in prison just because my son's not here. My word not do then?"

"But the duke!" said the runner feebly.

"Heavens, man! I'll deal with that. Look, here's fifty pounds bail for the girl." The earl drew a large paper banker's draft from his pocketbook and let it flutter down onto the desk. "You let her go now and I'll swear that the duke will have dropped all charges by mid-morning, or call me an ass!"

As the unfortunate runner did not want to be accused of calling a lord an ass, he reluctantly picked up the banker's order and nodded to Amos.

"Start to make the necessary arrangements, Amos," he said. "I'll clear this with the magistrate."

"Sir John Solmes, isn't it?" said the earl.

Constable Lennox nodded.

"In that case, I'll come along and help you. We're old friends—went to the same school. You sit there, child. I won't be long."

The earl led me to a chair by the fireside and handed me into it as if I were a fine lady.

"Thank you," I said hoarsely, bemused by this unexpected turn of events. How had he known I was here? And would he really be able to get me out?

In the interval that followed, all that could be heard in the office was the scratching of Amos's quill and the crackle of the fire. For the first time since yesterday afternoon I did not feel cold.

"Ready to go, my dear?"

In my exhausted state I must have fallen into a doze, for the earl was at my elbow before I knew it.

"Go?"

"Yes, child. You are free to go."

"She's on bail, sir," corrected Constable Lennox, looking at me with distrust. He clearly still suspected me of as yet unspecified crimes. After all, he had me down as the mastermind behind one of London's most fearsome gangs.

The earl ignored him.

"My carriage waits outside. We have a call we must make before I can return you home, I'm afraid, Catherine." The earl helped me to my feet. "Good morning." He tipped his hat to Amos and the constable and led me out into the sunlight.

"How did you know?" I asked once we were settled in his carriage. The earl tucked a large blanket around me and handed me a flask of warm tea.

"Sheridan. Last night he sent an urgent message explaining how you'd ended up in jail thanks to my miscreant of a son. I came as soon as I could, but I had to check that Jonathan had gone."

"So it's true—he has left."

"Yes, sailed this morning with a stiff breeze to fill his sails. You need not worry about him anymore, Catherine."

"It's Cat. Johnny calls me Cat."

"Does he indeed?" The earl smiled and ruffled my hair in the exact same gesture used by his son. "Well, here is one father who is mighty pleased that his offspring had the sense to choose you for his friend. That African boy—Pedro, isn't it?—told me all about your exploits this morning when he took me to the docks. We were just in time to see the *Potomac* heading out to sea."

I snuggled back into the blanket. "So where are we going now?"

"To get that fool of a duke to drop his ridiculous charges, of course!" said the Earl of Ranworth.

We arrived at the front door of Grosvenor Square just as the big house began to wake up for the day. Footmen were opening the shutters. A maid was scrubbing the doorstep as we made our entrance. She bobbed a curtsy as we passed.

Joseph, the footman, opened the door to us.

"My lord," he said with a bow, recognizing the caller. His eyes slid to the shabby urchin bundled up in a blanket and I saw a look of alarm flicker in his eyes, but when he spoke his voice remained calmly professional. "His grace is at breakfast. Shall I tell him you are here?"

"That won't be necessary," said the earl, striding past him. I hovered on the doorstep, uncertain as to my welcome across this threshold, until the earl turned back. "Come on, Catherine. You have to come too."

Joseph stepped forward. I thought for a moment that he was going to throw me out, but instead he said, perfectly politely:

"Would miss like me to take her . . . her cloak?"

"If it's all the same to you," I said in an embarrassed whisper, "I think I'll keep it on." Underneath I was hardly fit to be seen in these halls.

Joseph bowed. "Of course, miss."

I stepped into the foyer and saw a chest waiting at the bottom of the stairs.

"His lordship's," said Joseph in a low voice. "Off to school after breakfast, I'm afraid, miss." The footman gave me a significant look as if to say he was fully aware of the circumstances that saw me arrive there smelling of the sewer and that would drive his master off the premises.

"Avon!" The Earl of Ranworth strode on while Joseph and I hung back to have our brief conversation. He was opening door after door, looking for the duke. "Dammit, man, where are you?"

Joseph hurried to overtake him and opened a door on the far side of the foyer.

"The duke is in the breakfast room, my lord," he said, ushering us through. "Good luck!" he muttered as I passed.

The Duke of Avon was indeed at his breakfast, sitting at the far end of a long table draped in a snowy linen cloth. He had a newspaper propped up on the salt cellar in front of him and was tucking into a hearty meal of eggs and bacon. On his right sat a disconsolate Lady Elizabeth, who was toying with a piece of dry toast. Standing by the sideboard with his back to his father was Lord Francis. He was in the act of slipping a muffin into his pocket, and I guessed he was hoping to supply me with my own breakfast later that morning as his parting gesture.

"What the devil!" blurted the duke on seeing the Earl of Ranworth burst into the room with so little ceremony. He then spotted me and dropped his fork with a clatter. "What's she doing here? Joseph! Joseph!"

But Joseph did not come. I suspected that he had become conveniently deaf and was preventing any other servants answering the summons from his post outside the door.

"Cut that out, Avon!" barked the Earl of Ranworth. "You are not turning anyone—least of all this child—out of your house until you've heard me through. You've been a complete fool and thrown an innocent girl into prison. You would have murdered her too if I hadn't come to hear of it."

"What the . . .!" said the duke, unable to find the words to express his astonishment.

"She had that money to pay for my wretched boy's ticket to America. Your daughter—as kind and lovely a girl as a father could wish for—was ready to help Jonathan, for she cared more for him than those bits of glitter and gold that she had in her jewelry box—and you should be proud of her. As for your son, his only crime was to help a friend in trouble and find a safe passage for him. He is completely blameless."

"But, but . . ." The duke was looking from son to daughter, who both were staring at the Earl of Ranworth, openmouthed. They had been as unprepared for his entrance as their father. "But what has Lord Jonathan got to do with all this?"

The Earl of Ranworth gave a great groan as if it cost him much to admit his family's shame.

"The foolish boy only got himself charged with treason."

"Treason!" exclaimed the duke in astonishment.

"Yes, man. He is Captain Sparkler, of course. Stupid boy! Well, he is paying the price for it now. Some years in exile should knock that nonsense out of him."

"Captain Sparkler?" The duke was having difficulty keep pace with developments. He turned to Lady Elizabeth. "You knew this?"

"Yes, Papa," she said meekly.

"And is all this true?"

She nodded.

"My God!" exclaimed the duke, throwing his napkin onto the table and striding to the window. He looked out on the Square, trying to find counsel in the trees and grass.

"So you see, Avon, you've been a fool," continued the Earl of Ranworth. "You should go on bended knee to ask this child's pardon. Think what you would have felt if someone had put one of your own children into that hell pit, eh? But *you* did that, paying no heed to the pleas of your family. An innocent child, Avon! Look at her! And thanks to you she's passed the night in a cell with one of London's most hard-bitten criminals."

The duke turned his eyes to me. I must have made a sorry sight in my blanket. Was he finally convinced or not?

"Well, Miss Royal . . ." the duke began. He stopped and cleared his throat. "It does appear that I owe you an apology."

Despite myself, I let out a sob and crumpled into the nearest chair, tears of relief now streaming down my face. The Earl of Ranworth patted my shoulder comfortingly.

Lady Elizabeth leaped to her feet and clapped her hands. "Oh, Papa! You believe us now?"

He nodded. "I believe you. But why on earth didn't you tell me the truth—the whole truth, mind? All this rubbish about boxing matches and betting—what was I to think?"

"Well, sir . . . you see, sir . . . ," said Lord Francis, pulling on his collar as if it were choking him.

Lady Elizabeth saved the day. "But, Papa, look at poor Miss Royal! She's in a frightful state. The least we can do is make sure she is bathed and rested. Then you must take her back to the theater yourself and make sure everyone understands that she is blameless in this whole affair."

"You are right, as usual, Lizzie," said the duke, patting his daughter on the arm. "Miss Royal, I hope you will accept my apology and my daughter's offer to assist you now."

"Thank you," I said, struggling to control my tears. "I would be most grateful." I took a calming breath and smiled at Lady Elizabeth and Lord Francis, feeling the trails of salty tears on my cheeks.

I was free at last!

EPILOGUE

DIAMOND

I shall never forget my return home. The duke refused to let me skulk in by the side entrance but escorted me into the auditorium, followed by Lady Elizabeth on her brother's arm. There, to my astonishment, was gathered the entire theater company—and more besides! As my foot crossed the threshold, Peter Dodsley led the orchestra in a fanfare and everyone broke into applause.

Before I knew it, I was back among them all. Syd pulled me firmly away from the duke and into the middle of a scrum of his boys. I had my hand shaken, my hair ruffled, and my back slapped by so many that I lost count. Pedro elbowed his way to the front, and we gave each other a hug, needing no words to express our relief that we were together again.

"Order! Order, gentlemen!" laughed Mr. Sheridan as he extricated me from the Butcher's Boys. "I need this young lady for a moment. You'll get her back, I promise."

He led me up onto the stage, where the Avons were waiting by the grounded balloon.

"In you go, Cat," said Lord Francis mischievously.

"What?" I protested as he hoisted me over the side of the basket. Mr. Sheridan hopped in after me and gave a wave to Mr. Bishop. The ropes began to creak and I grabbed onto the rim.

"Are you sure this can take two?" I asked anxiously.

Mr. Sheridan laughed, showing no sign of concern as we were heaved over the heads of the crowd. "I thought you liked living dangerously, Cat."

"Now what gave you that idea?"

He grinned and turned to address his audience.

"My lords, ladies and gentlemen, now that we have our returning heroine center stage, the Duke of Avon would like to make an announcement!"

A hush fell in the theater. The duke stepped onto the forestage.

"I am sure you are all relieved to have your friend back among you after the distress of the last few days." He paused and coughed. "I would like every one of you to know that not a single cloud shades this young lady's reputation. It was all a stupid mistake on my part, for which I am most heartily ashamed and sorry.

"You should be proud of her. She will always have a welcome at my house and, I hope, here at yours."

"Hear! Hear!" shouted Peter Dodsley. Applause erupted again from all sides. Syd and his boys whistled. My cheeks were burning and I didn't know where to look. The upturned faces suddenly became very blurry.

Mr. Sheridan handed me a handkerchief.

"So, Cat, you did look after my diamond after all," he said softly as he gave me a moment to compose myself.

"Look after the diamond?" I blew my nose. "No, I did a hopeless job. I didn't even know what

I was looking after until it was too late. Shepherd's gang was convinced there was a real diamond by then and came looking for it. I had no time to let them know that there was nothing here."

"Oh, but there was."

"You mean the reward for Johnny? I suppose they would have accepted that gladly enough."

"No, I didn't mean that. They didn't realize that under my nose I had a real treasure that I had ignored all these years. You see, Cat, even with Captain Sparkler gone, I still have one treasure left in Drury Lane. I have my Cat— useful in a tight spot. I'll certainly bear you in mind next time I or any of my friends land themselves in trouble."

His words warmed me, thawing the last remnants of fear that lingered from my night among the disreputable and disgraced. I blushed at his kind words. No one at the theater had ever before said that I was of any value.

"So, are you ready to return to the party?" he asked.

"Party?"

"Yes, to welcome home Cat: the diamond of Drury Lane."

Balloon descends. Curtain falls.

ALL ABROAD—wide of the mark

ALL MY EYE—a load of rubbish

ALL UP WITH—doomed, finished

ANNE'S FAN—a rude gesture with thumb to nose
and hand spread (don't do this at a Bow Street
runner unless you want your ears boxed)

ARSY-VARSY—preposterous; it can also mean
"head-over-heels," bum upwards

BARTHOLOMEW FAIR—fair held in August at
Smithfield; the entertainments are spectacular—
rope-dancers, acrobats, wrestling . . . what more
could you want!

BEAK—magistrate

BEAU—sweetheart (and whatever that Billy says, I
don't have one)

BOW STREET MAGISTRATE'S COURT—a place you
definitely don't want to end up

BOW STREET RUNNERS—the magistrate's men
who police the streets around Westminster (not
my favorite people)

CARRIER—horse and cart that carries people and parcels, usually very slowly

COVENT GARDEN—fruit and vegetable market; there's also a theater of that name but we don't talk about it

CREEPER—louse, toady

DAGGLE-TAIL—slatternly woman

DONE A MIDNIGHT FLIT—run off

THE DROP—the gallows; a hanging

FLASH—showy

FLAT—someone easily fooled

THE FLIES—area above the stage where scenery and lighting is suspended

FOGRUM—senile old man

FROGGIES—a rude nickname for French people

FUNK—to back out, to fight shy

GERRARD STREET—a favorite street of writers, artists, and print sellers

GIMCRACK—showy but worthless

GOB-FULL OF CLARET—a bloody mouth

THE GODS—balcony seats

GREEN ROOM—place where actors wait to go on stage, so called because of the color of its walls

GROSVENOR SQUARE—high-class part of the West End of London

HEMPEN FEVER—death by hanging (the rope is made of hemp)

HOG-GRUBBER—mean, nasty, sneaking person

HOYDEN—boisterous girl

ISLINGTON—country village, north of London

JARVEY—driver of a hackney cab

JOHN BULL—the British nation; the government

LAID UP IN LAVENDER—pawned

MARYLEBONE FIELDS—open land just north of Oxford Street

MOONSHINE (a load of . . .)— insubstantial rubbish

NIPPING-JIG—dance of death on the gallows

NOSEGAY—little bouquet to hide bad odors (and there are plenty of them around my neighborhood)

NOT WORTH A FART—you don't really need me to explain this, do you?

THE PENNY SEEMED TO HAVE DROPPED—to suddenly realize or understand something

THE PIT—lowest level in the theater, frequented by gentlemen and those aspiring to be counted in that class

THE POOL—moorings in the Thames

PORTER—a dark beer

PRIG—self-righteous know-it-all (as well as lots of other meanings I won't repeat)

RETICULE—a small, drawstring purse

THE ROOKERIES—also known as St. Giles, a dangerous district you should avoid if you want to emerge with your possessions, teeth, and hair intact

SCARPERED—run away

THE SERPENTINE—a lake in Hyde Park

THEATER ROYAL, DRURY LANE—the best theater in the world. And my home, just off Covent Garden

TOGS—clothes

TOWER OF LONDON—fortress and prison

WAPPING—the docks (keep an eye on your valuables)

WITH KNOBS ON—even more; that goes double!

THE WRONG END OF THE STICK—misunderstanding; being confused